SARAN[illegible]

Saiswaroopa Iyer is a best-selling author celebrated for her evocative retellings of epic heroines. Her acclaimed novels *Draupadi* and *Rukmini* reimagine two of the Mahabharata's most compelling women, bringing their voices, choices and dilemmas into sharp contemporary relevance. As a Stree Shakti awardee (2022), she is known for her ability to combine meticulous research with narrative intensity, carving a niche as one of the foremost voices in Indic mythological fiction.

Alongside her literary journey, Saiswaroopa has over a decade of professional experience across academia, startups and venture capital. Currently, she serves as Program Lead—Writing, Courses, and Communication at INDICA, where she is setting up the Writing Centre and spearheading initiatives to nurture the next generation of authors and communicators. She is also associated with Chanakya University, where she taught creative writing, communication, and entrepreneurship, mentoring students to discover and refine their voices. Saiswaroopa is the curator of LitTales by The Verandah Club, India's largest immersive literature and cultural carnival for children.

Through her books, teaching, and program leadership, Saiswaroopa continues to explore the transformative power of stories—whether through epic retellings, contemporary fiction, or by empowering others to write their own.

SARANYU

Surya's Wife

Saiswaroopa Iyer

RUPA

Published by
Rupa Publications India Pvt. Ltd 2025
161-B/4, Gulmohar House,
Yusuf Sarai Community Centre,
New Delhi 110049

Sales centres:
Bengaluru Chennai
Hyderabad Kolkata Mumbai

This is a work of fiction. Names, characters, places and incidents are either the product of the author's imagination or are used fictitiously and any resemblance to any actual person, living or dead, events or locales is entirely coincidental.

P-ISBN: 978-93-7003-253-8
E-ISBN: 978-93-7003-964-3

First impression 2025

10 9 8 7 6 5 4 3 2 1

Printed in India

Contents

Author's Note

Of all the central tenets of Hindu belief system, one of the foremost is the cyclical aspect of Time, Space and Creation. Writing the story of Saranyu has hence given me the opportunity to explore this tenet in a narrative detail. The story of Devi Saranyu (Sanjna as she is known in Puranic narratives) and her wedding to Lord Vivasvan makes for a turning point in the cycle of creation for she becomes the mother of Manu Vaivasvata (Shraddhadeva or Satyavrata), the progenitor of mankind for the current Manvantara. Considering that Manu Vaivasvata is the progenitor of mankind in the cycle of our existence, Devi Saranyu becomes our foremother. We exist because of her. The beauty of mortal life in the framework of Srishti, Sthiti and Laya is explored in many dialogues in his novel.

The story also gave me an ample platform to explore the concept of Devas, Daityas and Daanavas more from the underlying belief system of these clans rather than from a one-dimensional view. Devas symbolize sustenance and stability, the order and balance for the Universe to go on, while Daityas symbolize ambition. The Deva way of thinking puts the larger good above individual wellness, while the Daitya way of progress seeks to outgrow the shackles of conventional thinking. But when Asura way prevails, ambition sacrifices larger good, and Dharma, the Cosmic Balance, comes under threat. The Avataras of Lord Vishnu have largely taken place to restore this balance and direct ambition towards sustenance.

Coming to the Avataras of Vishnu, the popular memory of

their order has somehow followed a Darwinian pattern from fish to man, which is NOT the right chronological order. Lord Vishnu blesses Satyavrata (Shraddhadeva in this book) in the form of a fish to instruct the king to guide the creation through to the next Manvantara. Saranyu, being the mother of Shraddhadeva, is also the niece of Daitya King Virochana, who participated in the great churn of ocean, implying Kurmavatara predates Matsyavatara. Also, Virochana is the son of Prahlada, which also implies that Varaha and Narasimha Avataras took place before Kurma and Matsya. Though the story of Saranyu is not closely related to the story of any Avatara, it takes place at a crucial time of Manvantara Sandhya (referred to in this novel as the Great Twilight), in between the Avataras of Vishnu—between the Kurma and Matsya to be precise.

While this is about the external story of Devi Saranyu, very less has been explored about her own internal journey. From an unsure wife married to a God whose radiance she could not bear, to becoming the mother of a Manu, hers should have been a compelling spiritual journey from self-doubt to self-realization. Hence, Saranyu's is not a typical story of good winning over bad or gods killing demons, but of the self, rising above differences to see the Universe as a whole. It is a story of true evolution.

From a creative perspective, it is a new experience for me, for all my previous books have been more or less rational explorations of episodes from Mahabharata and Rig Veda. But this is the book where my creative abilities needed to transcend the reimagination on Bhuloka and manifestation of the realm of Gods and their counterparts. Completing this story itself is a blessing of those Gods who indulged my reimagination and creative liberties, and I shall forever be grateful to Them for manifesting in this little literary exploration of mine. I pray that the readers who pick this book also find themselves a tad closer to those Cosmic forces.

Prologue

He was the Great Grandsire.

He was the Creator.

He was the Guardian of All Knowledge, the spouse of the Goddess who embodied the Highest Knowledge.

Lord Brahma glanced at the Cosmos. It had emanated from Him. And it would eventually merge with Him. His four heads overseeing the four cardinal directions, He delighted in what one would call an intermission during the day's activities. Brahma smiled.

His days were incredibly long, or so to those in the thirteen worlds below him. A day for Brahma meant fourteen cycles of Creation, each cycle reordering according to Rta, the Cosmic Order, and realigning its activities and dynamics to Dharma, the Cosmic Balance. Each of the fourteen cycles functioned as a Manvantara—Era of Manu. Each Manvantara comprised seventy-one cycles of Chaturyugas, totalling 852,000 Deva years. The rules and order for each Manvantara fell upon the shoulders of the presiding Manu. Six Manvantaras had passed of the day. The Creator's day was reaching its zenith as He enjoyed the Manvantara Sandhya or Great Twilight—the interstitial period between two Eras of Manu.

Brahma sensed the shift in the dynamics of the celestial bodies that revolved around him. The Cosmos awaited its next Manu. Who would it be? The change in Manvantara also meant the arrival of the new Indra, King of Gods. Brahma's lips twitched at the ends. Manojava Vaasava, the current Indra, would be happy to retire. The son of Vasu had shouldered the responsibility of King of Devas for the last Manvantara, named after Manu Chaakshusha, and was looking forward to making way for the next one. The signs of fatigue were clear. Brahma chuckled to himself at the life cycles repeating themselves rapidly even before midday passed—the day or Kalpa was named after Shweta Varaha, the Great White Boar, one of the glorious forms of Lord Vishnu, the Sustainer of the Cosmos. Brahma sat up straight on his seat, the Eternal White Lotus. Things needed to be set into motion. The Universe awaited its new guardians. His sweeping gaze came to a graceful pause at a certain reddish ball of fire in the distant skies.

The Great Grandsire smiled.

The Great Twilight

The hues of the sky changed in a rhythmic sequence. Holding down the Celestial hammer, Saranyu gazed at her father's reaction. In her right hand, she held a newly forged weapon, shimmering and glowing in reaction to the orbs of primordial energy entering into it from the sky.

'Father!'

'Stand back!' Tvashtra, the Divine Architect, instructed as they both held the weapon steadily till Dyaus, the Guardian Entity of Skies, finished his task of bringing the weapon to life.

Saranyu nodded and set aside the weapon, aware of their next step. The Deva weapon came to life, its intricate designs dancing with the essence of cosmic energy. Her father, Tvashtra, moved to the other side as together, they wove ethereal strands into the weapon's core. The glow diminished as what was once energy, acquired a shape.

'Father, why are we fashioning these weapons?' Saranyu asked the question she had wanted to since a while. This was the time she knew he would answer her, for his task had come to fruition.

'Ah, child, we live in unusual times,' Tvashtra replied, his voice laced with excitement and melancholy. 'Our Brahmanda, this Universe, is passing through a Great Twilight.'

Saranyu furrowed her brow. 'Great Twilight? The interstitial between the eras of two Manus? The time of cosmic transition?'

'Yes, child,' Tvashtra smiled. 'Indra, the Saptarishis, and other Gods retire, making way for new, chosen and deserving incumbents to ascend to their positions.' He paused, taking a moment to admire his daughter's craftsmanship before continuing. 'Brahma Himself entrusted me with the position of Divine Architect, commanding me to keep the arsenal ready for the incoming pantheon.'

Saranyu smiled with pride and gazed at the weapon before turning again to her father. 'Who would be the new Indra after Lord Manojava? More importantly, who would be the new Manu?'

Tvashtra fell into deep thought as he covered the weapon with red fabric. 'According to hearsay, the youngest son of Devi Aditi and Kashyapa is the Destined One.'

'Purandhara—the one who was born with an arrow in hand, and at his very birth had demanded to know who stood with Dharma and who did not?' Saranyu recalled witnessing the birth of the one who could be the next Indra.

Her father replied with a nod and a shrug, signalling some uncertainty. 'There is also some speculation that Bali, the son of Virochana, could be the Destined One too!'

'Bali? A Daitya?'

'Remember the boon bestowed upon the Daitya King Prahlada—that he would be the grandfather of a future Indra?' Tvashtra frowned as he wondered what destiny had in store. *If the fiery Purandhara and the ambitious Bali were to contend for the coveted position...* Tvashtra tried hard to shake off the visions of possible disasters from his mind.

'And who would take the position of Manu, the great son of Chaakshusha?'

Tvashtra smiled at her curiosity. It was time she asked the question. What was destined had to come to fruition. Yet, the father in him feared the uncertainties embedded in the certain destiny. *O, the ways of the Creator!* His gaze fell upon the covered weapon. 'Work still remains on the weapon, Saranyu,' he grinned. 'The Luminous Son of Devi Aditi must still bestow his *tapa*—cosmic heat—on the weapon for its forging to conclude.'

'Vivasvan, the Luminous One, the eldest son of Aditi,' Saranyu muttered as she touched the weapon, its hue resembling the dark sky, the Celestial Energy now in its form—a mass capable of destruction that she was yet unaware of, and not interested in learning about either. Her interest lay in helping her father channelize cosmic power to manifest itself in shapes. And destiny took each fruit of their labour to its rightful agent. If at all she was intrigued by anything, it was with the fact that Tvashtra always kept her away from the sessions when he worked with Vivasvan.

The Luminous Daystar's radiance was a topic of discussion among all the celestial women Saranyu had interacted with, including her friend, Danava Princess Sachi Poulomi. Though Saranyu had noticed that of late Sachi was more intrigued by the youngest son of Aditi than the eldest one. 'This time, I want to witness the work of Lord Vivasvan, Father,' Saranyu declared, hoping to not give him an opportunity to turn down her request. She sensed Tvashtra frown and open his mouth to protest. But something around changed. The gentle breeze transformed into an ominous gust.

The realization hit them both at the same time. Tvashtra moved closer to the weapon. 'Saranyu, you know what to do.'

'By all means.' Saranyu brought her hands together, chanting the primal syllables in the order that he had taught her. She moved her hands, letting a grey orb emanate from her. The odourless smoke permeated the Forge space for a moment, and Tvashtra beamed at the transformation. The orb paled into nothingness but not before leaving them surrounded by lookalike weapons of various sizes, camouflaging their original piece of work out of the sight of the unexpected guest, Virochana, the Lord of Daityas and brother of Tvashtra's wife, Rechana.

'Virochana!' Tvashtra greeted him, his practised cordial smile masking any signs of his earlier unease.

'Uncle Virochana.' Saranyu approached him like any affectionate pampered niece would.

'Saranyu, Brother Tvashtra,' the Lord of Daityas beamed, his affectionate voice betraying undertones of something inexplicable. Saranyu could sense the dissonance, as could her father. 'Ever since my dear brother-in-law Tvashtra was given the responsibility of forging divine weapons, we have been bereft of his presence. So, this is where you fulfil your destiny.' Virochana's gaze slid along the length and breadth of Tvashtra's forge. 'Interesting,' Virochana mused. 'I'm certain these new Gods will be pleased with your creations.'

'Then my purpose would have been fulfilled, indeed,' Tvashtra said, his voice firm and unwavering. 'These weapons are meant only for those chosen by Lord Brahma, the Creator himself.' Tvashtra motioned with his hand towards the exit. 'Have you met Rechana yet?'

Virochana seemed to consider Tvashtra's invitation to the inner chambers. The tension in the air thickened as an unspoken challenge was exchanged between them. The Lord of Daityas smiled, offering no further confrontation. Instead, he bowed at the creations of his brother-in-law. 'I had to meet Visvarupa.' His gaze turned intense. 'And of course, my beloved sister.'

'What would the Lord of Daityas want to speak about with Visvarupa, the interim Guru of Devas?' Saranyu frowned at the thought of Virochana meeting her twin brother.

'Saranyu?' Tvashtra silenced her. 'I was just telling you about the Great Twilight between two eras of Manu.'

'Just as I was educating Bali.' Virochana mentioned his son. 'And about the need to relook at the age-old rivalry as something to be relegated to history.' He smiled. 'After all, my son is destined to lead the Gods according to the blessings of Lord Vishnu Himself when He saved my father, assuming the form of Narasimha! Hence, no harm in Bali spending some time with Vishvarupa and Lord Manojava himself.'

As the Lord of Daityas followed Saranyu's father into his inner chambers, Saranyu breathed a sigh of relief. She had no desire to follow the men. There was something sinister about Virochana's façade. And the assurances about the Great Twilight being the time when old rivalries could be suspended did not work. Glancing at her own work—the array of the many illusory weapons—Saranyu smiled to herself. She would stay back and safeguard the weapons instead. It was possible that the Lord of Daityas had brought someone with him to discreetly spy on the Divine Forge. That was when Saranyu felt another shift in the energy around. Her senses felt an unusual pull in a direction she could not comprehend, as a glow blinded her vision.

The Luminous One

The chamber was filled with an ethereal glow, as if the very walls were carved from the signature radiance. Rays of golden light danced through the air, casting intricate patterns on the floor. Saranyu's vision cleared as the patterns on the floor glowed. She looked up at the next visitor to her father's forge. 'The Luminous One!'

Vivasvan's radiant form stood tall and proud, his eyes shimmering with an intensity unique to him. 'Daughter of Tvashtra,' Vivasvan acknowledged, his gaze warm and steady. 'I can guess you've had visitors.' His gaze swept through the maze of illusory weapons that Saranyu's work had manifested before resting upon the red fabric that covered the real weapon. Saranyu stared, astounded by the ease at which he had seen through her illusion.

'Father is particular about following Lord Brahma's mandate of protecting the weapons till their rightful owners are declared.' She smiled, feeling drawn to the tranquil yet intense spark in his eyes. The power in his gaze drew a part of her out of her form. The illusory weapons melted into nothingness, leaving only a couple of newly forged weapons in front of them.

Vivasvan approached the weapons, his gaze lingering on each of them. He closed his eyes and took a deep breath, summoning the immense power within him. The air in the chamber grew thick with heat. Beads of sweat formed on Saranyu's brows as she watched, rooted to the spot. 'By the power of my fiery essence,' Vivasvan began, his tone intensifying. 'May these weapons be infused with the might of the sun!' He intoned as he raised his hands. A torrent of golden flames erupted from his palms, engulfing the weapons in a blaze of divine fire.

The weapons seemed to come alive under Vivasvan's touch, their forms twisting and contorting as they absorbed the Sun God's energy. The chamber became a symphony of crackling flames, hissing metal, and the steady hum of divine power.

'Truly magnificent,' Saranyu marvelled, oblivious to the blur that engulfed her. As Vivasvan's flames danced around the chamber, the daughter of Tvashtra stood entranced by the spectacle before her. Her celestial beauty was marred only by the faint furrow on her brow, a lingering testament to her struggle to find her place in the Brahmanda. *Can my purpose ever match his?*

One part of her reminded the rest of her that Tvashtra had told her to stay away from his forge when Vivasvan visited. Possibly, her presence was still undesirable when the Luminous Son of Aditi worked his magic upon the Deva weapons. Despite herself, Saranyu willed herself to wait, drawn to Vivasvan's radiance and power, the shivers running down her spine intensifying with the energy emanating from him. 'Is it possible for one being to hold such strength within them?' Saranyu wondered, unable to tear her gaze away from the mesmerizing scene.

Vivasvan remained focused on his task, channelling his fiery essence into the weapons. As the weapons continued to transform under his touch, the chamber seemed to come alive with the force of Vivasvan's power, and hummed with divine potency.

The air grew thick and heavy, making it harder for Saranyu to breathe as she continued to watch. 'Who am I in this grand design?' she asked herself, her thoughts a tumultuous storm of doubt and wonder. 'Am I but a mere apprentice and observer, or do I have a greater role to play?'

Though the questions swirled in her mind, Saranyu could not escape the magnetic pull of Vivasvan's power. As the Luminous One worked tirelessly, oblivious to her presence, she found herself yearning for a connection with him

'The weapons are now imbued with tapa,' Vivasvan declared, his voice echoing through the chamber as he finally lowered his hands, signalling the end of the ritual. 'May they bring courage and righteous power to those who wield them.'

'Thank you, Lord Vivasvan,' Saranyu replied, bowing reverently. The weight of her own uncertainty pressed down upon her, even as the allure of Vivasvan's brilliance beckoned her closer. The moment seemed suspended in time, as if the Universe itself held its breath. Saranyu's curiosity gave way to an overwhelming sensation, a mix of awe and unease as she gazed at Vivasvan's radiance. The heat emanating from him grew more intense, seeping into her very being, igniting a fire in her soul.

'Too much...it is too much,' she whispered, her voice barely audible, even to herself. Then she felt her legs give way, before collapsing on the floor.

'Saranyu!' Tvashtra rushed in that very moment.

Vivasvan turned towards the disturbance, his penetrating gaze sweeping over Saranyu's prone form. 'Saranyu!' he exclaimed, rushing to her side.

'My child! You were not ready!' Tvashtra exclaimed, cupping her usually glowing face, now losing its essence. 'Luminous One, she should have been warned!'

'Take her to the Daitya Guru, Tvashtra,' Vivasvan urged, concern etched on his radiant face that betrayed guilt. From the corner of his eye, he saw the Lord of Daityas, Virochana, Devi Rechana, and Vishvarupa, Saranyu's brother, rush in. 'Guru Shukracharya alone possesses the knowledge needed to revive her. Don't waste any more time.'

ᔓ

The Guru of Daityas was a figure of immense wisdom, his countenance fierce yet tempered by an underlying gentleness—a duality that had earned him the respect of Devas and Daityas alike.

'Daitya Guru!' Tvashtra bowed. 'We seek your aid. My daughter, Saranyu, has fainted due to the overwhelming energy and heat radiated by Lord Vivasvan.'

'Ah, I see,' Shukracharya nodded, his expression softening as he approached Saranyu's still form. His glance at Tvashtra revealed many emotions, unspoken allegations and indignation. But the Guru of Daityas knew how to prioritize things. 'Fear not, Architect of Devas, the power of *Sanjeevani* can revive your child.'

'Thank you, wise Guru,' Tvashtra replied, relief washing over him.

Without hesitation, Shukracharya knelt beside Saranyu, his fingers deftly weaving an intricate pattern in the air above her body. As he worked, he chanted what Tvashtra understood as life-giving incantations, calling upon the power of the Sanjeevani herb to revive her. The herb seemed to dissolve into a shimmering mist that enveloped Saranyu, its essence seeping into her very being. A soft, radiant glow suffused her form, and her chest began to rise and fall with the gentle rhythm of her breath.

'Awaken, child,' Shukracharya commanded gently. 'Saranyu,' his eyes met hers as she stirred back to consciousness. 'You are safe now.'

'Wh...what happened?' she murmured, disoriented and weak.

'Your spirit was overwhelmed by the intensity of Lord Vivasvan's energy,' Shukracharya explained, helping her sit up. 'Fortunately, your father brought you to me in time.'

'Thank you, Daitya Guru,' Saranyu whispered, her eyes glancing around, till she found her father's relieved face. 'Why can't I withstand Lord Vivasvan's radiance?'

Neither the Celestial Architect nor the Guru of Daityas seemed ready with an answer. Shukracharya rose, shifting his gaze towards her father. 'I bid that she rests now. Let her stay at Daitya Loka till she recovers completely.'

'Daitya Loka?' Saranyu exclaimed even as Tvashtra dropped to his knees by her bedside. 'Father? Are we in the abode of Daityas?'

'Only Shukracharya could revive you!' Tvashtra muttered, gently stroking her dishevelled hair. 'Rest here, child. Your mother too shall stay back here to watch over you.'

As Saranyu's strength gradually returned, so did the memory of her encounter with Vivasvan. She recalled the overwhelming radiance of the Luminous Daystar, the heat that seared her soul, and the fascination that led her too close to his divine presence. A shiver ran down her spine. 'Why can't I withstand Lord Vivasvan's radiance?' She knew that this puzzle had to be solved, that her question warranted an answer.

Whispers in the Dark

The Luminous Daystar's warmth barely reached the dimly lit chamber in Daitya Loka. He yearned to know of her well-being through the thick walls that separated their abodes. Bitter winds whispered through the cracks in the walls, brushing against Saranyu's frail body as she lay on a bed of silken cushions. She shivered, her strength yet to return to its full potential since her recent ordeal. Time seemed to slow down at Daitya Loka, and her physical state only added to her mental turmoil. Saranyu ached to get back to her father's forge, the only place where she had found some sense of purpose before the very first meeting with the Luminous Daystar had thrown her into a questionable state of existence. How could she feel so drawn to him and yet feel so distant?

The presence of her mother Rechana only added to her pain, for the sister of the Lord of Daityas now entertained a new idea—pushing Saranyu closer to the Daitya heir Bali, who would visit her to check on her health with annoying regularity.

The chamber door creaked open. Saranyu cringed, bracing herself for yet another awkward meeting with Bali. But when she opened her eyes, she found herself staring at the familiar figure with three heads. 'Vishvarupa!' She sighed, smiling weakly at her twin. Vishvarupa, stepped inside, concern etched on his three faces. His first face wore an expression of deep worry, the eyes darting around the room, taking in his sister's frail state. The second face was calm and observant, its sharp eyes scrutinizing every detail. Meanwhile, the third face remained engrossed in reciting soothing Vedic hymns, a serene smile gracing its lips.

'Ah, dear sister,' he said, his voice a blend of a gentle wind and a thunderous storm. 'How does it feel now?'

'Brother,' Saranyu managed to whisper, feebly raising a hand towards him. He crossed the room in two strides and knelt beside her, placing a delicate touch on her forehead, assessing her condition.

'Still weak, I see,' he muttered, frowning. 'But fear not, your strength shall return soon. The Daityas are skilled healers. You are in the right place.'

'The *right place*?' she mumbled, uncertain of his words. Her gaze shifted to his alert face, watching it carefully for any signs of deception. 'Strange words for the Guru of Devas to use for Daitya Loka.'

The second face of her twin frowned while the other face smiled. 'Ah, well,' he hesitated for a moment before continuing, 'It is the time of the Great Twilight, little sister.' Both the faces smiled at her, though the second one followed the first after a moment's delay. 'Daityas could be the next Devas. Prince Bali could be the next Indra.' He paused and beamed at her as she continued to frown. 'Maybe it is time to set aside old rivalries and forge new alliances. Prince Bali, for instance, has shown great interest in your well-being.'

'Prince Bali?' Saranyu's brow furrowed, suspicious of the idea of a friendship with the Daitya Prince. She glanced once more at Vishvarupa's middle face, the one that never failed to see the truth, seeking reassurance.

'Indeed,' he affirmed, his voice steady and confident. 'He has been most attentive, ensuring that you receive the best care possible. I believe we may be witnessing the beginning of a fruitful relationship between the erstwhile Devas and Daityas.'

Erstwhile Devas? Saranyu stared at her brother, her thoughts churning like a stormy sea. The Great Twilight or anything else notwithstanding, she could not bring herself to trust the Daityas. But she also knew that Vishvarupa was wise, his three heads representing the balance needed to navigate such treacherous waters. Could it be that he saw something in Prince Bali that she did not? Or was he merely blinded by the prospect of an alliance?

'Rest now, dear sister,' Vishvarupa whispered, brushing away a stray lock of hair from her face. 'We shall speak more when you are stronger. Trust me.'

Saranyu's eyes narrowed, her gaze flitting to Vishvarupa's alert head. She managed to mask her scepticism from her brother's perceptive head, but the unease lingered, coiling within her. As if on cue, the heavy doors of her chambers swung open and their maternal uncle, Virochana, Lord of Daityas, entered with a flourish.

'My beloved niece,' he exclaimed, his voice a mix of warmth and authority. 'Glad to see you recuperating! And Vishvarupa, welcome to Daitya Loka. This is the first visit of yours after you became the interim Guru of Devas.'

'Uncle Virochana,' Vishvarupa nodded. 'I could not hold back myself after I heard about Saranyu. And thank you for your care.'

'Of course, dear child.' Virochana's eyes twinkled like far-off stars as he took in the sight of his niece, still weak but recovering. 'Her health is of utmost importance to us all.'

Saranyu sensed it. The wordless exchange between Virochana and Vishvarupa, and she could only guess its contents. With a nod of understanding, they turned towards the door, making their way to Virochana's private chambers.

'Rest well, Saranyu,' Virochana called over his shoulder as they departed, leaving her alone once more.

But Saranyu's curiosity would not be quelled. Giving the men the lead of a few moments, she rose from her bed, despite her body protesting, and followed them. Her footsteps were silenced by her innate mastery of illusion, each step lighter than the one before.

She trailed them through the grand corridors of Daitya Loka, her heart pounding in her chest as she kept her distance, following their footsteps that echoed along the marbled floors. Finally, they reached Virochana's chambers. Saranyu pressed herself against the cold stone wall, masking her presence from the ever-alert guards, and peered through a latticed window.

Inside, the two were soon joined by the Guru of Daityas, Shukracharya, his robes shimmering like liquid silver. They sat together, their voices hushed but intense as they discussed matters of great import. Saranyu strained to catch fragments of their whispers that slipped through the lattice. Her breath caught in her throat as she listened.

'Brihaspati…difference of opinion with Vasava…' Shukracharya murmured, his voice thick with hidden agendas.

'…the outgoing Indra won't even suspect… Vishvarupa can do something that was even inconceivable…' Virochana added, his words sending a shiver down Saranyu's spine.

She knew then that something was amiss. Was Lord Manojava aware of Vishvarupa's presence at Daitya Loka? If the Guru of Daityas and the Guru of Devas were to meet even for a diplomatic convention, it would seem odd for it to happen in the absence of another Deva representative. Something about their conversation held secrets that could change the very balance of power within the realms. Saranyu invoked a chant taught by her father to subtly close the distance between her and the trio so that she could hear better.

But before she could glean any more information, an alertness seemed to come over Vishvarupa, his middle head cocking in her direction sensing an eavesdropper nearby. Saranyu's heart raced, but her identity stayed camouflaged as she retreated into the shadows just as her brother's gaze flitted towards the window.

Heart pounding and mind reeling, Saranyu walked back to her chamber, her steps quick and silent. She found her thoughts mired in worry and suspicion, unable to shake off the feeling that the Universe and thus her life were on the brink of transformation.

As she entered her chamber, she felt the familiar presence that had set her heart into a different kind of flutter. The golden glow filled the chamber, dispelling the frigidness that seemed to be the signature of the Daitya Loka. The churning within only strengthened as she recognized the presence.

'Lord Vivasvan!'

The Shadow Shield

Saranyu's heart pounded wildly as the luminous form of Vivasvan manifested in her chamber. His eyes...they were the last things she had seen before falling unconscious in her father's forge. This very moment, she felt him close her eyes with his hands, the contact drawing out a gasp from her.

'Don't try and look into my eyes, Saranyu.' She held her breath for a moment before letting it out and nodded. 'Forgive me, Saranyu,' Vivasvan said, his voice a warm whisper. 'I did not realize my radiance would have such an effect on you. You are good at camouflaging. Why don't you set up a sort of translucent shield that can allow us to see each other and also protect you from any *after-effects*!'

'A shadow shield!' Saranyu thought aloud and manifested the same. The effort did take up much of her still-depleted strength. His hand slid from her face and she traced a circle in the air with her finger, creating a translucent cloud that seemed to dim his glow. She met his gaze, savouring the warmth of his concern.

'You gave us all a scare!' Vivasvan beamed. 'I hesitated a million times, not wanting to put you through the same ordeal, but I *had to* see you!'

'Luminous One! Is it safe for you to visit Daitya Loka at this juncture? That too just to check on me?'

'The times are different now, Daughter of Tvashtra.' Vivasvan beamed at her concern. 'Besides, you cannot expect me to sit back and do nothing when you fainted due to me.'

Saranyu pursed her lips, swallowing back the protest that

she did not blame him for her condition, the strange condition that made her insufficient to withstand his radiance, something her father and twin brother could do effortlessly. A part of her felt flattered at his guilt and concern. She wanted to continue the conversation instead of reassuring him of her condition, and sending him away.

'Has my father completed work on the weapon?'

Vivasvan nodded, the depth in his eyes seeming to stretch across aeons. 'Yes, Tvashtra's creation is complete. He is on his next one.'

Saranyu nodded, her heart fluttering at the chance to linger in his company a little longer. In these moments, it was as if the boundaries between Gods and the Martyas—mortals, Devas and Daityas, blurred, opening up a realm of possibilities.

'Your father's skill is unparalleled,' Vivasvan continued, his gaze never leaving hers.

Saranyu's chest swelled with pride but also with a strange sense of longing—to be part of something greater, to stand alongside Vivasvan and her father. It stirred a fire deep within her soul.

'May I ask what the weapon is capable of?' Saranyu enquired, her curiosity piqued.

'That is a secret for now,' Vivasvan replied with a knowing smile. 'But I assure you, it will be a force to reckon with.'

'Your words fill me with hope and anticipation, Lord Vivasvan.'

'Hope is a powerful force, Saranyu. It can mend broken hearts and bridge the gap between worlds.' His eyes sparkled with the light of a thousand stars as he spoke, his voice resonating with wisdom.

'May our hope guide us through these uncertain times,' Saranyu whispered, her heart yearning for more than just the conversation they shared.

'Isn't it strange,' Saranyu mused, 'that during the Great Twilight, a Deva may now enter the Daityas' abode? And even

Daityas stand a chance of becoming Devas?' The shadows around them seemed to dance with flitting possibilities.

Vivasvan raised a brow at her words but quickly masked his doubts with a smile. 'Yes, these times are full of surprises. But no matter what happens, the core of sustenance, of Dharma, remains the same. And Dharma can flourish only if peace can be maintained between our people.'

Saranyu admired his diplomatic approach, but her thoughts wandered back to their earlier conversation about her health. She sensed Vivasvan's hesitation, his concern for her well-being. A soft warmth spread across her chest as she realized that he was genuinely worried for her.

'Is there any way...' Vivasvan began, his voice almost a whisper, '...for you to integrate this protective shadow with yourself, so that you can withstand my radiance, so that we may continue to meet without causing you harm?'

A secretive smile tugged at the corners of Saranyu's lips. She relished his eagerness to see her again; his vulnerability endeared him to her even more.

'Perhaps,' she replied coyly. 'I shall speak to my father, Tvashtra, about this. He might have a solution.'

Their gazes met for a brief moment, an unspoken promise passing between them. But just as quickly, the moment was shattered by the sound of footsteps echoing through the halls.

'Vivasvan, you must leave,' Saranyu whispered urgently, fear gripping her heart. 'Bali is coming.'

'Come on!' Vivasvan lingered, his gaze unwavering. 'Let him come. I do not mind being noticed by the Daitya Prince.'

'Please,' Saranyu pleaded, 'for both our sakes, leave.' But she was too late. The Daitya Prince had entered the chamber.

The tension in the room crackled as Bali and Vivasvan locked eyes, their expressions a wordless challenge. Vivasvan's light was alien to the frigid atmosphere of Daitya Loka. Concerned at the situation spiralling out of control, she stepped between them, keeping her voice light and cheery to ease the tension. 'The Luminous Son of Aditi feels so needlessly responsible for my state that he could not help coming down to Sutala Loka,' she explained, forcing a smile on her face. 'I assured him that he shouldn't blame himself for my feeble state.'

The Daitya Prince frowned, his eyes flitting between her and Vivasvan before finally relenting. A thinly veiled snigger appeared at the edge of his lips. 'Needlessly, yes.' He chuckled, gazing at Saranyu. 'Lord Vivasvan need not bother about your well-being, Saranyu,' he said slowly, each word measured and deliberate. 'You are now under Daitya care.'

Vivasvan, unfazed by Bali's words, met his gaze directly, his shoulders squared and chin raised. 'Her well-being is indeed my responsibility as well,' Vivasvan replied, his voice firm but calm. 'For I look forward to working with Saranyu and her father Tvashtra on crafting more weapons for our mutual benefit as the Universe readies itself for a new age.'

As Vivasvan spoke, Saranyu caught a flicker of surprise in Bali's eyes, that was quickly replaced by a neutral expression. It seemed the prospect of working together had given him pause, and she couldn't help but feel a small spark of triumph within her.

'Very well,' Bali said at last, his tone guarded. 'If it is for the greater good.' He smiled again at the uninvited guest. 'Sutala, the realm of Daityas, can do with some luminosity once in a while.'

Saranyu let out an inaudible sigh, alternating her gaze between both. Vivasvan made no move to make a polite exit. Nor was Bali in a mood to leave him alone with Saranyu. The onus was on her to diffuse the awkwardness of the situation. 'Now that you are here, you may also meet the Guru of Devas.' She glanced at Bali, who suppressed the haul of his brows but not before she caught sight of it. Vivasvan betrayed no surprise even if he felt it.

'Lord Vishvarupa would, of course, rush to check on his sister.' Bali beamed wider than he had done a moment before. 'And he is always welcome in his maternal grandparents' house.'

Saranyu sensed the defence issue from the Daitya Prince's lips in an uncharacteristic hurry and looked at Vivasvan, who seemed to stare into vacuum before meeting her gaze, though for a brief moment. The Luminous Daystar brought his hands together and stepped back. 'Shall take your leave then. The interim Guru of Devas deserves his family time too. Convey my regards to him.' He gazed pointedly at Saranyu before meeting Bali's eyes more for a customary farewell before his form melted into nothingness.

It did not take Saranyu much to realize that Vishvarupa's presence had sown a seed of scepticism in the mind of the Luminous Son of Aditi. Just as she had hoped.

'Care for a tour of Sutala?' Bali's smile was more relaxed after Vivasvan's departure.

'Would have loved that.' Saranyu smiled back weakly. 'But the Princess of Danavas had sent word that she would visit me any moment today.'

'Sachi is coming?' Bali frowned before Saranyu pretended to struggle to retain her balance. Bali guided her to the bed. 'I am afraid it was irresponsible of the eldest son of Aditi to come this close to you when he knew that it was his radiance that had harmed you in the first place!' Saranyu felt a cloud cover her sight. This time it was not the one that she had created but something that the choking in her chest had brought forth. The cloud melted into a teardrop that she brushed away. Vivasvan's radiance was the source of energy for the entire Universe, *save her!* And that hurt her more by the moment.

She had to speak to her father. And she had to do it at the earliest.

The Fated Yearning

Saranyu's heart pounded in her chest as she returned home, the moments of her encounter with Vivasvan fresh on her mind. The fragrance of the blooming champaka flowers did little to still her inner turmoil. The Luminous Daystar made her yearn for him. At the same time, he overwhelmed her, making her doubt the reason for her existence. The connection she felt in his presence was undeniable. Yet, her condition had no solution.

As she entered her chamber, Saranyu could not help but notice how mundane everything seemed. The walls painted with intricate murals of celestial beings seemed pale compared to the vividness of Vivasvan's presence. Her silken bed, once a place of respite, now seemed inadequate to contain the whirlwind of emotions she felt within. Her limbs heavy with exhaustion, Saranyu lay down on her bed and closed her eyes. She had made a hasty departure from Sutala, much to her mother's consternation. Rechana was unwilling to cut short her visit to her natal home. And Saranyu did not press her mother to return with her. On the pretext of homesickness, she had headed back to Deva Loka. The journey weighed on her. In an instant, sleep claimed her like a powerful wave, pulling her into the depths of a dream world. There, she found herself surrounded by blinding light again.

'Vivasvan,' Saranyu breathed, her voice trembling even in her dream. 'This is torment!'

'The solution lies within you, Love.'

'Don't tell me to hold up a shadow. I resent a third presence between us!'

'The shadow is a part of you, Saranyu.'

In that moment, she felt the intensity of their connection, as if they were two celestial bodies drawn together by an unseen force.

'Tell me, Saranyu,' Vivasvan said, his voice deep and resonant. 'Do you feel it too?'

'Feel what?' she asked, her breath hitching in her throat.

'The undeniable pull between us?' he whispered, his face inching closer to hers. 'We are destined for each other.'

Saranyu's heart raced as his radiant luminosity enveloped her. It was as if she had been plunged into a pool of liquid light, with her entire body warmed by his divine presence. The sensation was both exhilarating and terrifying, filling her with an overwhelming mix of emotions.

'Vivasvan,' Saranyu stammered, struggling to find the right words. 'I–I don't know what to say.'

'Say nothing,' he replied, his lips brushing against her earlobe. 'Let your heart speak for you, Saranyu.'

And so she did. For the first time in her life, Saranyu allowed herself to be vulnerable, letting her heart guide her actions. And she embraced Vivasvan, their bodies fusing together like molten gold.

'Stay with me, Vivasvan,' she whispered, her voice barely audible. 'Don't let this moment end.'

'Time is but an illusion, my love,' he replied, his breath hot against her neck. 'In our hearts, this moment will last forever. But the Universe needs something more…'

'From us?'

The smile was elusive. But the spark in his eyes was a mix of determination and compassion. And his beautiful face gave way to a flood of light that blinded her again.

'Lord Vivasvan!'

Saranyu awoke with a start, her heart pounding as the memory of Vivasvan's warm touch lingered on her skin. She knew she had to speak to her father Tvashtra. The conversation was long pending. Gathering courage, she rose and hurried towards his Forge, following the trail of the scent of incense and burning metal.

'Father?' she called out softly, stepping into the dimly lit room.

'Saranyu! You are back?' Tvashtra let go of his tongs and gathered her in his arms. 'Your recovery isn't complete! What brings you back this soon, child? Is Rechana back?'

'She is still at Daitya Loka.' She hesitated, biting her lip. 'Father, I–I must speak to you about something important.'

The frown on the face of the Celestial Architect told her that Tvashtra had a clue about what was bothering her.

'Vivasvan visited me when I was at Sutala,' she began, her voice trembling slightly.

'And he asked you to erect a shadow screen between you both so that you are safe from his…radiance!'

Saranyu pursed her lips but did not avert her gaze from her father. 'How do you know? And what do you know?'

Tvashtra let out a sigh and turned around as though his work would give him respite from the conversation that obviously made him uncomfortable. 'You aren't ready for this, Saranyu.'

'And given your protectiveness, I will never be!' The words tumbled out of her mouth before she could stop them. It was only when the Celestial Architect froze and turned around to face her that Saranyu felt guilty of letting her exasperation get the better of her.

'Saranyu…'

'Why should I feel this pull towards the one whose radiance overwhelms me?' A sob shook her. Something in her father's unmoved expression betrayed helplessness. 'I don't know why I exist? I have neither the power that a Deva wields, nor the ambition of a Daitya. I cannot bear to lock my eyes with the Luminous One my heart feels bound to. As though Brahma had a sadistic streak in Him when He created me!'

Tvashtra heard her out, offering no interruption. Her father wasn't a man of empty solace. He knew the power of his own thoughts and words, for, those were the seeds of his manifesting. 'Come child,' he led her to a seat, pausing as if he were weighing his next words.

'You were not born without a purpose, Saranyu. Your ability to manifest that shadow shield between you and Lord Vivasvan should have told you that. The power to withstand the radiance of the Luminous One is within you!' He paused again before uttering the inevitable. 'You both are destined for each other, and for the Universe. But...'

'My inability to withstand him...'

'And your ability to construct that...'

'For the sake of the Three Gods, I hate that screen between us! It is an intrusion!' Saranyu burst out. 'It is just proof of my insufficiency. Like a dark side of myself mocking at me!'

'Now, now, Saranyu.' Tvashtra stroked her hair, an uncharacteristic indulgence overtaking him. 'I am aware of what destiny holds for you. But with the challenges before us and now the curious ability to put up that screen that you seem to have mastered, we can only hope to uncover the secrets of your hidden strength with time.'

Saranyu leaned back against the seat and rested her head in both her hands. Her spirit was draining faster than the physical drain she had felt at the impact of Vivasvan, the whirlwind of emotions she had experienced in his presence. A strange mix of excitement and trepidation filled her heart, but she knew without a shred of a doubt that she was willing to risk everything for the chance to see him again.

Tvashtra left her with her thoughts and went back to his work. The clanging of metal striking metal echoed through his workshop as Saranyu watched her father work. His skilled hands moved with precision, forging weapons of divine power that would tip the balance between gods and demons. The scent of molten metal and burning embers filled the air.

'Father,' Saranyu began hesitantly, her eyes never leaving his skilled hands. 'This shadow screen that I could manifest, is there a chance it can become a source of trouble? If yes, can I control it? Will you train me to?'

Tvashtra paused his work to consider her question. He knew the challenge she faced, but he also saw the determination etched on her face. Sighing, he wiped his brow and turned to her. 'Very well, my daughter. I will teach you what I can, but we both know playing with this new ability of yours is going to be fraught with challenges.'

Saranyu beamed her gratitude as her father went on to explain a rigid regime of austere practices to follow, about blending into and resonating with the five elemental forces—earth, water, fire, air and space—drawing out in the process the cosmic potential to achieve what she sought to.

'Are you ready to do this, my child?'

'Understood, Father. I am.' Saranyu replied, her voice steady and resolute.

'Lastly,' Tvashtra cautioned, his eyes narrowing with concern, 'do not let your emotions cloud your judgement. Vivasvan's power is immense, and you must remain focused and vigilant when in his presence.'

'I promise to be cautious, Father,' Saranyu assured him, her brow furrowed with determination.

'Good,' Tvashtra nodded, a hint of pride in his eyes. 'Now, let us return to our work. There is much to be done, and I missed your assistance!'

As the sounds of hammering and forging resumed, Saranyu began to assist her father, her energy returning at the thought of doing her favourite task, right in her father's workshop. The expression on Tvashtra's face told her that something else had been bothering her father. 'What is it, Father?'

'There is this question of Bali.' Tvashtra sighed. 'Your mother is not going to give up without a fight.'

Saranyu hesitated for a moment, remembering her brief encounter with the Daitya Prince. And yes, Rechana's will was indomitable. 'But you said we were meant to be. Will mother challenge the will of Brahma Himself?'

'I hope she does not!' Tvashtra chuckled, though a part of him could not help fearing that the Daitya Princess would do her best to question even the Creator.

Saranyu took up his Celestial hammer, prompting him towards the next step of his smith work. Soon, the sounds of metals clashing and fires roaring in the distance drowned the unrest in both their minds. Saranyu couldn't help but steal one last glance at the skies where the Luminous One shone bright. If the purpose of her life was to be fulfilled by his side, she vowed to push herself to be resilient enough to achieve it.

Somewhere in Bhuloka

The flames danced to the reverberating chants of the *Adhvaryu* and other Rishis supporting him. There were seven of them in all—Sumedha, Viraja, Havishman, Uttara, Madhu, Sahishnu, and Atinama—the Guardian Rishis of the receding Manvantara. After a long time, the ground had become propitious for the *Yajna*. The Rishis remembered the ravaged state of Mother Bhumi before she was rescued and revived by the God of Gods in his Yajna Varaha form. Restarting life was a priority. And the Yajna was meant to propitiate the Gods to aid the process. The Prajapatis—Progenitors of Creation—had given their blessings. Maharishi Sumedha continued to chant, pouring oblations through the pair of *Sruk-Sruva* that he held.

And then the tranquillity around them was shattered.

A deafening cacophony of war cries and clanging metal pierced the air. Something fell into the sacred fire, arresting the ritual midway!

'Bali!' Sumedha's eyes turned crimson.

'Who do you seek to strengthen through your chants in these times of the Great Twilight, Maharishi?' The Daitya Prince bellowed as his minions surrounded the premises.

Sumedha's gaze narrowed. Arguing with Daityas was of no use, especially on the matter of performing Yajnas. Still, the Maharishi suppressed his rage. 'When the Great Twilight gives way to the Great Dawn again, the mortal realm needs to be revived, Prince of Daityas. It is by the order of Lord Brahma and by the blessings of the Prajapatis that this ritual was conceived. As the Guardian Rishis, we are performing our Dharma.'

'Are you sure you are still the Guardian Rishis?' Bali sneered. 'As you said, Sumedha, it is time for the Great Dawn to usher in change. And the change will be Daityas assuming their roles as the rightful guardians of all realms.'

'Our oblations are for the Devas. It does not matter if they are from the womb of Aditi or Diti.' Maharishi Sahishnu attempted to reason with the Prince of Daityas, but Sumedha signalled him to not engage with Bali.

'I assume that the Daityas are here to finally learn about the ritual of Yajna.' Sumedha's lips twitched. 'But looks like the son of Bhrigu forgot to instruct you on how to behave when you come seeking knowledge.'

The Daitya commanders advanced by a yard, but Bali raised his hand signalling them to fall back. 'The outgoing Guardian Rishis, I hope, haven't forgotten that the energy channelled into the Yajna should instead be preserved during the period of the Great Twilight. Of course, Guru Shukracharya has trained us well to wrest control when others forget their limits!'

It was then that lightning struck Earth. The Rishis and Daityas looked in its direction as it was followed by the earth-shattering thunder. A presence made itself visible.

'Someone seems to claim that they know better than the Creator and the Prajapatis!' The words were harsh, but the voice reverberated through the wilderness, covering the ravaged state of Goddess Bhumi. The entity took form to reveal a radiant being, not a day older than thirty. A smile broke out on the tense faces of the Rishis. The lips of the Daitya Prince too curled, but in contempt.

Purandhara, the youngest son of Aditi; Vivasvan's youngest brother; the most valiant one, and the incumbent Indra as had been predicted at the time of his birth, stepped forward, his form lighting up the darkness left by the dying flame. Bali sneered inwardly and shared a discrete signal with four of his generals who seemed to retreat. Purandhara stationed himself between the Rishis and the Daityas while the skies continued to pound the earth with lightning. Maharishi Sumedha and the others seemed to relax for a moment before the four minions of the Daitya Prince lunged at the youngest son of Aditi and Kashyapa. Purandhara raised his javelin just in time as another bolt of lightning struck, throwing his assailants afar.

'Please refrain from turning the *Yajnasthala* into a needless battlefield!' Sumedha intervened and held Purandhara's arm. A drop from the skies fell upon Sumedha's face, followed by many more. The drizzle and breeze intensified into a downpour.

'The Devas have heard you, great ones!' Purandhara beamed at the rain. *The first rain in Bhuloka since aeons!*

'The incumbent Indra has shown his prowess!' It was Rishi Sahishnu. Purandhara smirked at Bali.

'Incumbent Indra indeed!' Bali sneered. 'Your arrogance shall be your undoing, young one,' spat Bali, his eyes narrowing into sinister slits as he regarded his celestial foe.

'Arrogance?' retorted Purandhara, an amused grin spreading across his face. 'No, my great grandnephew! Confidence. Leave this place, Bali,' warned Purandhara, his tone firm. 'Today, I spare you out of respect for the blood that connects us. But do not mistake my mercy for weakness.'

As Bali's forces retreated, he locked eyes with Purandhara, his expression dark with unspoken threats. Then, with one final snarl of defiance, Bali disappeared into the shadows.

Unseen by the retreating Daityas and the Rishis, a pair of doe eyes trained themselves upon Purandhara. As if sensing the gaze, Purandhara turned in the direction. She hastily retreated into the shadows. But the youngest son of Aditi had sensed the alien presence, and came for her. She had not much choice than to melt her form into thin air and recede. Sachi Poulomi, daughter of the Lord of Danavas, had strayed into Bhuloka, but little did she know that she would see *the one.*

Deva Loka in Peril

'No! I can't believe it!' Saranyu gasped as she navigated through space alongside her bubbly-eyed companion. 'You went to Bhuloka alone? And I missed all the action because I was fixated on fine-honing the razor edges of this strange spherical weapon that Father was working on!'

'You, unlike me, Saranyu, are this "obedient daughter"!' Sachi giggled. 'And the consequence—the obedient ones miss out on all the excitement!'

'All it would take for this statement to no longer hold true is one misadventure!' Saranyu smacked Sachi on the forearm, and they broke into laughter. Their mirth was short-lived. They noticed something odd as they approached the realm of Devas. The golden-hued gates of Deva Loka stood ajar. Saranyu exchanged a cautious glance with Sachi as they traced their path lit by a constellation of flickering stars that seemed to wane by the moment.

'Is Bali up to no good again?' Sachi exclaimed as Saranyu hushed her. Something was amiss. The air that was usually vibrant with the chorus of mantras, adding to the vitality of Deva Loka, now bore a haunting silence.

'Welcome back, children,' greeted a Deva guard, his voice a mere whisper, burdened with fatigue. A shimmering spear lay beside him, its light dimming. 'Is this the daughter of Danava Puloma?' The guard frowned but let them pass. He knew that the Indra himself had summoned her, and Sachi had sought out Saranyu to accompany her.

They crossed the garden path following the fragrance of the blossoms of the Parijata tree and entered the radiant court of Sudharma. The court was relatively empty save for the King of Gods and two others. Saranyu frowned at Bali's presence in Deva Loka but hastily transformed her expression to a cordial acknowledgement after she saluted Lord Manojava, the Indra. She could sense Sachi barely being able to control her surprise on seeing the third man—Purandhara, the incumbent Indra as many Rishis hailed him.

'Welcome, children.' Lord Manojava nodded at the two young ladies. He showed Sachi to a seat to his left and looked at Saranyu apologetically. Saranyu understood that something private was about to be discussed and backed away. 'You could have a word with your brother Vishvarupa, while I resolve this, Daughter of Tvashtra.'

'Now, why are the two supposed Indra-designates of the future interfering with the activities of the Saptarishis?' Saranyu heard Lord Manojava speak sternly as she hastily retreated from the court. Sachi would fill her in on the details, though Saranyu had guessed that the Danava Princess was going to testify against Bali. Making her way to the quarters of the Guru of Devas, she saw a Deva guard stumble as the ambience around them suddenly turned dark.

'Are you alright, Sire?' Saranyu rushed to steady him. The guard nodded, in part grateful and in part apologetic. 'Is something wrong?'

'With the presence of the Daitya Heir and the Danava Princess at Deva Loka, the balance is bound to be threatened.' The guard shrugged.

Saranyu frowned at his mistrust of Sachi. 'But we noticed something wrong even before I accompanied Lady Poulomi inside the gates.'

'You are right.' The guard shrugged again. 'Perhaps the Great

Twilight is slipping into the Dark Night. Things are bound to come to an end. Are you headed towards your brother's quarters, My Lady?'

'I expected the Great Twilight to be a vibrant time of ushering in the future, filled with healthy contentions and installation of newer Gods,' Saranyu remarked, her voice steady despite the quiver of apprehension that danced along her spine. The dark atmosphere of Deva Loka was uncharacteristic, unnatural; it was certainly not a feature of the Great Twilight.

'Every dawn is preceded by a span of darkness and shadows of fear, Daughter of Tvashtra,' the guard replied. His gaze reflected the embers of a battle fought for long yet not won.

Saranyu pressed on, her silken robes trailing behind her, the jewels on her body emitting a pale glow that struggled against the encroaching gloom. As she meandered through the celestial groves, the usual harmonious hum of Deva Loka was replaced by an unsettling quietude. The gardens, once ablaze with flowers of unearthly hues, were now eerily still, their colours muted, as if the very essence of life had been leeched out of them.

'Even the flora senses the turmoil,' Saranyu mused to herself, brushing her fingers lightly against a withered Parijata blossom. 'What has befallen you, Deva Loka?'

Saranyu told the guard to return to his position, and walked around the garden, trying to fathom the reason behind the sudden gloom. Her heart throbbed with the rhythm of uncertainty, each beat adding to her restlessness.

She navigated the hallowed corridors of Deva Loka, realizing a profound disconnect. 'Has the conflict with the Daityas in the last Manvantara drained us so much? Is Deva Loka experiencing the fatigue now?' she wondered inwardly, a pang of sorrow knifing through her resolve. 'Can it be rejuvenated before the rein of the next Manu? Or is the Universe headed towards a sinister darkness?' Her connection to this realm was intrinsic, bound by blood and duty; the thought of it faltering filled her with an ache that tugged at her very soul.

'Deva Loka will endure. The Trimurti shall not let us fail,' she reassured herself with a silent prayer amidst the tumult of her thoughts. But even as she went over those words, doubt crept into the recesses of her mind. She approached the official quarters of Vishvarupa, the interim Deva Guru, her determination a flickering flame in the growing dusk of uncertainty. Perhaps, she would find the answers here.

Saranyu stood still as the thought entered her mind; something was even more amiss at the entrance of Vishvarupa's quarters. Her gaze surveyed the surroundings and rested upon the Deva guards. Unlike the other guards that she had met on her way in, these ones seemed unaffected by the uncharacteristic fog around them. Something churned in Saranyu's mind and she invoked the shadow shield, rendering herself invisible.

Nice to see you hale and hearty, dear sister. The mirthful chuckle of an alien voice rang out, but in her mind.

'Who is that?'

Don't worry, your presence is masked. I, your shadow, am ensuring that.

Saranyu froze. Did her shadow have a voice of her own? She shook her head and hurried towards the gates, closely observing the Deva guards.

They are Daityas in disguise! Her shadow echoed within her chest! *You are right, they are imposters. Our twin is up to something…interesting!*

The voice of her shadow sounded like an apparition. Saranyu halted and gathered herself. She had manifested this shadow. She was its creator and owner and she would show it where it belonged. 'Intelligent one, here is a challenge for you. Go in and find out anything you can about what Vishvarupa is up to, without alerting that second head of his if you can.'

And in a moment, Saranyu felt lighter. The imposter Deva guards sensed her presence. One of them walked up to her, his hands coming together. 'Salutations, Daughter of Tvashtra. And apologies. Your brother is engaged in a ritual, so he does not want to be disturbed midway. Can we take a message?'

Saranyu hesitated. So, the shadow had deserted her and had hopefully entered the quarters, hoodwinking these guards. 'Is it so?' She pretended to ponder in front of the guards. 'Will it take time? Who else is there with him?'

The guard exchanged an uncertain glance with his companion. 'We are neither aware, nor at liberty to divulge anything even if we were, My Lady.'

Saranyu nodded and took a step back. 'Fine, I shall linger around for a while and then leave if it takes too long.'

Oddly, the guards did not seem to mind her strolling around the premises as long as she kept away from the chambers. Before long, her mind picked the presence. The shadow was back.

Our brother, Vishvarupa, the shadow's laughter forced a pause, *in his quest for power, conspires with those the Devas stand against—the Daityas. He performs a dark ritual to deplete our divine essence, weakening the Devas from within. Isn't this exciting, sister?*

The Universe seemed to tilt on its axis. Saranyu grasped the armrest of a nearby chair for support, her knuckles whitening. The air felt charged with a maelstrom of unspoken curses. How could her twin, born of the same father, forge such treachery?

'Stop laughing! Does he not realize the chaos he invites?' An incredulous Saranyu's question hung between them.

Power blinds even the sharpest of visions. The shadow hummed as though it were singing a song. *And in his blindness, he sees only the throne he covets. If Bali becomes the next Indra by hook or crook, he shall enjoy the position of Guru of Devas for eternity!*

Saranyu clenched her jaws, the muscles taut with the effort to contain the whirlpool of emotions that threatened to consume her. Her loyalty to the Devas wrestled with the love for her brother—a battle as old as Creation itself.

'Then we must act,' she declared, her resolve hardening like the weapons her father forged for the Gods. 'We cannot allow his ambitions to doom us all, and the Universe along with that.'

You are such a spoilsport! The shadow murmured, adding to her annoyance. Saranyu had to speak to her father again. At this rate, it was a matter of time before the shadow entity went rogue! *Act with caution, Sister. To confront Vishvarupa is to open old wounds that may never heal.*

Saranyu felt the weight of her predicament settle upon her shoulders like a mantle of stars—beautiful but heavy with purpose. The choices she made would shape the future of Deva Loka and beyond.

'Old wounds must sometimes bleed anew to cleanse the poison within,' she said in a fierce whisper. 'You may go now. I'll take it from here.'

This was fun. Call me more often, dearest sister!

Sighing partly with relief at the welcome silence that followed the shadow's departure, Saranyu prepared to confront the fraternal bond that had turned venomous, ready to sacrifice her peace for the greater Cosmos.

The sun had begun its descent, casting an aureate glow upon the ornate Gopurams of Deva Loka, when Saranyu stood at the edge of the celestial gardens. The once vibrant air of Deva Loka, pulsing with the energy of a thousand hymns, now felt like a fading echo, a feeble whisper of its erstwhile glory.

Saranyu's heart plummeted, the gravity of their plight anchoring itself in her chest. Her gaze drifted skyward. The early stars had begun their nightly vigil. They seemed to flicker with uncertainty, mirroring the turmoil in her heart. 'Affection or duty,' Saranyu whispered to herself as her thoughts spiralled inwards, 'twine together like the roots of the sacred banyan, each vying for the nourishment of my soul.'

She thought of Vivasvan, the Luminous Daystar, feeling the warmth that had begun to thaw her once-guarded heart. Now her love for him clashed with the loyalty she bore her kin. Saranyu clenched her fists, feeling the calluses born of wielding celestial weapons and crafting potent elixirs. 'Such is the burden of those who stand between worlds,' she muttered softly. Closing her eyes, Saranyu reached inward to the wellspring of power nestled within her core—the gift of her celestial lineage. With her heart fortified by love and duty, she readied herself for the invocation, prepared to summon the one whose light could guide her through the impending dusk.

'Beloved Vivasvan…the revered in the three worlds, the Bhuloka, Bhuvar Loka, Deva Loka.' The words escaped her lips, a silent prayer carried on the breath of desperation. 'Guide me,' she implored, her plea rising. 'Your radiance has never led anyone astray. I stand at the crossroads of destiny, beseeching your wisdom.' She breathed, 'Guide me, my love, through the path of Rta, the Cosmic Order, and Dharma, the Cosmic Balance.'

The air seemed to shimmer, responding to the resonance of her yearnings. She felt his warmth encircling her, banishing the chill of doubt that had engulfed her heart.

A gust of wind swept through the grove, stirring the flames into a frenzied dance as if echoing her inner turmoil. The scent of jasmine and sun-dried grass wafted in, evoking memories of days spent basking in his golden embrace.

'Saranyu,' a soft voice resonated from the depths of her being. It was not the casual voice of her shadow, but her own, as though the clouds had lifted from her mind. 'Choices forge chains or wings. What binds you may also set you free.'

Saranyu took a deep breath, releasing it slowly as if to dispel the fog of uncertainty. She stepped closer to the flame, her silhouette merging with the fiery glow. In her mind's eye, she saw Vivasvan's chariot blazing across the sky, his divine countenance serene amid the celestial expanse.

'Your silence speaks louder than the thunder of war drums,' she said, almost smiling despite the gravity of her situation. 'You trust me to choose wisely, even when the path is shrouded in doom,' she affirmed, her voice carrying a newfound conviction. 'For our love is the kindling that fuels the courage within me.'

Saranyu turned away from Vishvarupa's residence, her steps echoing with purpose. She would not let fear dictate her fate. The time had come to confront the darkness, with Vivasvan's silent blessing as her guiding star. The golden hues of Deva Loka dimmed as Saranyu's heart ached at the thought of life without Vivasvan. The vibrant gardens where they once strolled, now seemed like a mere echo of their love, wilting under the weight of her dread.

'Is love not the force that holds the stars in place?' she mused, her gaze piercing the twilight canopy above. 'Then let it be the power that upholds us through this strife.'

'Vishvarupa, flesh of our flesh, has cast his lot with the shadows,' Saranyu continued, her words cutting through the silence of Deva Loka. 'He drains the essence of our kin, leaving us bereft of might.'

The air shimmered again as if responding to her call, the very fabric of reality awaiting the response of the Day Star. Tension hung heavy, the prelude to the storm that threatened to rupture the delicate balance between Devas and Daityas.

'Only together can we mend the fissures wrought by deception,' she implored Vivasvan, the urgency of her message carried on the wings of a prayer. 'Join me, My Sun, before darkness claims the throne of day.'

A tear escaped her eye, tracing a silver path down her cheek, an offering of vulnerability to counterbalance the strength she projected. It fell to the ground, a tiny, glistening star amidst the shadows of doubt.

'Please,' she breathed, her heart a drumbeat in her chest, waiting for the symphony of his reply. And there, in the hush of anticipation, Saranyu stood resolute, the embodiment of hope in the face of the unknown.

As the light of dawn crested the horizon, spilling onto the pathway, casting long, ethereal shadows, Saranyu closed her eyes. She waited for Vivasvan, for the touch of radiance that would break the silence and illuminate her path forward.

Betraying a Brother

The silence that followed felt like an eternity, a void where hope teetered on the edge of extinction. Saranyu's resolve, however, did not waver. She clung to her faith, to the belief that Vivasvan, the All-Seeing, would not forsake her in her hour of need. He would not fail the mantra that he was supposed to abide by.

The sacred syllables cascaded from Saranyu's lips, resonating through the clearing. The air around her fell into a rhythm, charged with the energy of her mantra as if the very atoms were aligning with her will. The mantra echoed off the trees, wrapping Saranyu in a cocoon of sound, a protective barrier that shielded her from the chaos brewing beyond this sanctuary.

The invocation progressed, the connection with Vivasvan strengthened, a thread of light spun from her essence towards the heavens. Her mind's eye pictured the solar deity, resplendent and fierce, a beacon of hope amidst the gathering darkness of deceit.

And then, there he was, a brilliance banishing the shadows and bathing her in warmth. Vivasvan descended, his presence an inferno of comfort and might; his form both ethereal and solid, a God manifest yet untouchable—the paradox that was divinity itself.

The joy of seeing him was short-lived, for Saranyu had to invoke the protective shield that had now grown a voice, mind and identity of her own! But the time wasn't suitable for her deliberations. *Chhaya! My Shadow.* She called out in her mind, and sooner than expected came the answer. *Here I am, Sister!*

And what a magnificent mate have you been fated to have!

Saranyu ignored the giggle that followed in her mind and trained her gaze on Vivasvan. 'Luminous One, I bring grave news, a truth that tears at the fabric of our realm. Only you can show me the way.'

'Speak, Saranyu,' Vivasvan commanded, his eyes—a blend of compassion and unforgiving blaze—fixed upon her.

Her gaze did not shift from the God before her, finding solace in his unwavering light. 'Vishvarupa...he…betrays the realm of Devas!' she said hesitantly, the finality of her words hanging in the air, heavy with consequence.

Vivasvan's countenance, previously a warm daybreak, acquired the ominous hues of a looming storm. His aura, once a comforting presence, now pulsed with an intensity that caused the air itself to quiver. 'Betrayal?' Vivasvan's voice boomed, echoing across the Celestial Plane. 'How deep does this treachery run?'

'Deep enough to shake the foundation of Deva Loka,' she replied, her words painting the picture of a heaven on the brink of chaos. 'He conspires with the Daityas, feeding them secrets that could unravel our defences.' His face set with resolve, Vivasvan affirmed, 'The Cosmic Balance must be restored. The Cosmic Order depends on it.' The Deity's golden brow furrowed, the skies above mirroring his frown with the gathering dark clouds. Anger and concern warred on his countenance, a storm brewing within the depths of his radiant eyes. 'But the action must be from your side, Saranyu. My task is to bear witness!'

'I should take action,' Saranyu repeated. 'Confronting my brother may not be a wise idea. We know not about the forces of the realms of Atala, Vitala, Sutala, Talatala, Rasatala and Patala that may be assisting him.'

'Indeed,' Vivasvan nodded. 'We must be swift, yet cautious. Vishvarupa is cunning, but we have the light of truth on our side. We will expose his machinations and have them undone. Go, love,'

Vivasvan instructed, his eyes alight with the flames of foresight. 'Inform the King of Gods, Lord Manojava, of Vishvarupa's misdeeds. I shall make sure that truth comes to light.'

'Yes, Indra must be warned,' Saranyu's words cut through the serenity of the grove. 'Vishvarupa's deceit runs deeper than the roots of the ancient Ashwattha. But the allegation is against the Deva Guru. Will Lord Manojava heed my words?'

'Trust me, he should not sit on the throne of Deva Loka if he refuses to see the truth.' Vivasvan smiled. 'Truth alone shall be your strength, Saranyu, as you are mine.'

A smile touched Saranyu's lips, fleeting as the first light of dawn, but it did little to ease the weight on her chest. She backed away as the form of her beloved disappeared from her sight, and traced her steps back to the court of the Gods.

Will you betray our brother now?

Saranyu realized that the quiet presence of her shadow sister had lingered beyond its utility. 'I am only bringing truth to light! I am no keeper of the three-headed man's treacherous secrets!'

But don't you want to consult Tvashtra once?

Saranyu's steps faltered for a moment. Yes, her revelation would leave the decision to the King of Gods and the possibility of Purandhara being an incumbent Indra did not assure any clemency. But that was the will of Vivasvan.

What if Father would want you to protect our brother?

'I don't need your counsel!' Saranyu brushed aside the lingering doubts caused by her shadow and hurried towards the court. The Deva guards raised a hand signalling her to pause.

'Devi, the long audience with Purandhara and Bali is still on!'

But Saranyu marched on. And the guards did not have the courage or the energy to stop her.

'Lord Manojava!' Saranyu called out, casting a wary glance at the audience in the relatively empty court of the King of Gods. She knew she had broken protocol. Purandhara and Bali frowned at the interruption while Sachi's eyes widened with concern. Saranyu ignored all three and steadied her gaze on the King of Gods. 'You need to come with me!' her voice partly pleading and partly urging. A part of her was in a hurry to set matters right before her own sibling bond could weaken her resolve. 'Please come with me right now!' The rest of it was a prayer that only her mind could articulate—which she hoped that the Indra would understand.

And he seemed to. 'Wait for me.' Lord Manojava signalled his two probable inheritors and the Danava Princess, and followed Saranyu.

'When did you know?' was his quiet question when they were out of earshot of the Daitya Prince. 'Just now as I sought his audience and came to know that he was up to this ritual...' Saranyu's face contorted mid-sentence, unable to find more words as her mind conjured up possibilities of what could follow now.

'Does Tvashtra know?'

Saranyu shook her head. They paused at the entrance of Visvarupa's quarters in time to see the three-faced interim Guru of Devas leaving his abode.

Saranyu's gaze met her twin's; a second passed in their mutual outcries of betrayal. Of course, Visvarupa's second head had alerted him about her betrayal. *As had her newly crafted shadow being alerted her of his betrayal.* She saw those eyes on her brother's middle face narrow as if to say she would pay for this.

O Sister! He seems angry! The shadow that always had a hint of scorn in her tone seemed to shrink further within her. *We betrayed him!*

Saranyu ignored the voice and tore her gaze away from her brother to train it back on the King of Gods. There would be a trial. And things were going to take a turn for the worse for her. Just that something happened in the next few moments that proved her half-right and half-wrong. She saw the King of Gods signal to his soldiers to surround Visvarupa. The three-faced god scoffed and gazed at the approaching Deva soldiers who collapsed without as much as him raising his little finger.

As though the exposition of his deception meant nothing.

Indra called for more reinforcements. Vishvarupa only shook his head as his third head continued to chant something that Saranyu had not heard before. She exchanged a glance with the King of Gods and he stepped closer. 'Too late, Saranyu.' Her lips parted as the rest of her froze. 'I'll hold him off. Warn Purandhara and Sachi to save themselves. I have a feeling Bali is with Visvarupa in this!'

Saranyu gathered herself and rushed out, seeing more Deva soldiers assemble. And she knew their fate! Even the power of Amrita that was supposed to give them immortality seemed to fade. She did not have to run for long as Purandhara and Sachi met her halfway. The youngest son of Aditi was rage personified. With chaos taking over, Saranyu did not have to tell him what happened. Purandhara tapped the floor beneath them with his javelin. 'Dear Eldest, Vivasvan! Pray, conduct the ladies to safety!'

Saranyu saw Vivasvan nod, first at his brother, then at Sachi, consciously avoiding her gaze. This time, she did not feel his usual scorching radiance. And the realization struck them both. 'My brother's ritual weakened you too?' Saranyu stared at the Luminous One whose fire seemed to have less than halved. Vivasvan shrugged with a slight smile as though he did not want to complain.

'It is spreading fast! The effect of his dark ritual!' Sachi gasped. The Danava Princess stood her ground even as Vivasvan and Saranyu turned to make a move. 'I'll go with you.' She told Purandhara, resting her left palm on her hip as though she wasn't ready to listen to anything else.

'The battle is going to turn dark.' Purandhara frowned. 'And it is no child's play, Daughter of Puloma!'

'Child's play? You are the youngest born among us!' Sachi retorted.

'We aren't a day younger or older than thirty!' Purandhara hissed. 'And do you want to discuss age-groups when a war with darkness is about to break out?'

'You started it!' Sachi did not back away even when Purandhara strode closer. 'Visvarupa has unleashed a dark energy that is weakening the Devas. Your eldest seems no exception. Vishvarupa's own sister is no exception! But you are not yet a Deva. I am a Danava. We are immune! Now stop fighting me and let's both fight him instead!' A spark erupted from Sachi, blinding Saranyu for a moment. As she blinked, the Danava Princess assumed her warrior form, donning an armour, brandishing a goad.

Purandhara said something but his words were drowned by the roar of combat, by the resounding clashes that spoke of a Cosmic Order teetering on the brink. And in the heart of that maelstrom, two beings embodied the eternal conflict between divine duty and the seduction of power.

Saranyu felt Vivasvan's hand on her back, steering her away from the mayhem. And Sachi followed an unwilling Purandhara, giving Saranyu a mischievous wink as they parted.

'That was...' Vivasvan suppressed a smile, '...fiery. She suits my little brother.'

Saranyu smiled while the heavenscape shuddered, throwing her off balance. Vivasvan hauled her up in a trice. Their gazes met again—hers full of yearning, his mirroring her longing. He smiled as though he did not mind losing his radiance for this while.

My precious coy sister, who is going to inform our father of the mayhem you helped unleash now? The shadow spoke within her. And that brought her back to the grim reality that awaited her. 'I need to rush to my father, Vivasvan,' Saranyu's voice choked with emotion. And the Luminous One had the sensitivity to lead her back to her father with no questions asked, letting her cope with her turbulence.

They had just reached the entrance of Tvashtra's abode when Saranyu felt her heart lurch as though a string that bound her soul to something had snapped. Her chest tightened, choking her breath. The All-Knowing Daystar let out a sigh before stepping closer to steady her. 'They killed him?' Saranyu gasped. The darkness that had engulfed the Cosmos started to wane.

'Let it be known,' the unseen cosmic voice proclaimed, 'that the one who betrayed the Devas met his end at the hands of the youngest son of Aditi!'

And the truth stood like a wall between them. 'Your brother killed mine,' Saranyu said, her words bereft of emotion. 'And I helped it happen!'

∽

Rechana's face was etched with lines of grief, her eyes pools of pain that refused to spill over. She stood at a distance, bidding her husband to not dare come any closer. Tvashtra's face looked as though he had lost the ability to feel. Saranyu froze at the threshold; neither of her parents reacted to her presence.

'Father, it was...' Saranyu fought the turbulence within that seemed to throttle her words. 'He was weakening the Guardians of the Cosmic Order with his dark rituals!' But she had not expected her brother to be killed.

'They killed the one they had instated as their Guru! Guardians of the Cosmic Order, indeed!' Rechana's unshed tears evaporated in the rage brimming in her eyes. 'Your kind continue to be pardoned and glorified for every slip they commit, while mine get punished for any action that questions or challenges the bias, Tvashtra!'

'Rechana...' Tvashtra approached his wife in a vain attempt to placate her. Saranyu rushed over to her mother but Tvashtra held her back.

'You!' Rechana shook her finger at Saranyu's direction. The sentence hung in the air as Rechana chose to not spell it out, but when Saranyu's mother turned away from her, it hurt more than any curse would have.

The saga of the Devas and Daityas would continue, fraught with trials and tribulations. No number of peace treaties, cross-alliances and truces or agreements seemed to put a definitive end to the conflict. Not even during the Great Twilight when both stood a fair chance to occupy key guardian positions for the upcoming Manvantara.

'Mother, I could not help it. The Deva soldiers were collapsing. The heavens were quaking! The Gods above us would not have brooked my silence!'

'Your blood,' Rechana spoke, her voice devoid of its usual warmth, 'is no longer mine to claim.' Each word fell like a hammer on an anvil, shaping a new, unwelcome reality.

Saranyu's heart clenched—abandonment, betrayal's cruel sibling, now stood before her. 'Mother, please—' she began, but Rechana raised a hand to silence her.

'Not a word,' the matriarch commanded. Her eyes darted to the side where Tvashtra stood, his form shrouded in a mix of defiance and disbelief. 'You and your father are... I cannot...'

Tvashtra took a step forward, his jaw clenching. 'Rechana, love, what Vishvarupa did, you know things would have come to this end even if Saranyu had not alerted the Indra.'

Saranyu sighed, slightly relieved at her father's understanding, even though he refused to meet her gaze.

'We can heal from this!' Tvashtra pleaded. 'Let us not lose the hope of staying together.'

'Togetherness?' Rechana's laugh was bitter, resounding in the air like the call of a raven. 'Look around you, Architect of Devas. Our togetherness lies severed like Vishvarupa's heads from his body.'

Saranyu extended her hand to placate her mother but froze midway at Rechana's forbidding gaze. 'Your daughter's choices have led us here,' Rechana continued, casting a sweeping glance at the sombre sky. 'And my choice is to return to the shadows from where I came.'

With a fluid motion, Rechana turned, her back speaking far more than her lips ever could. As she strode away to the abode of Daityas, each step seemed to echo with a finality.

Saranyu clenched her fists tight, her nails digging into her palms, drawing forth the sting of her own flesh. 'Rechana!' Tvashtra's plea, as desperate as it sounded, was in vain.

The figure of her mother did not falter, her silhouette gradually growing smaller, merging with the horizon until it vanished completely, swallowed by the distance.

Saranyu felt Tvashtra beside her, his presence a reminder that not all was lost. 'She will return,' he murmured, more to himself than to her. 'When the wounds have healed and pride has lessened.'

'Forgive me, Father.' Saranyu collapsed to her knees. Yet, her father refused to look her in the eye.

'I understand what you went through, child.' Tvashtra's voice was hoarse. 'I understand why you did what you did.'

'Then why don't you even look at me?'

The Architect of Devas drew in a long breath. Saranyu sensed that it had taken a humongous effort on his part to look her in the face again. 'I know who influenced you as well!' Tvashtra frowned. 'And who lost his cool at the wrong moment and let his thirst for battle drive him as he recklessly beheaded my son.'

Her father gazed into the horizon, his eyes plagued by vacuum. 'But Lord Brahma will bid me to continue making diplomatic efforts to maintain peace between Daityas and us. And my first attempt will be met with demands that I cannot fulfil.'

Saranyu looked up at her father, and rose to her feet. Her father didn't bother helping her get up, nor did he console her. When she saw him, the grief in his eyes was replaced with something else.

'Leave this abode, Saranyu. Claim your future with the one who brought you to this.'

The effect of his words numbed her enough to send her hurtling down the skies down to Bhuloka or even to the nether realms. Disbelief, shock, hurt shook her to the core, one after the other, numbing her emotions, freezing her to the spot. Till she felt a hand grasp her wrist.

Vivasvan, who had waited politely, found it prudent to intervene. 'Come with me, love.'

The Wedding

'I know grief. I'll not even pretend with false consolation, Saranyu.' Sachi stated, braiding Saranyu's hair. 'I remember Lord Vishnu's Sudarshana Chakra slicing through the head of my cousin, Svarabhanu.' The Danava Princess pursed her lips. Saranyu suppressed a sob and squeezed Sachi's wrist.

'My brother and your cousin, both had crossed the line,' Saranyu said, staring at the distant skies. Outside the chamber, the hustle of preparations seemed to have picked up pace. But both Sachi and Saranyu spent a few moments in silent camaraderie.

It was the Danava Princess who recovered first, and turned her attention again to setting Saranyu's curls right as she helped fix a string of celestial blossoms, weaving them along the length of her lustrous hair. 'I should be in good cheer, Sister, and so should you try.' Sachi let go of the braid she had expertly woven and turned Saranyu around to face her. 'Today is the day of your dreams.' She gave an animated smile that finally forced a twitch on the corners of Saranyu's lips too.

'The day of my dreams, indeed,' Saranyu grimaced. 'Marrying the one I had always looked upon with awe and wonder, but without the blessings of those who birthed me. Does this not seem precipitous?' Saranyu's voice trembled, her eyes reflecting the shimmering gardens around them, alive with the hum of divine beings preparing for the grand event, yet distant from the vibrance.

'Lord Manojava has sent for Vasu Prabhasa, your grandfather. Grandparents' blessings are twice as strong as those of parents,'

Sachi announced in a prophetic tone. 'Don't ask me which Rishi said so. It is just the order,' she grinned.

This time, Saranyu beamed back. Her gaze slid along her long plait as Sachi went about adorning her with select pieces of jewellery from the pile that lay beside her. Lord Manojava had been sympathetic to Saranyu and had taken care of every little requirement of the bride as a father would have. Saranyu's gaze turned stern before she softened it with some effort. 'Any news of Purandhara?'

Sachi stilled, a cloud of sorrow passing over her otherwise lively face. Saranyu immediately regretted asking her the question. A moment later, though, she felt it was her duty as a friend to let Sachi express her grief. Purandhara had leapt into battle well before Indra could even denounce Vishvarupa formally, and had sliced off the three heads of the erstwhile Guru of Devas, thereby ending the possibility of his candidature as the next Indra. The youngest son of Aditi argued that every Deva had come under the influence of the dark power of Vishvarupa's ritual, and that beheading the traitorous Guru was the only way to remove the spell. The debate on his fate had raged on even as Saranyu struggled to deal with her parents abandoning her, though under the care of the one she loved. *And who loved her back in his own way.*

'He has retired to the abode of Mother Bhumi to atone,' Sachi stated as Saranyu heard the unspoken words: *I shall wait for him.* The Danava Princess was again quick to recover, bringing her characteristic cheer back into her eyes. She led Saranyu towards the golden bronze surface, to her own reflection.

A cascade of silk was draped over Saranyu's shoulders, dyed in hues of sunrise—coral, amber and gold. The delicate fabric clung to her form, accentuating her divine grace. Jewellery encrusted with rubies and diamonds gleamed against her skin, each stone catching the light with every movement, echoing the stars that had watched over her since time immemorial.

'Will I be enough?' she pondered inwardly, her mind a whirlwind of thoughts as complex as the cosmic patterns that governed the Universe. 'Am I truly prepared to stand beside the Luminous One?' Yet, amidst the flurry of preparation, a surge of elation coursed through her veins. This was more than a marriage; it was a confluence of powers that had to have its influence in shaping the destinies of all who dwelled within the three realms. She only had to discover what her role was.

And with that, Saranyu stepped out of her chamber, greeted by the fanfare of celestial music and the awe of countless Devas who had gathered to witness the union. The air was thick with the scent of jasmine and sandalwood, mingling with the heady aroma of incense that burned in golden censers.

Saranyu's heart raced as she took tentative steps through the corridors of the celestial palace, her hands lightly brushing against the intricate carvings of ancient legends that adorned the walls, where every corner whispered tales of eternity.

'Child,' a deep voice resonated, halting her mid-step. Saranyu could have screamed with joy. Tvashtra stood before her, his eyes reflecting wisdom born from epochs of creation and destruction.

'Father!'

The Celestial Architect would have embraced his daughter were it not for a warning from the Apsaras following Saranyu that he might ruin the bride's dress and hair. As his calloused palm brushed his daughter's face lightly, Tvashtra's expression turned solemn. 'You are the embodiment of beauty and vigour, Saranyu. But the life ahead is one of fierce flames and blinding light.' Saranyu looked at him, her expression earnest, her eyes widening at the revelation. 'The effect of the dark ritual on Devas will wane soon. And your state in the presence of Vivasvan will again be affected.' Had Saranyu not known her father better, she might have interpreted his words as a curse.

'But the wheels of destiny have already been set in motion, Father.' She gazed into her father's eyes, her face tranquil and resolute.

'We weave, forge and weld our destiny each day, with our own choices and actions, child,' Tvashtra said, moving closer, his own garments rustling softly with the weight of cosmic dust. 'The Sun God—your Vivasvan—is not just a consort. He is a force of nature, relentless and all-consuming. Being his wife will demand more than love, Saranyu. It will demand a part of your essence, a share of your radiance.' Tvashtra continued, his tone a mix of caution and care. 'Are you ready to shine alongside him, yet be distinct? To be a comfort in his solitude, yet not lost in his shadow?'

She listened intently, absorbing her father's words. 'Is anyone ever truly ready for such a transformation?' she asked, her gaze drifting towards the heavens visible through the open archway.

'I pray that Time will be a friend, and guide you on the way forward, my child.' Tvashtra blessed Saranyu, placing a hand on her shoulder, grounding her amidst the whirlwind of celestial anticipation. 'Learn the dance of his flames, let your light grow in its own time. There is power in patience, Saranyu.'

Saranyu nodded as a flicker of doubt that had been consuming her internally, surfaced in her eyes before they turned resolute again. 'I will learn, Father. I will adapt. I must.'

'Adaptation is the way of the Cosmos,' Tvashtra acknowledged, a faint smile gracing his lips. 'Then carry this advice close to your heart: let your love be the anchor, but never the chain. Preserve your essence, for it is what drew Vivasvan to you, and it is what will sustain both of you through aeons.'

With a deep breath, Saranyu resumed her path toward the sanctified grounds where her life would forever be entwined with Vivasvan's. The sound of her anklets chimed with each step, a melody of resilience and hope that echoed through the vastness of the realm of Devas. Her father had not abandoned her as she had feared. But there was no denying that she was the reason behind the wedge that separated her parents even as she herself stood at the threshold of marital bliss. That cloud would always cast a shadow on the light that was meant to illuminate her life ahead. Soon, her retinue of celestial beings, Gandharva women singing, and handmaidens, caught up with her.

'Every bride gets butterflies in her stomach,' replied one of the handmaidens, her voice lilting with mirth, mistaking Saranyu's thoughtful gait for jitters. 'But you, Goddess, will soon soar alongside the Sun himself.'

Saranyu managed a smile, though her gaze shifted to the preparations outside, seeking solace in the spectacle unfolding before her. The sanctified grounds were alive with the vibrancy of the impending ceremony. Devas bedecked in ethereal attire moved around gracefully, their cheer, chants and chatter harmonizing with the tinkling of wind chimes and the soft hum of celestial veenas. Garlands of star flowers and moon blooms, strung between pillars of luminescent cloud marble, swayed gently, while the air itself shimmered with the magic of the occasion.

As the Sun began its ascent towards where she stood, Saranyu felt her breath hitch. Vivasvan descended from his golden chariot in the sky, and seemed to pause as if to bear witness to the moment unfolding below.

'Are you contemplating the horizon or seeking answers within it?' Vivasvan's voice was warm like the first light of dawn, dispersing all traces of uncertainty that seemed to cloud her face.

Saranyu's lips parted. 'Perhaps both,' she admitted, her gaze meeting his. Their eyes locked, an unspoken understanding passing between them, a connection that rooted deeper than the foundations of the Cosmos. Or so Saranyu hoped.

'Come,' he said, extending his hand, radiant with a soft glow. Hand in hand, they moved through the throngs of Devas who busied themselves with garlands and silks, ahead of Apsaras who giggled and teased at what some killjoys might have called a bold approach by the groom of the day who could not even wait for the bride to reach the holy fire pit. The hum of activities was a symphony of anticipation, each note resonating with the sanctity of the impending nuptials.

'Does it please you?' Vivasvan asked as they admired the intricate canopy under which they would be united in the eternal bond of *vivaha*. Its pillars were crafted from beams of sunlight, solidified into pillars of warmth.

'More than I could express,' Saranyu replied, her heart swelling with love. The structure was a testament to Vivasvan's realm—resplendent, unwavering. 'Yet, it is not the *mandapa* but the Luminous One beside me who fills my heart with joy.'

'Even when the world spins faster than we'd like?' he enquired, his brow furrowed with concern.

'Especially then,' she quipped, allowing a playful smile to dance on her lips. It was an attempt to ease the weight of the moment, to brush aside the rapid pace at which they had been thrust together by destiny.

'Your smile,' Vivasvan mused, studying her face, 'is like the break of day, banishing any shadows of hesitation.'

'And yours,' she countered, her pulse quickening beneath the soft fabric of her costume, 'is the promise that no matter how dark the night, the Sun will always rise.'

The air shimmered with the resonance of divine music, a celestial symphony that wove through the constellation-draped sky of Deva Loka. A select few among the ones gathered knew of the new epoch that this wedding would usher in.

'Behold, the auspicious moment arrives,' pronounced a sage's voice as the Devas gathered in an orb of light, their radiant forms and eyes glimmering with eternal joy.

'My child, today you align your soul with the Keeper of

Daylight, the Lord of Planets and the Holder of Destiny,' said the officiating Rishi whose beard flowed like the river of Time itself. 'Let us begin the rituals,' beckoned the chief priest, his hands orchestrating the sacred fire that crackled with divine energy.

'May the Eternal Ones who prevail and preside through countless Great Twilights and endless Kalpas bless our path ahead,' Saranyu murmured, circling the flames alongside Vivasvan, the heat licking her skin—a reminder of the power she was binding herself to.

'May they illuminate our path,' Vivasvan responded, his hand finding hers, the touch sending a surge of warmth that fought against the cold fingers of doubt attempting to clutch her heart.

'Your glow outshines the fire,' she confessed, her voice steady, though inside her spirit wavered between elation and trepidation.

'Your radiance is the dawn that awakens my world,' Vivasvan returned, his eyes blazing with an intensity that could outshine the darkest eclipse.

As they completed the seven ritual steps, each stride a promise etched into the Cosmos, Saranyu felt her uncertainties recede like the tide under the pull of the new moon. Vivasvan's presence was a constant, his love the anchor in the vast ocean of her emotions.

The Devas hummed their blessings, a resonant chord that filled the space between the stars. And as the final notes of the heavenly music cascaded over them, Saranyu allowed the joy to eclipse her doubts, her soul alighting on the cusp of a new beginning with the Lord of Light.

The moment the final note of the celestial chorus faded, a hush settled over the divine assembly. Saranyu stood beside Vivasvan, her hands trembling like a leaf in the gentle breeze. Saranyu's breath hitched as she allowed herself to lean into his promises, her inner tempest quieting. She nodded slowly, the action setting free a cascade of golden flowers from her hair.

As they turned to face the priest, a venerable sage who had witnessed the turn of countless ages, the weight of their forthcoming vows seemed to solidify in the air around them. The Devas and celestial beings watched in silent reverence, aware that they were witnessing the confluence of mighty rivers of fate.

A symphony of conches and divine instruments swelled, echoing the triumph of love over apprehension. As Saranyu looked upon her husband, the Lord of Light, her spirit danced on the edge of a luminous future, their fates inseparably woven. Together, they stepped forward into the embrace of forever, to the unknown future of cosmic adventures yet to unfold.

Charaiveti – Way Forward

The celestial gardens of Deva Loka sparkled with a golden hue while bees buzzed with their melody and rhythm over flowers, almost reminiscent of the voices of Apsaras. Saranyu sat on a bench carved from luminous and fragrant sandalwood. Beside her sat the resplendent figure of Vivasvan, his aura resembling the first light of dawn. The couple were temporarily housed in one of the opulent mansions of the abode of Gods where every nock and corner brimmed with sensuous appeal, with the privacy that any newlyweds would deserve with just the support of celestial maids and guards who knew how to be discreet enough.

The ambience was quiet, yet resonant. Saranyu could not forget that while she sat in the lap of sensuous luxury and appeal, her mate having transcended those basal instincts, was an embodiment of the knowledge of enduring truth and order, of what lay beyond what always changed. 'Tell me, Vivasvan,' Saranyu began, her voice steady yet infused with an undercurrent of yearning, 'why must we endure this ceaseless Deva-Daitya conflict? Is it that both sides are truly seeking immortality? Or is the control of the Cosmos so alluring that one would conspire and kill their own kin?'

Vivasvan turned towards her, his gaze, though filled with tenderness, also deep and unfathomable. 'Immortality,' he began, the word hanging in the air like a soothing hymn, 'is not merely about enduring through the ages. It is about sustaining the equilibrium of the Cosmos. We Devas, we exist as guardians of this balance.'

Saranyu plucked a stray petal from a nearby lotus, twirling it between her fingers. 'But isn't there a certain beauty in mortality?' She watched as the delicate petal drifted downward, caught in the gentle zephyr. 'A finite life imbues each moment with meaning, does it not?'

'Indeed,' Vivasvan nodded, his lips curling into a thoughtful smile. 'To be mortal is to cherish every breath, every sunrise, every fleeting joy. Yet, for us Devas, it is different. Our existence stretches beyond the ebb and flow of time.'

'But what defines us, Vivasvan? Our experiences, actions, growth and love, or just the span of our lives?'

'Wise question, my love,' Vivasvan said, reaching over to grasp her hand in silent support. 'Perhaps it is only through understanding mortality that one can truly appreciate the essence of immortality.'

Saranyu looked up meeting his gaze, her eyes reflecting the complex turmoil of her existence, half-Deva, half-Daitya. 'And yet, the Universe is in a constant flux,' she mused aloud. 'Manvantaras change. Kalpas progress. Lord Brahma too retires and the Cosmos is sucked into Him. He wakes up to breathe out everything and recreates the Cosmos again. Where and what would we be in that new realm of existence? How can one remain unchanging amidst such transformation?'

'Change is the very soul of existence, Saranyu,' Vivasvan said, his gaze directed at the infinite sky. 'Our eternal, or let's say relatively immortal, nature allows us to guide and nurture these changes, to ensure harmony persists. Without us, chaos would consume all.' Vivasvan stared into the star-studded space around them, his gaze turning grave. 'Just that mortality seems to have disappeared, and is refusing to take birth again since Hiranyaksha ravaged Mother Bhumi. She who is the only one with the nurturing capability that can sustain multiple cycles of mortality now lies violated and barren.' The weight of his own words seemed to choke him. Saranyu traced her palm along his cheek and leaned closer. His hand wound around her, letting her breath soothe his chest.

'When the God of Gods rescued Mother Bhumi as the Great White Boar, did he not enable her to heal?' The quivering in her tone was not out of fear but out of empathy for the life-sustaining Mother. Vivasvan's arms tightened around her as though he felt her pain.

'Let us not make the mistake of assuming Mother Bhumi as a helpless woman, reeling under trauma.' Vivasvan brought his lips to Saranyu's forehead, his gaze still fixed on the skies where the blue-green sparkle danced. 'She might just be still disgusted at the extent of monstrosity that some can unleash on her, and is not yet convinced to birth and nurture another cycle of life.'

Saranyu attempted to nod, a part of her yearning to shift from the dialogue on the Cosmos and mortality, and just savour the intimacy of her luminous husband and test its limits. Vivasvan, though, still seemed lost in the legend of the past and the insights that time had gathered from history. 'It seems that before Hiranyaksha and Hiranyakashipu were born, Mother Diti who had them in her womb, had the inkling of the horrors they would unleash upon innocent beings. And she refused to birth them. So, she kept them caged in her womb for long, too long, till she could not anymore.' He paused, sensing Saranyu's growing discomfort and shifted his gaze to her eagle-brown pupils. 'But of the same Hiranyakashipu was born Prahlada, the greatest devotee of Lord Vishnu. And of Prahlada were born Virochana and your mother Rechana. Then from Rechana were you born.' He cradled her face in his large palms. 'I know that Mother Diti's guilt and pain would have reduced considerably.'

'This was a great attempt at wooing your half-Deva, half-Daitya wife, Lord of Light.' Saranyu winked. 'I am won over.'

The Sun beamed and pulled her into his lap. Then he turned

her over on her back, letting her bear the weight of his chest. 'I meant to say, Mother Prithvi may just need this gentle reminder that darkness will ultimately end in light. It is bound to. And she will heal to become the true Mother that she always has been.'

Saranyu arched her neck, letting his lips lend her their warmth. 'Maybe it is within this understanding that I shall find my place in this eternal conflict—between light and shadow, creation and destruction.' His eyes closed for a moment but then shot open. 'Yet, I am born of both worlds,' Saranyu said, turning to face Vivasvan, her stance firm, rooted like the ancient trees surrounding them. 'My Daitya blood courses through me just as strongly. Must I reject it to be part of this Cosmic Order you speak of?'

'Strength,' Vivasvan answered, tracing his thumb across her tensed brow, 'comes from embracing all parts of oneself. Your lineage grants you a unique perspective, Saranyu. One that is invaluable.'

'Your empathy, Vivasvan...it is balm to my troubled soul, so assuring!' Saranyu admitted, turning back to face him. Her fists unclenched as if releasing the last vestiges of self-doubt. 'I fear my darkness, but you...you see light where I see shadows.'

'Because there is light,' he insisted softly, 'even in the darkest of places. And sometimes, all it takes is for someone to remind us that it is there.'

His words cascaded over her like a cleansing river, washing away the sediment of her fears, leaving behind a bedrock of newfound confidence. Saranyu nodded, a silent vow etched in her eyes—a promise to herself to seek out the light within her darkness.

Their hands met, fingers intertwining, and Saranyu felt the truth of his assurance resonate within her core. She was not just Daitya or Deva; she was the harmonious convergence of both—a beacon of potential in this age-old conflict.

'Let us move forward, together,' Vivasvan spoke with conviction, his eyes reflecting the myriad stars above, 'for Dharma, the nurturing sustenance.'

'Together, for Dharma,' she echoed as his lips claimed hers. '*Charaiveti*.'

The Luminous Mate of hers perhaps had an inkling of the threshold she stood at, with a potential to lead the Universe towards the cusp of a new era. And he knew that she had to unravel many mysteries of existence in her journey. When they withdrew from the kiss, Saranyu saw in his eyes a myriad emotions. Empathy, assurance, love and deep compassion for the future he knew they would share. 'Love,' he tapped her chin. 'If you ever turn away from me…' he paused briefly as if to see the change of emotion in her eyes, 'I will find you.' If his lips hadn't curled, if his fingers had not been caressing her curves, the words would have struck fear.

'Was that a warning or an assurance?' she teased, tilting her face away from his lips.

'Make what you want of it,' he chuckled before his lips pulled at her ear, making her moan.

And the Cosmos braced itself for the next step beyond the Great Twilight.

Birth of Destiny

Saranyu clutched at the silken sheets with knotted fingers, as the next contraction shook her. Her body felt like a tempest brewed within, each contraction tearing through her. She breathed deep, trying to match the rhythm of her pain.

'Vivasvan,' she murmured, her voice barely rising. 'It is nearly time.'

'Stay strong, my love,' Vivasvan stroked her dishevelled hair, his warm hand wiping away the beads of perspiration.

'I hope they inherit your radiance and my…' Saranyu looked at her husband, the sudden inability to complete the sentence hitting her. The next wave of agony hit her, saving her from the current one raging in her mind. She would not succumb to doubt or despair, not at this moment.

'Your perseverance, love…' Vivasvan pulled at her arms, hauling her to a more comfortable position, willing her to look at him.

Was he being truthful or just compassionate towards the bride who trusted him? Was he considering her his equal or as someone who needed his refuge?

'Ah!' The cry escaped her lips as the force of creation surged and churned within her.

'Focus on me, Saranyu,' Vivasvan coaxed, his eyes pools of liquid amber. 'Look at me. You are the daughter of Tvashtra, the Architect of Celestial Realms. What comes out of this womb of yours will shape the destiny of the Cosmos too.'

Her gaze locked onto his, and for a fleeting moment, the world beyond their entwined souls ceased to exist. In those eyes, she saw reflections of the Cosmos—the birth and death of stars, the dance of planets, the eternal cycle of night giving way to dawn. And from there, from that celestial expanse, she drew her strength, and a vision of a future, however blurred. Her children, Vivasvan's children. Their children—they were coming to usher in a new era of the Cosmos.

'Shraddhadeva… Yama… Yami…' she whispered their names like a mantra, as if invoking them from the core of the Cosmos, her womb being a mere channel.

Saranyu bore down, her body a conduit between realms, every fibre of her being focused on the act of birthing. With a final, monumental effort, she surrendered to the natural forces at play, and the wail of a newborn pierced the air.

'Shraddhadeva, the one who does not swerve from the path of eternal truth, Satyavrata!' She heard Vivasvan's voice. The pride of a father intertwined with the pronouncement of a cosmic guardian, resonated in the intonations of his words.

'Again, Saranyu,' Vivasvan encouraged, his thumb caressing her clenched fist.

She gathered the remnants of her will. There was no room for fear; only the singular purpose of motherhood. As the second and third wave of cries joined the first, filling the chamber with the music of life, Saranyu slumped back into the pillows, her chest heaving with exhaustion and elation.

'Yami, the Nurturer of Life and everything that is beautiful… Yama…' Vivasvan paused as though he too was struggling for words to describe his vision of his youngest. Saranyu feebly opened her eyes to read her husband's expression. What looked like shock morphed into grave understanding before he smiled. 'The Impartial One, free of biases, the Guardian of Dharma!'

And there was something that he did not reveal about her third child. 'Beautiful,' she breathed, the word a prayer of gratitude. 'Aren't they beautiful, Vivasvan?'

The pain had been indescribable, transcending mere physical sensation to touch upon something profound and sacred. But now, cradled in her arms, swaddled in starlight, were three miracles—flesh of her flesh, bound to her by more than just blood.

'Indeed they are,' Vivasvan agreed, his voice thick with emotion. 'Just like their mother.'

Saranyu's gaze lingered on the three infants nestled against her chest. Her heart, still thundering from the ordeal, now raced with concern of a different kind. The firstborn, Shraddhadeva, had eyes that shimmered like twilight, almost a symbol of the times he was born into, with an unusual hue around his golden irises typical of Deva progeny. Yama bore an aura that seemed to still everything around him, as though he brought the past, present and future before him, his tiny brow already furrowed in what appeared to be contemplation or judgement. Yami, the girl, slender, vulnerable, and yet with a spark that showed that she was here to prevail, gurgled with a tiny smile. Her touch held a warmth that surpassed the expected gentle heat of Deva offspring.

'Look at them, Vivasvan,' Saranyu whispered, her voice tinged with awe and an edge of fear. 'They are...unlike any other.'

Vivasvan leaned over, his face breaking into a smile as he regarded his children. 'Different yes, but in such wondrous ways.'

Saranyu's hand trembled as she stroked Yama's cheek. 'But it is not just their appearance, or their auras. They are not fully Deva. There's something else... I can feel it. Could it be my Daitya heritage?'

Vivasvan's brow furrowed at her observation as though he did not approve of her wave of doubt. Saranyu saw him brush Yami's head almost protectively as if to compose himself. 'Even if that is so, Saranyu,' Vivasvan smiled, taking her hand in his, 'they hold the promise of a new era, owning everything that went into making them. Fear not their uniqueness, love.'

'Yet, the world judges those who deviate from norms,' Saranyu countered, her thoughts careening like wild deer. 'Will they be feared? Shunned? Will Lord Manojava bestow Amrita on them? Will the lingering shadow of conflict shape their place in this Cosmos?'

'Let the world learn to appreciate the cosmic complexity, than cling to the simplicity of a single thread,' Vivasvan replied, his thumb grazing her knuckles in a soothing rhythm.

'Simple for you to say, my love,' she responded, her voice laced with uncertainty. 'You are the sun, revered and mighty. But I—'

'You are their mother,' Vivasvan interjected firmly. 'You bear both the *light* of wisdom and the *shadow* of strength. They will inherit this balance, and it shall spur them on in their path ahead.'

Saranyu sighed, watching Shraddhadeva's chest rise and fall, as she took in Vivasvan's assurances. Her doubts lingered even as she struggled to understand why the infinite love of the Lord of Light was never enough to make her feel at ease.

'May it be as you say,' she murmured, her eyes tracing the delicate lines of destiny etched upon her children's faces. 'For their sake, I shall hope...and believe.'

'Each soul is born with its purpose, Saranyu,' Vivasvan said, his voice gentler. 'The Universe does not make mistakes. Our children, they are no exception.'

She turned to him, her eyes brimming with questions that teetered on the edge of fear. 'I just don't want my lineage to become their burden.'

'We shall teach them to rise above it,' Vivasvan replied, his gaze steady. 'They will be stronger for it, just as you will be, for them and for me.'

'Stronger or isolated?' Saranyu whispered, tracing a finger along Yama's tiny hand.

'Those who shape cosmic destiny always have to pass through the rite of isolation. Their own *tapasya* begins with cutting the self from the Universe, and culminates in making them integrate with each other.' Vivasvan countered, moving to cradle her chin in his hand, guiding her to meet his eyes. 'Come on, Saranyu, they are *our* newborns.'

Her Lord never put a reproachful thought into words. She knew even if he were annoyed by her doubts, he would not voice it given her state. She felt his lips descend on her forehead, the kiss almost like a silent plea to set her doubts to rest. She closed her eyes, not wanting to ruin a father's celebration.

Saranyu's thoughts spiralled inward, diving deep into the well of her own lineage. She was of two worlds—Deva light and Daitya shadow. It was a duality she had wrestled with all her life. She silently implored the Gods that her children be spared her inner strife. Would they inherit her resilience or her restlessness?

'Look at them, beloved,' Vivasvan urged, lifting Yami in his arms. 'Do they emanate anything but hope and joy? They are unique, yes, but they are also divine.'

'Divine,' Saranyu echoed, allowing the word to roll off her tongue like a prayer. In it, there was hope and an invocation for protection. She closed her eyes, hoping that she could share his conviction. His belief in her, in their progeny, was a fortress against the siege of her anxieties. But could a fortress stand unshaken forever?

'May they inherit your radiance, Vivasvan,' she murmured, opening her eyes to watch the golden light play across the room, casting halos around her children. 'May it guide them when the shadows from my past reach out to touch their future.'

For the umpteenth time in the short span of their marriage, Vivasvan repeated what he would always tell her, 'Shadows and light are not adversaries.' His tone did not betray the exasperation that she thought it would. A part of Saranyu actually hoped to see his emotions, his ire over her nagging self-doubts, something that would signal the finite nature of his patience. But neither his radiance nor his patience showed signs of hitting the bottom.

And for some reason, this did not sit right with her. 'Together, they create the balance of the world. Our children will embody this truth,' Saranyu heard him prophesy.

Nestling in the crook of Vivasvan's arm, she felt the taut strings of her worries loosen if only for a short while. Her breath came easier, syncing with the rhythmic rise and fall of her infants' chests. There was comfort in Vivasvan's certainty, a promise in his embrace that spoke of unconditional support.

∽

Time flew and Saranyu found rhythm in bringing up her children, nurturing and teaching them the ways of the Cosmos and about those who guarded it. She taught Shraddhadeva the language of the ancients, delighting in his quick mind. To Yama, she imparted lessons of fairness, watching his sense of right burgeon. And with Yami, she practised the art of leadership, seeing her daughter's innate ability to inspire.

Saranyu spoke with a heart swelling with love, 'Our children, Vivasvan, they are growing fast to assume their rightful roles.'

'I can see that,' Vivasvan replied, warmth suffusing his words. 'Well done, Devi. They are ready to forge their paths, powerful and unapologetic in their truth.' The Lord of Light took an additional moment to let himself experience the joy of seeing his progeny grow. 'About time they met the King of Gods, Saranyu,' Vivasvan urged gently, extending his hand. 'The future beckons.'

'This soon? Are they that ready?' Saranyu frowned, turning around to cast a glance at her children. It did not seem as though much time had passed since she had held them as infants. Deva progeny did not take time to grow.

Vivasvan let out a chuckle beside her. 'They will never be ready unless they are ready.' He held her hand. 'The Universe awaits them, love.'

∽

Time that seemed to fly past when she reared her children, suddenly seemed to slow down to a standstill as Saranyu and Vivasvan waited in the opulent gardens of Deva Loka. Their children were in the court of Sudharma, having an audience with the King of Gods, Prajapatis, Saptarishis and other primal Devas.

'Am I late?' The chirpy voice at the southern entrance made Saranyu look up and turn. She beamed at her old friend, Sachi, who had come to lend her the much-needed moral support, and embraced her.

'What happened?' The other male voice boomed from the northeastern gates.

'Talk about the timing of these two!' Vivasvan whispered to Saranyu, who froze at the new entrant, while he beamed at Purandhara. 'How does your tapasya fare, little brother?'

'How I wish I could say what you wish to hear, Eldest,' Purandhara said, jaws clenched before letting his own vulnerability show. He turned to Saranyu, his gaze softening. 'I never got to apologize to you, Devi.'

Saranyu gave a stiff nod; her brother-in-law did not seem too keen to earn her forgiveness for killing her brother. Nor did he show any inclination to explain himself. Almost as though what he had done was his job. Deva Loka had not fully recovered from the debilitating strike it had suffered under her brother's covert rituals. She noticed Purandhara's gaze survey the garden. She did not fail to see his eyes pause briefly as they landed on her friend.

'The waters have receded further from when I visited last in Bhuloka,' Sachi remarked. 'The cooling that happened after that fateful day of Vishvarupa's dark ritual also seems to have helped the land. The wild growth shows signs of colours and blooms.'

Saranyu did not know if Sachi was defending Vishvarupa's actions to Purandhara or just trying hard to mask her attraction.

'Unforeseen consequences,' Vivasvan mused. 'But what will

happen to this nascent life on earth when our radiance is back in its full glory?'

'If the understanding of heat that I gained during my tapasya means anything, heat or radiance is not what was holding back life,' Purandhara replied. 'Mother Earth needs to recover and rediscover her rhythm of nurturing the cycle of life. And She will.'

'How long are you in Deva Loka, brother-in-law?' Saranyu asked, even if only to overcome the awkwardness between them.

'I will need to go back to Bhuloka soon.' Purandhara looked at her, again without a hint of apology or hostility. 'Guru Brihaspati has agreed to take up his position as Deva Guru again.'

'That's a feat!' Vivasvan patted Purandhara. His secret hope did not go unnoticed by Saranyu. Vishvarupa's episode had created an undesirable vacuum during the Great Twilight: Bali, given his devious involvement, had to be immediately disqualified from being an incumbent Indra, while Purandhara had to give up aspiring to the position for committing the grave sin of *Guru Hatya* by killing Vishvarupa—a development that Lord Manojava, the outgoing Indra, would not have been pleased to handle as he had looked forward to training his successor well before retiring. 'Lord Manojava would have been relieved.'

Before they could discuss further, a shift in the wind alerted Saranyu to the arrival—of her children, and of the Gods and Rishis who had come to assess them. The moments from her sighting her children to when they came close to her seemed to last an eternity. 'Can you sense anything by their expressions? I mean they don't betray any emotion. Not even Yami!' She asked her husband. A look at Vivasvan's face told her that he knew of the result long ago. Long before this event. Long before their birth. Probably long before he had married her. 'At times, it is a blessing not to know what happens in the future.' She did not know why she said this. Perhaps it was the indignation of trying to look unaffected. And it only amused him. Saranyu straightened up as Lord Manojava stepped ahead from the group, sharing a knowing glance with Vivasvan before turning to her.

'Your first born, Daughter of Tvashtra, is endowed with a thirst for the knowledge of both the *iha* and the *para*—the transient and the intransient. And that…'—the pause was not one of hesitation or even of deliberation over the choice of words, but of the gravity of his pronouncement, '…makes us Devas and Rishis hope for a possibility of his…'

'Was my first-born given Amrita or not, Lord Indra?' Saranyu felt Vivasvan grip her wrist. And she saw the King of Gods signal to her husband that her interjection was fine. Given that she had betrayed her own twin for the greater good of Gods, and of the Universe, she had earned some tolerance for an outburst or two. Or more!

'To answer your question, not today, child.' Lord Manojava did not mince words. Nor did he attempt to placate her. 'There were things of immense gravity that the council deferred for a consultation with and pronouncement from the Lord Creator Brahma Himself.'

Saranyu turned frantically to her husband. The Lord of Light did not seem to have a reaction save for a smile that could be taken for courtly courtesy or detachment that was possible for the one that ruled over all knowledge along with light. Beside him, Purandhara's eye roll gave away his opinion of the outgoing Indra. Had they been alone, Saranyu would have heard her brother-in-law utter words such as *indecisive*, *procrastinator. No wonder the Cosmos is stuck in a never-ending era of the Great Twilight.* If not for the awkwardness over Visvarupa's killing, Saranyu would have whole-heartedly resonated with the youngest son of Aditi.

'How about Yama and Yami?'

'Your children have forged a unique cycle of purpose, Saranyu.' Lord Manojava beamed. 'Yama wants to safeguard the balance and has earned himself the position of a Dikpala. He shall protect the South.'

'But the South spells death,' Saranyu let out an anguished cry.

'We can worry about death when there is life...' The King of Gods' wide grin proved that he seemed to find his quip humorous, '...life that can be duly nurtured by your youngest one, *if* and *when* it takes root.'

The Trial of Radiance

'Tentative!' Saranyu let out an exasperated sigh, unable to suppress her disdain. 'Their future hangs in balance! And Deva, you let it be so!' She lashed out as they returned from Indra's abode. Purandhara had offered to take the children to a tour of Bhuloka and Sachi had followed them, promising to keep Yami company. Saranyu was thankful for she did not want her children to witness her vent her ire on her husband. 'You did not speak a word, Vivasvan!'

'Saranyu.'

'They aren't Devas.'

'Dikpalas are Devas.'

'You refuse to see the plain truth, Luminous Lord! It is my Daitya lineage that has come into play again... It is… For once, stop placating me and look at what it has done to our children, Deva!'

Vivasvan held her gently by the shoulders, turning her to face him. 'Pray, love. I need you to hold on to patience and hope. Our children will not disappoint us. Ever. Trust me, Saranyu.'

Saranyu looked up, meeting his gaze, tears blurring her vision. 'But I have let them down. I have let you down.' She let out an anguished groan. Vivasvan cupped her face, and she swallowed the rest of her words. They were going to be harsher than anything that she had said to him in the past. 'Stop giving me false hopes, Vivasvan. The least you owe me is the truth, however harsh. Remember Vishvarupa! This rivalry is never going to heal. We, the children of mixed heritage, have to live with the harsh fact. It is never going to end.'

'Saranyu!'

Anger was never a trait of her husband, but the moment was one where his never-ending patience seemed to wear thin. His forehead creased in an uncharacteristic frown and his eyes turned crimson. Saranyu though was past caring, the copious tears in her eyes blurring her sight. And then it happened. The skies quaked and the Universe tilted dangerously before finding a new equilibrium. An orb of brightness washed over the endless space around them. Vivasvan turned at the new light, sensing the celestial transformation. It was something that the Deva Loka would celebrate—a moment of jubilation, stability and direction in the tricky waters of the Great Twilight.

'Brihaspati, the Deva Guru, has ascended to his rightful position again!'

And it struck him. He turned back to meet her gaze as Saranyu still reeled from the shock of seeing his anger for the first time, and the momentous celestial change.

'Vivasvan, Deva!'

'Don't meet my gaze!' His hand blocked her eyes as the scorching heat engulfed her. A burst of light hit her vision before the world went dark.

'Saranyu!'

She must have lost her balance for Vivasvan's arm was her only support till he led her to the couch in their inner chambers, making her lie down. She lost count of the time that her consciousness gave her as a much-needed break, before she opened her eyes again.

'Saranyu! Thank the Creator!' Sachi rushed to her side as did Yami.

'Mother!'

Saranyu looked around for Vivasvan, but he was nowhere in the chamber. The skies outside shone with a brightness thought to be of the past. She could sense the ethereal beings of Deva Loka celebrating the return of the Deva Guru. The realm of the divine had gained the protection of their preceptor. As fate would have it, her spouse's radiance had attained its past glory. And it made him unbearable to her. Saranyu let out a sob as Sachi gathered her in an embrace.

'Testing times, my dearest friend. Stay strong, Saranyu.'

Saranyu composed herself. She was the daughter of the Celestial Architect. Tvashtra had taught her to invoke the cosmic forces, weld matter and craft tools of meaningful purpose. She had not seen her father for a while but the skills he had imparted to her remained with her. Turning to Sachi and Yami, she instructed, authority back in her tone. 'I need to be alone.'

Sachi gave a slow nod and backed away while Yami persisted, grasping her mother's hand. Saranyu softened, 'Leave now, child. You will see your mother recover soon.' She smiled, trying to be the reassuring being that a mother had to be. She needed that time alone.

Saranyu pursed her lips before chanting, trying to invoke the shadow self whose presence she had hoped would never be needed.

Now you remember me, Sister?

The voice was rebellious, laced with contempt as it uttered the word 'Sister'.

Saranyu frowned, offering no response. She would silence that rogue voice, weld the shadow to herself, and solve the problem of her marital life forever.

∽

'I am Saranyu. I am the daughter of Tvashtra, wife of Vivasvan, Mother of a future Dikpala.' The words summing up her energies and associations were spelt out to the Cosmos.

'The responsibility of nurturing the future protectors of the

Cosmos lies with me!' She whispered her will, the decision igniting a force within her core. 'I cannot, I will not let this be my destiny.' She closed her eyes, summoning every ounce of courage from the wellspring of her lineage. Visions of her children, mighty and resplendent, danced before her inner eye, stoking the fires of her determination. To see them rise, to ensure they had the guidance they deserved, she would walk through the inferno of transformation.

'Are you prepared for what such an attempt may cost you, daughter of Tvashtra?' The question was her own, a reflection of the doubts that had been her constant companions.

'The cost is immaterial when weighed against the duty I bear,' she answered defiantly, her gaze fixed on the horizon where Goddess Bhumi shone in Her characteristic blue-green sparkle. 'Let the Guardians of the Universe, the Creator Brahma, the Sustainer Vishnu, the Destroyer Shiva bear witness; I will not falter.'

With those words, she stepped back resolutely from the brink, her silhouette etched against the canvas of the skies

'May the Gods guide me,' Saranyu implored, her voice barely above a whisper. 'For I walk into the crucible, to emerge reborn or not at all.'

'O Agni, Purifier of All, lend me your flame,' she intoned, her voice steady despite the fluttering in her chest. 'O Vayu, Bearer of Breath, guide my resolve.'

'O Indra,' she murmured, invoking the name of the King of Gods, 'let your might be with me.' Saranyu grasped a slender rod of pure gold, a conduit for the celestial forces she sought to harness. 'O Father,' she whispered, not as a part of any ritual but as a daughter's plea, 'stand with me this day.'

At her invocation, flames sprang forth, encircling her with a ring of fervent heat. The air shimmered, reality bending at the edges of the inferno she had crafted around herself.

'By the ancient compact, I invoke thee, Tvashtra's fierce alchemy!' Saranyu cried out, her voice rising above the roar of the fire. The gold rod in her hand thrummed with power, its glow intensifying until it seemed as though she held a part of the sun itself.

'Transform and temper, forge anew!' With a swift motion, she plunged the rod into the basin, unleashing a torrent of mystical energies that coiled around her like serpents made of starlight. 'Chhaya! My shadow! Be united with me!'

Pain seared her body, a thousand needles pricking every inch of her being. Her cries mingled with the crackle of flames, yet Saranyu held firm. She owed it to herself, to her loving spouse and to their children. 'Endure,' she commanded herself, feeling her essence fray and reweave under the relentless force of the solution. 'For them. For all.'

Tears evaporated before they could fall; her skin glowed with an otherworldly luminescence, a testament to the transmutation she was undergoing.

'Let it be done,' she breathed, and the world turned white with the divine fire.

The divine fire that had consumed Saranyu's senses now ebbed, leaving an eerie silence in its wake. She opened her eyes cautiously, half expecting to see the remnants of her own body scattered like ashes upon a celestial wind. Instead, she found herself whole, her breath coming in ragged gasps as though she had been reborn from the very flames that had sought to consume her.

'Am I...?' she began, her voice a mere whisper against the stillness of her sanctum.

'Alive? Yes, you are, sister dearest,' came the response behind her. Saranyu froze. It came from behind her. Not from within. She whirled around, her heart a wild drumbeat. Standing before her was a figure identical to herself, down to the intricate patterns of the henna adorning their shared skin. The lookalike, Chhaya, gazed back at her with eyes that mirrored her own confusion.

'Chhaya?' Saranyu stammered, her mind reeling as she struggled to comprehend the impossibility before her. 'This, this…!'

'Yes, Chhaya, I like that name!' the doppelganger smirked, her tone imbued with a sense of wonder. 'And thus it feels to have an existence of my own!'

Saranyu's knees buckled beneath her; she braced herself against the pillar behind her. This was not what she had intended, to split her being and give life to another entity, yet here stood proof of the raw power she had unleashed.

'What trickery is this?' Saranyu screamed. 'You were supposed to weld into my core! Merge with me!'

'No trickery, Sister,' Chhaya said, stepping closer with a fluid grace that seemed both familiar and alien. 'We are two halves of a whole, yet distinct. Do you not feel it, Saranyu? The lightness within you, as if a burden has been lifted?'

Indeed, Saranyu did feel an unaccustomed ease, as if part of her spirit had been severed, taking with it the weight of her past struggles. But this cleaving brought forth a new kind of turmoil, one that gnawed at the core of her identity.

'By the Grandfather Brahma! What have I done?' she murmured.

'What have you done?' Chhaya echoed, tilting her head inquisitively. 'You did not mean for this to happen, but this is destiny, Sister. It seeks to give me my rightful marital life with our beloved husband! Don't you see the marvel!'

'A marvel, or a curse?' Saranyu pondered aloud, her hands trembling.

'Are you afraid?' Chhaya enquired, her voice laced with concern that Saranyu wasn't sure was genuine. The shadow-turned-new-being scoffed. 'During that phase of fated convenience when Vivasvan's radiance simmered down, you *conveniently* forgot about my existence! Yet, here I am, to assist you through your tightrope walk of marital life.' The gleam in Chhaya's eyes belonged to another world—*the realm of Daityas!*

'Come, sister dearest,' Chhaya offered, extending a hand that shimmered slightly, as though not entirely of the same substance as Saranyu's own flesh. 'Let us discover what destiny has in store for us!' In that outstretched palm, Saranyu saw not only the image of her physical form but also the embodiment of her deepest desires and fears. The potential for both chaos and harmony lay within this being who had sprung from her essence, and in that moment, Saranyu understood the duality of her own nature made manifest.

'But your presence... It splits my identity, fractures what I thought was whole,' rued Saranyu.

'Split or multiplied?' Chhaya challenged gently, her feet barely touching the floor as she circled Saranyu.

'Multiplied?' Saranyu scoffed under her breath, her thoughts a whirlwind of doubt and defiance. 'You are an echo, not a being in your own right.'

'An echo with form and purpose,' Chhaya countered. 'I can do what you have found burdensome. Isn't that why you sought Father Tvashtra's solution? To ease your load?'

Saranyu took a step back, her chest tightening. 'Yes, but not to create another entity! Not to divide my soul!'

'Consider this,' Chhaya said, her voice soothing. 'I possess your resilience without the shackles of your past. I am what you desire to be—unburdened, unfettered by the chains of legacy. Let the past be, Sister. Let us not be at odds,' Chhaya implored, signalling truce for the first time, reaching out her hand once more, its outline shimmering with a strange luminosity. 'Together, we could be formidable.'

Saranyu hesitated, feeling the pull of kinship and the push

of fear simultaneously. To accept Chhaya's hand would be to acknowledge her existence fully, to acquiesce to a future altered by her very creation. Could she share her life with this spitting image of herself, born of desperation? Her soul cried out for solitude, for the simplicity of being one, not two.

With a deep breath, Saranyu lifted her chin, steeling herself against the uncertainty that gnawed at her resolve. 'Time...' Her voice trailed off as she stared into the future, seeing the various paths leading to it now split before her. 'Time will tell if this is a blessing or a bane,' Saranyu murmured, more to herself than to Chhaya. She withdrew her hand, not yet ready to bridge the gap between them, not yet ready to embrace the sister born of her spirit. For now, she needed to wrestle with the reality that her solitary journey had taken an unforeseen turn. 'And Chhaya, your manifestation, is a phenomenon I am yet to comprehend.'

'My manifestation…' Chhaya's words seemed like an echo of Saranyu's, 'is not a phenomenon beyond comprehension, Sister, but of admission—that you need me.' Chhaya's eyes narrowed. 'And yet, you hesitate to face the truth. You refuse to embrace it.' She hauled a brow and shrugged. "So here I am. A part of you, yet a complete me!"

Saranyu watched her lookalike, studying the intricate patterns of her attire, different in shade but identical in design, the gravity of their situation reflected in each word, each glance. 'You possess my face, my form,' Saranyu whispered. 'But the essence that animates you is woven with threads foreign to my soul.'

'Indeed,' Chhaya nodded, a smile touching the corners of her lips. 'Your own essence which you always doubted, almost despised. Result, the one ability you possessed to bear the radiance of Vivasvan is no longer a part of you!'

Saranyu clenched her fists, the gilded threads of her garments digging into her skin. 'Think of your children, Sister,' Chhaya urged, her dark gaze seeming to focus on the distant sky. 'In relinquishing your position, you grant them continuity, stability.'

Saranyu rose, pacing the length of the chamber, her shadow mingling with Chhaya's. 'I have borne the mantle of responsibility since the dawn of my consciousness, but to yield it...'

'...is to show the greatest strength,' Chhaya completed her thought, standing up to meet Saranyu's troubled gaze. 'Act not out of pride, but love.'

'Love,' Saranyu repeated, the word carving out clarity from her tumultuous thoughts.

'Think about it, Saranyu. You can barely meet Vivasvan's gaze.' Chhaya's words were hard facts. Yet, an invisible dagger pierced through Saranyu's chest. 'The resulting imbalance in the household is bound to affect your children. Can Shraddhadeva, Yama and Yami grow up to fulfil whatever glorious roles you hope they can, when they see their mother failing to stand up to their father's radiance? This incompatibility between their parents... won't it fill them with bitterness even before they take on their destined mantles?'

'Enough!' Saranyu raised her hand, facing her ethereal twin. 'You win this, Chhaya,' she conceded, biting her lower lip. 'And what of you, *Sister*? What do you desire?'

'Desire is a human affliction,' Chhaya said with a serene smile. 'I wish only to fulfil the purpose for which I was conjured.'

Saranyu's chest swelled, a tangle of admiration and sorrow. In Chhaya, she saw the resolve she had always wielded like a shield. 'You shall take on my role in the household of the Lord of Light?'

Her lookalike shrugged with a grin. 'Neither the Lord of Light nor his children will feel your absence, Sister.'

'Then let it be so,' Saranyu declared, her voice steady despite the tremor that threatened to break through. 'For the sake of my children, for the continuation of our lineage, I bestow upon you my role.'

'Then I shall serve as their guardian, as their mentor,' Chhaya vowed, her voice a solemn melody.

'Until time deems otherwise,' Saranyu added, releasing Chhaya's hand. She turned away, her gaze lingering on the fading light that filtered through the chamber's windows. A new era was dawning, and though her heart was heavy with the sacrifice, it was also buoyant with the hope that her children would thrive under Chhaya's watchful eyes.

With a final, lingering look at Chhaya, Saranyu stepped toward the threshold of the chamber, knowing that with each step, she walked further away from the home she once thought inseparable from her being, and closer to an uncharted destiny. She turned and saw the ethereal gardens that were in eternal bloom.

'If you ever turn away from me, I will find you.' It was a playful threat that her luminous spouse had intoned when he had taken her to his bosom in the hours of their marital bliss.

'I know that you know everything, Deva.' Saranyu's lips quivered as she caught sight of the distant red ball of fire on the horizon. 'I leave it to you—whether you wish to let me go, find me and reclaim me, or leave everything to the hands of Time.'

∽

Saranyu's steps echoed through the hallowed corridor leading to Tvashtra's sanctum. She owed him this visit before she yielded herself to the future. And she deserved answers, perhaps this time, before she let uncertainty claim her existence. She paused before the ornate threshold, inhaling the mixed scent of matter and metal manifesting from her father's craft.

'Father,' she barely whispered. 'Hear me out one last time.'

Tvashtra hurried out of his workshop, his wrinkled forehead bearing proof that he had turned his solitary existence to an incessant phase of work.

'Saranyu?'

'Something unexpected has transpired,' she began, not letting him or herself give in to the moment of an emotional reunion. 'In my pursuit to resolve my…insufficiency, I have... created another.'

'Another?' Tvashtra's brow creased ever so slightly, betraying his curiosity.

'Chhaya,' she uttered the name; it felt like relinquishing a part of herself. 'She is me, yet she isn't. And I…' Saranyu paused, gathering the shards of her resolve, '…she takes my place, playing me, even as we speak.'

'She takes your place?' Tvashtra repeated, his brow furrowing. 'You entrusted your… everything to this...manifestation?'

Saranyu nodded, trying to appear resolute, while her hands trembled by her side. She clasped them together to still their betrayal.

'Does Vivasvan know?' Tvashtra asked, his gaze piercing through her façade.

'Perhaps,' Saranyu admitted, allowing vulnerability to colour her tone. 'And I hope he shall ensure that Chhaya provides the children what I no longer can.'

'And what do you seek to do now?' The Celestial Architect made no attempt to hide his concern, even disapproval.

'I need to work on my own lack, Father!' Saranyu clung to his arms, finally letting the pressure in her chest dissolve.

'My child!' Tvashtra kissed her forehead and framed her face in his calloused palms. 'You lack nothing.'

'Except the ability to look My Lord in the eye when I have done no wrong!' Saranyu sobbed. 'Show me the way out of this predicament now, Father. I cannot let Chhaya impersonate me for eternity!'

'The solution is tapasya, child.' Tvashtra fought back his instinct to cringe. 'That was not what I would want for you as your father. But when our efforts and interventions fail, the way forward is to surrender to the All-Pervading Shakti in the Cosmos and forge your will with the hammer of your resolve and the tongs of your devotion. Go forth to Bhuloka, child.'

Shadow in the Household of Light

Bhuloka

In the twilight of dawn, where the first rays of Vivasvan's radiance had yet to kiss the earth, Saranyu stood resolute amidst the tangled wilderness. 'Tapasya,' she whispered to herself, the word slicing through the morning stillness. 'It is through fire that gold is strengthened.' Her bare feet tread softly on the fallen leaves as she ventured deeper into the heart of the forest. 'May I emerge from this crucible, not just as Saranyu, Daughter of Tvashtra, consort of Vivasvan, but as a being transcendental, and yet whole unto myself.' Her declaration hung in the air, a solemn vow to the deities that watched over her. 'May this tapasya be my chisel, and my will the sculptor's hand.'

With those words, Saranyu returned to her meditation, the inner tempest quelled for now, her heart fortified with newfound insight. The journey ahead would be demanding, but within her pulsed the nascent beat of transformation—a rhythm that promised to reshape destiny itself.

Except that her tapasya was not going to be like that of others. Saranyu could not afford to stay rooted to a spot and hope to remain hidden from the gaze of Vivasvan. She had to keep moving along the surface of Bhumi, escaping his rays. There would come a day when she would face him. She promised herself. She would face him as his equal. But the day would come after she reclaimed

what destiny had denied her. She would reclaim that part of herself which would empower her to meet his gaze.

'And that is my will and resolve, Gods of the Universe, Goddess who rules over the Multiverse!' She looked up, willing the forces, seen and unseen, to grant her the form that would keep her moving.

The trees bowed gently as if in reverence to her conviction, and the wind carried her resolve across the land. 'Here, where the world's eyes do not pry, I shall unearth the power within me that slumbers,' she affirmed, gazing at the sky where her husband would soon blaze in his celestial path. 'Even you, my beloved Deva, must understand this solitary journey I undertake.'

She knelt on the soft bed of moss and closed her eyes, summoning the inner fire that had dimmed under the shadow of her roles. Her breath became a silent rhythm, a dance of the life force that prepared her for the rigours ahead. 'Agni, Divine Purifier, lend me your strength. Help me acquire the form that will take me along the circumference of Bhumi and keep with the night.'

Her body remained still, a statue carved from flesh and bone, yet her mind traversed realms unseen. 'Guide me, Shining Ones,' she called out to them, her voice a mere breath in the silence. 'Bear witness to this transformation.'

And the Gods seemed to bless her resolve, at least the first step, she mused as she felt her ethereal form morph into something swift and energetic—four legs to keep pace with the moving earth, a silky mane that would remind one of her celestial beauty, and a gaze that pierced the darkness ahead and gave her the vision required to move forward. She had turned into a mare, an Ashvini, the feminine form of an Ashva, almost like an earthly descendant of Uchchaishravas, the Lord of Equines, that was born out of the churning of the Great Ocean. And the mare journeyed into the night even as the day pursued in her wake.

A tempest raged, both within and without. With the wind behind her, the mare journeyed along at her celestial speed, matching that of the seven steeds that pulled her husband's chariot. The soil beneath her felt the familiar warmth. The grass softened under her hooves. The land she tread on experienced a wave of coolness in the nights that contrasted with the heat of her husband's heightened radiance during the day. Saranyu's tapa gathered within her the heat left by Vivasvan in his wake.

Who among you is chasing who, dear child? The soil beneath her seemed to ask.

Rest among us, dear Mother. The creepers of wilderness seemed to invite her. *We shall shield you from the eyes of your Lord if that is what you seek.*

Saranyu smiled her thanks and continued on her way. Fatigue was unknown to her, at least to her equestrian body fashioned out of her resolve, and the blessings of the Gods who were with her. In the emotional cycle of heat and cold, vast expanses of arid land experienced precipitation. Rain hammered down upon the sand, and rivulets and streams snaked through the underbrush of where she tread. In every round of her pilgrimage along the sphere of earth, Saranyu would experience a new growth of life, of wilderness transforming into something brighter and softer, into blooming creepers and nurturing trees, into grasslands interspersed with streams of water that flowed from the endless rain. It was as though every nook and corner of the mass ruled by Bhumi Devi awaited her footsteps and responded to them with a new spring of something more beautiful. In her sparse moments of rest and meals, Saranyu would experience the hospitality of the elements around her.

'Am I truly prepared for what awaits me at the end of this journey? Is there an end to this journey in the first place?' The questions clawed at her, seeking chinks in her resolve. She shivered, not from the damp chill that clung to her skin but from the realization that the greatest adversary she faced was her own uncertainty. 'Had the All-Knowing Luminous One failed to recognize the shadow from the light?' She pondered aloud, the vulnerability in her own voice startling her. 'Do they not even feel my absence?'

'Enough!' the stronger side of the mare would neigh against the noise of the storm as she forced her attention back to the present, to the sensation of the earth beneath her, solid and enduring. 'I am here to forge a new strength, not wallow in sentiments.'

'Yet, are you not also a mother, a partner? Can one part of your being simply eclipse the others?' The internal dialogue was incessant, each question a reflection of her conflicted self.

'Balance,' she declared to herself, the term a mantra to anchor her wavering spirit. 'In the mastery of the self lies the harmony of all roles.'

The rains subsided gradually, giving way to a pleasant dry spell when the moon shone brighter. The expanse looked festive, on sky and on earth. A gentle breeze caressed Saranyu's cheek, whispering secrets of ancient sages who had walked the path before her, who had sanctified the places she trotted along, as though their sheer presence had contributed to the transformation of Bhumi like her own unique tapasya in motion did.

'What wisdom lies in their silence?' she mused, her gaze following the dance of leaves caught in the wind's embrace.

It was then that she ventured into unexplored parts of the wilderness, leaving the hospitable grasslands. Perhaps the mare in her thirsted for adventure and encounters—encounters with Rishis and *tapasvis* whose presence could silence the nagging uncertainty within her. She had met the Saptarishis whose mere presence was believed to dispel misery. She had heard of others whose existence kept weakness, fatigue and negativity at bay. But as the forests grew thick enough to block the ray of the Sun,

Saranyu's search was met with empty wilderness. She trotted on, through the changing terrain, at times pausing in dark caves and dense groves when the rest of the land was awash with the golden rays of her beloved. She came out in the nights and made the most of her journey, admiring the silvery light of Chandra, the moon, a delight that made her crave the company of her luminous mate, a delight, she realized feeling a sense of pity, that her husband would never be able to indulge in for his very brilliance would drown that of Chandra's. Perhaps the indulgences that were denied to him by virtue of his role and existence did not mean much to him, for Vivasvan was an entity that embodied not just light that made things visible to the eye, but also made the nuances of eternal knowledge clear to the mind.

'Vivasvan,' she intoned as the first ray of the Sun touched her forehead. 'Even as I toil to escape your gaze, I seek you to illuminate my inner spirit. There has to be a destination to this circular journey. And that destination is by your side, with no flaw etched on my soul.'

By now, changing terrains and weathers were a constant that Saranyu encountered. So were the changing aspects of what she partook as meals to keep her equestrian body going. The earth seemed to yield fruits and roots, seeds and grains of tastes that were unique. '*Annam Brahma*,' she murmured, acknowledging the divine in her nourishment. '*Raso Vishnu. Bhokto Maheshvarah*.'

The pleasantness of autumn faded into long dark nights, into a phase where Saranyu could slow down her pace though a chill of a different kind tore into her skin. 'Tapas is the fire, and I am but raw ore,' she reminded herself, seeking the heat within to keep herself guarded. 'Heat and cold alternate with each other; monsoon and autumn contradict one another, while summer and winter may vie with each other for their effect to pervade the earth, but little do these temporary children of time influence Mother Bhumi, for she remains constant, despite the ravages of time and what they bring in their wake.'

And so the dance of day and night continued, a relentless pursuit of spiritual metamorphosis. Saranyu shed layers of her former self like leaves that fall to enrich the soil from which new life springs.

With each passing day, nature had something new to manifest to her. Saranyu was becoming the embodiment of the wisdom that the Cosmos chose to unfold before her even as her own self transformed, yet stood firm, unyielding as the mountains, fluid as the river, and radiant as dawn.

Encounters

The terrain sloped and the ascent became harder, but what greeted her hooves was the soft tingling of snow. The chill around was daunting but the heat of her resolve prodded Saranyu on till she realized solitude was no longer hers. Mother Earth signalled a presence and the mare paused. A Gandharva, a celestial musician, with wings that shimmered like morning dew on spiderwebs, alighted before her.

'O Daughter of Tvashtra,' the Gandharva spoke in tones as melodious as the veena's strings. 'Your gait is the rhythm from which the world has found enough solace to weave the dance and song of life. Yet, tell me, what rhythm beats within your heart when you think of those left behind?'

Saranyu's breath faltered. The faces of those she loved flitted in her mind's eye—Vivasvan's radiant gaze, her children's laughter. Her hooves dug deeper into the snow.

'Love,' she confessed, her voice barely audible, 'is the harmony I long for. Yet, I cannot allow it to be my undoing, or that of those for whom I am responsible.'

'Strength lies not in detachment alone, Devi,' the Gandharva intoned, his wings rustling softly, 'but in the wisdom to place the melody of affection into the monotoned hymn of duty.' With a nod, the celestial being disappeared, as if he had merged with his own song, leaving Saranyu with a heart both heavy and enlightened.

Hours melded into days, the chill around her too warming up and the terrain before her showing colours of the changing season again. Saranyu admired the new gift of nature to her eyes—valleys of blooms that sparkled as the silver crescent turned into gibbous and then to a full ball of ethereal glow. Saranyu started her downward journey, back into the thick growth, experiencing the greetings of new forms of life. Some stayed rooted to where they were born. Some ventured around with legs of their own. Some flew distances, long and short, only to land back on the soil where they belonged. The company of life churned a different kind of nostalgia in her heart.

'Am I forsaking my duties as consort and mother?' She grappled with the question, her throat constricted. 'Is my quest for self-improvement but a guise for selfishness?'

'Who speaks of guilt amidst such a valorous pursuit?' The voice rumbled like thunder, commanding yet unseen. An echo resonated from the surrounding trees. From the shadows stepped forth a Yaksha, stout and stern, his eyes gleaming like polished coal.

'A guilty conscience is the shield of the weak,' Saranyu retorted, steel in her tone. 'I wield mine as a sword, cutting through illusion to seek truth.'

'You speak with the courage of a warrior,' the Yaksha acknowledged. 'Yet, remember, the fiercest battles are often waged within the silent chambers of one's own soul.'

The entity melted back into the darkness, leaving Saranyu to ponder over his words amidst the chorus of the night creatures. Memories of her family danced before her like flames—warm, inviting, yet painfully out of reach. 'May even this longing solder my essence,' she resolved, her voice a mix of pain and power, 'as fire refines gold.'

Yet, even as she spoke, tears betrayed her, furrowing down her cheeks, each droplet an ocean of love and sacrifice. Saranyu shook them off. She would not succumb; she could not, for she was forging her tapasya not just for herself, but as a legacy for all who would follow her path. 'Let these trials sculpt me,' she whispered into the silence, 'into a vessel worthy of the divine.'

Surya Mandala

The golden rays of dawn washed across the heavens, but the glow fell flat in her presence. Chhaya stood at the threshold of the celestial palace, her silhouette a spitting image of Saranyu's. But while Saranyu's presence had always been a comforting beacon of warmth and strength, Chhaya's was tentative, her eyes betraying the weight of the mantle she had assumed.

'Mother?' The voice of Yama cut through the morning stillness, laced with confusion.

Chhaya turned, offering a smile that did not quite reach her eyes. 'Yes, child,' she replied, though her voice lacked the resonant timbre of Saranyu's.

'Will you not lead the rites today?' Yama enquired, his young face crumpled with worry.

'Of course,' Chhaya said, stepping forward. Her hands, though steady, felt alien performing the sacred gestures that Saranyu had done with effortless grace.

As she moved through the rituals, her thoughts were tumultuous. *Am I just Saranyu's substitute, an unwanted part of herself that she discarded to pursue something better?* She quelled the doubts, knowing that her role was vital to maintaining order and balance in the household of the Luminous God while Saranyu sought her enlightenment.

Vivasvan watched from afar, his distant resplendence a mask of serene acceptance, but his heart churned like the fiery surface of his celestial body. He missed Saranyu's vibrant energy, her unwavering certainty. With Chhaya, everything seemed a pale imitation.

'Father,' Shraddhadeva approached him with Yami in his tow, concern etched on their youthful faces. 'Is everything alright with Mother?'

'Why do you ask so, children?' Vivasvan smiled, seeking the tranquil equanimity that usually graced his first-born's face and the vivacious sparkle that had danced in Yami's eyes.

'She seems different, as though something has changed,' Yami uttered, her gaze alternating between Chhaya's silhouette and her father's gaze.

'Change is the only constant,' Vivasvan responded, his voice an echo of the depth of space. 'Even the sun must sometimes be shrouded by the jaws of Svarbhanu.'

'What is bothering her? Why doesn't she tell us?'

'We must give her the time she needs,' Vivasvan stated, not betraying his knowledge of what had transpired, though he too longed for Saranyu's return. A part of him wanted to pursue her. The rest of him held back, in quiet acceptance that the separation was a phase of strengthening what existed between them.

Chhaya performed her duties diligently, but her touch lacked the authenticity of the true matriarch that was Saranyu. The attendants whispered among themselves, while the children grappled with the subtle yet lasting differences in affection, guidance and authority.

'Tell us a story, Mother,' the children would implore in the evenings, seeking the comfort of tales spun from the threads of wisdom and magic.

Chhaya would comply, narrating epics and legends, her voice weaving images of gods and demons, of valour and virtue. Yet, the children sensed the lack of lived experience in her storytelling, the absence of Saranyu's heartfelt connections to ancient lore.

'Your stories are nice,' they would say, politeness masking their yearning for Saranyu's animated recitations.

'Thank you,' Chhaya would respond, her heart aching with the awareness of the gap she could not bridge.

Late at night, when the palace lay draped in the velvet cloak of darkness, Vivasvan would find Chhaya gazing at the dense forest, her figure bathed in the milky moonlight.

'Are you well, Devi?' Vivasvan would ask, remembering not to take the name that did not belong to the woman before him but unwilling to expose the secret that his beloved chose not to share with him.

'I am,' she would reply, turning to face him. 'Just contemplating the enormity of this responsibility, of being your spouse.' Chhaya looked at him with a keen expression that Vivasvan knew never belonged on Saranyu's face.

'You give your best; we all are witnesses to your endeavours,' Vivasvan assured her, though his gaze wandered to the stars, searching for the essence of his absent consort.

'Appreciated, but not sufficient,' Chhaya whispered to herself after Vivasvan departed, her words dissolving into the cool night air.

As the days melded into weeks, the inhabitants of the luminous mansion adapted to the change, accepting Chhaya's presence and ways as the new normal, without recognizing her truth, yet always with a sense that things were somewhat amiss.

The Guru beneath the Banyan

Bhuloka

Saranyu journeyed on with no clear intent about her destination, through the ancient forests. The number of times she had walked over the same place though in darkness should have made the land familiar to her. Yet, nothing seemed to be so. The trees hung close, their limbs intertwining like an intricate web of destiny that seemed to hold her in a relentless grip of introspection.

'How should I know where this takes me. Am I destined to undergo these endless cycles forever?' Her voice was barely a whisper, yet it seemed to ripple through the silence, reverberating within and without. 'Have I failed them, my family? Did I willingly give up when I should have fought more?' The words felt bitter, yet they poured out like libations upon the earth—honest and raw.

'Would they be as lost as I am?' Saranyu whispered to herself, moving through the foliage of the thickets that blocked her way. The forest listened, its only response being the rustle of leaves and the rhythmic chirping of the various life forms that moved, including the six-legged creatures that remained hidden but whose chirping was loud enough to echo through the forest. From the cacophony, it seemed as though the forest understood and even echoed Saranyu's tumult, but could do nothing more to resolve it.

'Mother Goddess of the Multiverse!' Saranyu murmured to herself. 'There has to be some way I can overcome this limitation.' She paused beneath the weight of her own enquiry, her gaze

shifting to the star-studded skies. There were times she hoped that one of those celestial beings would betray her presence to Vivasvan, and that somehow, he would come and reclaim her. Yet, she could not make herself stay back till the day broke and let him see her.

'Perhaps,' she continued, wrestling with the thoughts that ensnared her, 'what matters is not the answers we seek, but the courage to ask the questions.' Her nose sniffed through the blossoming bushes offering a medley of fragrances—the divine artistry of beings that reigned over this forest and who were at their hospitable best, if not capable of ending her pain.

'Every step I take,' Saranyu confessed to the forest, 'I fear it leads me further away from my children, from the mother I am meant to be.' Yet, the branches swayed, as if urging her onward. 'Guide me, guardians of these forests,' she implored, closing her eyes to better hear the wisdom of the woods. 'For I am but a wanderer in search of light—the light from within.' And though the trees spoke in an undecipherable language—of rustling leaves and creaking boughs—its sounds provided solace in the solitude of her quest.

Saranyu's breath grew ragged, her heart pounding against her ribcage. The whispers of the forest had fallen silent, replaced by the drumming of her own pulse in her ears. 'Where do I belong? Am I so lost,' she murmured, 'that even the winds refuse to answer?' A sudden rustle startled her as if the wind heard her. Saranyu turned and trotted in the direction of the sound. The rustle seemed to move further. She followed the sound, as though under the spell of an invisible being guiding her somewhere. The wind and the forest seemed to work in tandem, clearing the way for her. Saranyu cantered through the thickets, wondering where she was letting herself be taken by these mystical paths that never existed in the past.

'Who are you? Where are you taking me? Show me a sign,' she implored, pausing to lean against the gnarled trunk of a banyan tree whose branches extended like the many arms of the All-Pervading Mother, embracing the Multiverse in an eternal dance of creation and destruction. But Saranyu felt neither created nor destroyed—she was suspended in between, trapped in her liminality.

Her legs trembled, not just from the countless circumambulations around Mother Bhumi, but from the weight of uncertainty that bore down upon her shoulders. She feared her own footprints might soon swallow her whole, leaving nothing but a mother's sorrow embedded in the soil.

'Ancestors, great sages of the past, do whisper through the leaves, guide this weary traveller,' she begged. Though her plea hung heavy in the air, the only response was the flicker of a leaf spiralling downward, landing at her bare feet

And with that whispered invocation, the forest seemed to inhale deeply, holding its breath along with Saranyu, before exhaling a breeze that caressed her face with the faint touch of solace. She heard the rustle again. And again. The unseen force guiding her through the paths seemed to signal the end of her momentary respite. There was something unexplored, undiscovered. And it seemed to be calling out for her. Saranyu felt the paths open up again and cantered forward.

The tangled forest gave way inward for eternity, as though it were letting her pass through an unsolvable maze into its depth, to an unexpected sanctuary that felt as safe as a mother's womb to an unborn child. Saranyu paused, clearing the dry leaves with her hooves. A luminous haze settled among the foliage, illuminating the edges of each leaf and blade of grass with a gentle radiance that soothed her tired eyes.

'Is this real?' Her words slipped through her lips, barely making a sound, but it carried through the clearing like an echo. She stepped forward, her movements reverent in the hallowed space, drawn to the heart of light where it pooled most brightly.

There, under the banyan tree that seemed older than the soil it was rooted to, sat a figure whose youth belied his presence. Facing the South, he seemed like the embodiment of serene wisdom, eternal and enduring, his posture relaxed yet commanding, as if he were the axis on which the Multiverse turned. His eyes were half-closed in meditation, yet Saranyu felt seen, truly seen, for the first time in aeons.

Her gaze swept across the tranquil clearing, before settling on the four Rishis encircling him, their flowing white beards a sign of the millennia they had seen. *Such a young Guru guiding disciples much senior to him in age and experience?* They sat in the *padmasana*, their spines erect, their gazes fixed on their handsome and youthful preceptor. No one spoke aloud. Yet, each of them seemed to be engaged in his own conversation with the young preceptor. And his silence seemed like the multitude of answers they needed. His left leg rested upon his right knee while his right leg rested upon what one could mistake for a rock, but which was a dark dwarf gazing at the world around him menacingly. It seemed as though if he loosened the grip of his sole over the dwarf, the latter would engulf the Universe with his darkness. Yet, the Rishis sat around, unaffected by the malice of the dwarf, for their faith in the power and protection of their Guru overrode their fear of the malicious entity.

'Pray, who are you all?' Saranyu's voice barely rising above the rustle of leaves under her tentative steps, hesitant to let out any sound that might disturb this balance of quietude.

'Seekers of truth,' one replied, his own reverent eyes landing upon her with compassion before they turned to the Guru. 'Like you.'

Saranyu felt her throat tighten up as she drew nearer, each footfall a silent plea for understanding. She had to make an effort to calm her heart so as to not challenge the rhythm of the stillness that pervaded everything around them. She watched a butterfly alight upon the knee of the eldest Rishi, whose smile greeted the creature with a silent benediction.

'Welcome, Saranyu, you have come to the right place,' the Rishi intoned softly, his gaze rising to meet Saranyu's approach. The others nodded in unison, their acknowledgement stirring the air with a warmth that beckoned her closer.

'Am I...worthy of receiving His teachings?' Doubt ran through her words.

'Ah,' another Rishi spoke, his voice the timbre of wind through autumn leaves. 'It is not about worthiness, but readiness. Are you ready, child?'

'Ready?' Saranyu echoed, the question unfurling in her mind. Was she ready? To confront her fears, to embrace her flaws, to seek her purpose from the tangle of her own conflicting emotions?

'Had you not been ready, you would not have reached here,' the third Rishi chuckled, his fingers sketching patterns in the air, patterns that danced with the promise of unlocking profound secrets.

'The forest does not question the river's right to flow. Nor should you question your path to wisdom,' added the fourth Rishi, his eyes aglow with the fire of compassion. 'Every soul has its season to flourish, moment to ascend, to realize the eternal truth that prevails beyond the changing dimensions of space and time.'

'Pray, Guru of Gurus, let this be my season,' Saranyu declared, her voice growing steadier with the conviction that had begun to sprout within her. 'Teach me, so that I may live it and teach in turn.'

With reverence, like the Rishis, Saranyu took her place in the circle. Her heart that had been pounding with trepidation, now aligned to the surreal rhythm of the surroundings, tuning itself to receive and experience the abstract yet eternal knowledge under the watchful gaze of the handsome Guru.

His eyelids did not move from their half-closed state. Yet, His smile seemed to welcome her, revealing depths of understanding that transcended time. His unaffected tranquillity revealed the trove of wisdom that He embodied, as though He Himself was the panacea to every ailment that ever existed in the past, the present and the future, beyond the beginning and end of time, as though it was His guidance that kept the multitude of realms in knowledge and conscious motion. Saranyu's eyes lit up briefly before all the emotions within her churned and precipitated, flowing out of her eyes as an oblation.

'Lord Dakshinamurthy, heed my prayer,' she said, her curiosity melding into reverence. 'I am Saranyu, seeker of truths too heavy for my soul to bear alone.'

Your path has led you here, Saranyu, as all paths do, in time. The words did not come from His lips but from the very Cosmos that seemed to be the tree that sprouted from the seed that lay within His person as He willed the dimensions of space and time, weaving the narratives of illusions and realities that bound the destinies of everything that was created, with Him being the sole entity that was free from the bonds. *What burdens your heart?*

'Lord, I am lost,' Saranyu willed her body to change back to her celestial form and confessed, folding her legs beneath her as she sat on the soil. 'I am a wife who cannot stand by her husband's side, a mother who fears she is failing her children, a daughter of the heavens who cannot find her place among the stars.'

Each star shines at its appointed hour, Saranyu. The words echoed in her ears though His lips remained closed, the soft light dancing in His half-closed eyes. *And every mother's love is the constellation that guides her children home.*

'Yet my love feels like a storm—fierce and uncontrolled.' She clenched her fists, the weight of her doubts grounding her to the moment.

Even storms are part of the divine dance. His unspoken words reverberated within her, His calm unwavering. *Embrace your nature, for in acceptance lies the power to transform fear into strength.*

'Can one truly change the essence of their being?' Saranyu's gaze sought His, a flicker of hope amidst the shadows of uncertainty.

Change is the only constant, the constant being the part of you that is unaffected through change! Lord Dakshinamurthy's voice spoke from within the depths of her own being. *In the vast expanse of Creation, you are both the sculptor and the clay, the disciple and the preceptor, the child and the mother, if only you see through the illusion of difference between the cause and the result. You are the One. Mould your destiny with compassion and courage, child.*

'Compassion for myself seems like a distant shore,' Saranyu admitted, her voice tinged with the pain of realization.

Let the river of self-acceptance carry you there. He encouraged her silently. *For in accepting our own selves, we become the lighthouse for others lost at sea.*

'Thank you,' she said, a tear flowing down her cheek. 'Easier said than done to go soft on myself, but the lesson of acceptance you gave me…is a beacon in my dark solitary journey.'

The clearing was bathed in an otherworldly hush, as if the very air held its breath. Saranyu's eyes flitted from one Rishi to another, absorbing the weight of their collective wisdom. The sounds of the forest seemed to retreat, leaving behind a canvas of silence so profound it pressed upon her ears like the softest silk. Saranyu's lips parted, but her words clung stubbornly to her throat. She swallowed, trying to dislodge the knot of apprehensions that had taken up residence in her chest. Her gaze met Lord Dakshinamurthy's—His eyes a tranquil pool, reflecting patience and infinity. 'Yet, I cannot help feeling lost, My Lord, lost in finding my role. I have been fortunate to receive the love and compassion of my husband and yet fallen short of the

merit to stand by his side. I am lost!'

'Loss is but the path to discovery,' one Rishi intoned, his fingers with an elder's grace.

Saranyu paused, and then shook her head, abandoning her inhibitions. 'My steps falter.'

'Even the mightiest river begins as a hesitant stream,' another Rishi offered, his tone soothing like the rustle of leaves.

'In His presence, Daughter of Tvashtra, let your doubts flow,' urged a third Rishi, his voice as resonant as the distant thunder.

'Flow,' she echoed internally, letting the word seep into her being, travel through her veins. 'To flow is to live, to move beyond the confines of the self.' Her heart took solace in the metaphor; rivers did not fear their twists and turns.

Your flow will find its way. Lord Dakshinamurthy's silent words struck a chord within her, vibrating through layers of uncertainty.

'Lord, each day is a battle with shadows,' Saranyu confessed, her eyes reflecting the turmoil within. 'Shadows of doubt that cloak my love in fear, shadows of failure that obscure the joys of marital union and motherhood.'

Shadows exist only where there is light. Lord Dakshinamurthy responded gently, his words floating to her through the medium of quietude.

'Ironically, the spouse of the Lord of Light struggles to find the light within,' she admitted, her fists clenching at her sides. 'I let darkness overpower my light and take my place, as I ran away like a coward. Where can I find my light?'

You are the giver of light and the embrace of darkness—the balance that nature itself seeks. Lord Dakshinamurthy's gaze fell briefly upon the menacing dwarf pinned under His right foot. Avidya *seeks to set boundaries of finiteness, keeping the seeker engulfed in its temporary narrative. When the seeker realizes that she is the seer and the knower, finiteness itself fades.*

Saranyu absorbed His unspoken words, feeling them resonate deep in her marrow. Her clenched fists uncurled, her fingers brushing against the soft earth as though drawing strength from its enduring spirit. 'When the seeker realizes that she is the seer and the knower…' the words echoed within her, the concept unfurling in her mind like a lotus at the first ray of the Sun. 'Fraught with my imperfections and limitations, where can I seek that infinite?'

Lord Dakshinamurthy's smile was tender, a reflection of the compassion that the Rishis too exuded through their silent vigil. *It is through embracing your imperfections that you will ascend, Saranyu. Perfection is not the absence of flaws but the harmony within them.*

Saranyu stilled as she internalized the profound truth. Across from her, the Rishis sat in quiet contemplation, their presence a comforting support woven from the threads of timeless wisdom.

'Harmony,' she whispered, envisioning her fears and hopes dancing in tandem with a celestial rhythm. 'I seek the courage to dance to this rhythm, to be the mother my children deserve.'

Courage is already yours. Lord Dakshinamurthy assured her within, his silent voice serving as an anchor for her wavering spirit. *For it takes courage to stand before us, to voice your vulnerabilities, to yearn for growth.*

'Then I shall hold on to it,' Saranyu vowed to herself, sitting a little straighter, the invisible chains of self-blame finally beginning to loosen their grip. 'And I will wield it to carve a path for myself and my children.'

Let your love be your chisel, and your will, the arm that guides it. The wisdom of ages was encapsulated in Lord Dakshinamurthy's simple words.

'Love and will,' Saranyu repeated, letting the implication seep into her being. A newfound determination simmered in her, her heart beating in tandem with the pulse of the Universe. Yet, her legs refused to stand on their own. Saranyu did not want to let go of the stability and safety of the surroundings where she did not feel her lack and insufficiencies gnaw at her spirit. Even a momentary distraction from the eternal Guru's serene face, she feared, would push her back into the same never-ending cycle of self-doubt. Lord Dakshinamurthy's form was stoic, like an ancient tree untouched by the ravages of time, yet His eyes shone with a kindness that spanned aeons. He observed Saranyu, her soul laid bare before Him and His disciples the Rishis.

One more thing, Saranyu. Each being in this Cosmos, Lord Dakshinamurthy continued, His unspoken sermon unaffected by her lack of readiness to be convinced, compassionate at her inertial mind still pushing her towards self-doubt, *embodies the Universe itself. You, Saranyu, are not just a mother; you are creation and strength, you are the nurturer of destinies.* Her gaze rose to meet his, the gravity of his words anchoring her fluttering heart. *Your children, my child,* he continued, *do not merely need your protection—they thirst for your wisdom, your joy, your passion. They seek to witness the Universe through you.*

Saranyu felt a tremor within, as if these words were awakening dormant seeds of potential planted long ago. She shifted on her feet, the foliage beneath seeming to lend her its steadfastness.

Stop running away from what you feel are imperfections, insufficiencies, anything that makes you feel less than what you truly are... Lord Dakshinamurthy advised, his soothing yet authoritative voice resonating in her ears. *Embrace instead the perfect moment of now—where you are their guide, learning and growing alongside them.*

The Rishis nodded sagely, their serene faces reflecting the moonlight that filtered through the leafy canopy above.

Perfection is an illusion, a mirage that leads one away from the beauty of imperfection, she pondered internally, her thoughts intertwining with the Great Guru's teachings.

Your journey, He said, *will be fraught with trials, but remember, the lotus blooms most beautifully from the deepest mud.*

Saranyu watched a leaf spiral to the ground, its descent a dance of surrender to the natural order. She felt her fears, once heavy as stones, become like that leaf—weightless and free.

Seek not to shield them from life's storms, but to be their anchor in the tempest. Teach them to find serenity in chaos, strength in vulnerability... And meaning in mortality, He said, each word a beacon illuminating her dark thoughts.

'Anchor... Serenity... Strength...' she repeated silently, her inner voice steady and clear. Her stance became rooted.

Look upon yourself as the Divine does, Lord Dakshinamurthy concluded. *With eyes brimming with compassion and pride for the soul that braves existence.*

A smile stole across Saranyu's lips, timid at first, then blooming like the dawn. In his reflection, she saw herself—not as fractured or failing—but as whole and radiant, a bearer of light amidst darkness. 'Thank you,' she whispered, her voice no longer trembling but imbued with certainty. 'I see now—the love I hold for my children will be their greatest lesson.'

With those final words, a sense of purpose coursed through her veins, potent as the Ganga herself. Saranyu stood, a mother transformed, ready to return to her children, her spirit alight with the eternal flame of guidance and love. Kneeling on the verdant ground, her hands pressed together in a gesture of deep reverence. 'My gratitude knows no bounds.'

Gratitude is but the seed of wisdom—jnana, Lord Dakshinamurthy replied, his voice the gentle rustle of leaves in the wind. *Nurture it with action—karma.*

Saranyu rose to her feet, the weight that once hunched her shoulders was now lifted by an invisible force.

As she turned to face the four Rishis, their eyes met hers not as strangers, but as kindred spirits, guardians of ancient truths. 'Your presence has guided me to the light of understanding,'

Saranyu said, each word a petal unfurling in the sun.

'Remember, Saranyu,' one of the Rishis intoned, his voice like the distant call of a conch shell. 'The paths we walk are many, but they all lead to the same horizon.'

Her heart sang with their blessings. Within her bloomed a quiet resolve, delicate yet unyielding. She would no longer be the tempest-tossed leaf; she was now the river, carving her destiny through the stone of hardship.

'May your journey enrich the Cosmos,' another Rishi whispered, his smile as warm as the dappled sunlight filtering through the foliage.

'May it be so,' Saranyu responded, her gaze lingering on the serene figure of Lord Dakshinamurthy. His silence was her final benediction, a profound stillness that held more power than a thousand words.

The soft glow of the clearing seemed to pulsate in time with her heartbeat, and as she stepped beyond its sacred boundary, the light did not dim. It followed her, a guardian luminescence, guiding her path back to her children, back to the life that awaited her transformation.

'*Om*,' she breathed out, the primal note that contained all the love and wisdom bestowed upon her. The syllable that had Everything within. The forest absorbed her vow, the leaves whispering tales of a mother reborn, ready to weave her destiny through the Great Twilight.

Children of Twilight and Flame

Surya Mandala

Chhaya's silhouette loomed on the birthing couch as she grappled with the burgeoning life within her. Her breath came in short, sharp gasps. Each contraction spoke of the change that her progeny would bring forth into the Universe. Her and Vivasvan's progeny.

'Focus on your breathing, Chhaya,' the midwife prodded her on gently.

Chhaya complied, steadying herself against the silken cushions on the swan-shaped couch as more midwives supported her. 'They will come. Those who will change the old rules and bring forth a new era!' Chhaya replied through clenched teeth, her words etched with pain and power. 'And I shall ensure it!' Her declaration was punctuated by another wave of contractions, potent enough to bend time, it seemed. Chhaya gasped in between her ragged breaths. The midwife reminded her to stay calm.

Chhaya's hands grappled with the edges of the couch, her knuckles whitening with each new wave of pain. Her sari, drenched in sweat, clung to her skin. She summoned images of her unborn children, drawing strength from the unspoken bond they already formed. They were not merely extensions of her flesh, but spirits chosen by the Cosmos, each fated to leave an indelible mark upon the Universe.

'Remember, children,' she murmured internally, envisioning

their essence within her. 'You are born of perseverance, cradled in resolve.'

With every contraction, visions of her children's future danced before her mind's eye—mighty rulers and wise scholars, perhaps those who would challenge destiny. This thought steeled her resolve, transforming her cries into chants of resilience. 'I am the crucible,' she affirmed, 'from which legends will rise.'

'Push, Chhaya!' the command cut through her concentration. There was no room for doubt, no space for fear. Only the relentless push of life towards light.

'Mother of Infinity!' she groaned, anchoring herself to the legacy of those who had birthed worlds before her.

'Again!' insisted the voice, urging her to the precipice of creation. With a warrior's cry, she bore down once more, the echo of her voice mingling with the whispers of ancient hymns resonating in the ether. 'Ah!' The sound was both a release and an invocation, a call to the forces that knit the fabric of existence. And then, just as suddenly as the tempest had risen, there was calm—a serene quietude that filled the chamber like the first breath of dawn. 'Give me the one who will set the order for the new Universe! Give me the Manu of the next aeon!'

The celestial midwives were taken aback by her instructions instead of the prayer she should have offered to the Gods watching over the act of creation. 'Strength and power, my children, is our heritage,' she vowed silently, feeling the sacred bond connecting her heart to theirs

Swirls of indigo and gold danced on the walls, casting a celestial glow over the birthing chamber, where ancient mantras pulsed through the air in a hypnotic cadence. The chants invoked the protection of divinities, their sacred syllables weaving an invisible shield of solace and strength around mother and children alike.

'Let them come forth...' Chhaya breathed out.

With a grace born of untold ages, the first child came forth into the world, a boy with the sheen of twilight upon his skin. 'Saavarni,' Chhaya declared, recognizing the soul of a leader in his steady gaze, even as his tiny fists curled like budding lotuses ready to bloom. 'You shall usher the Universe into a new era. You shall reign over its law, order and protocols. You shall be the Manu!'

Barely a moment passed before another wave of contractions signalled the arrival of the second child—a dark-hued boy with a contemplative air that reminded her of Yama. The uncharacteristic lack of emotion in his eyes even as Chhaya cuddled him in her arms left her stupefied for a while before she recovered. 'Shani, with eyes as dark as the monsoon clouds, your path may be profound and you shall reign over the destinies, backing up your father!' Shani's cry pierced the air with a resonance that hinted at the deep influence he would exercise over the Universe.

The celestial midwives betrayed their discomfort and tried their best to mask it as they gathered the newborns in their arms when a third contraction wracked Chhaya's already spent body. 'Tapati,' Chhaya groaned, envisioning the stream of life that would flow from her daughter's hands. 'Embodiment of vitality and light! A life-nurturing river, you, like your brothers, will safeguard order and destiny!' Chhaya would have wanted to shower more blessings, invoke the power of the Cosmos to bequeath infinite strength and might to her newborn progeny. But her monumental exertion was apparent in her wavering consciousness.

'Welcome, children,' she whispered, her voice a gentle caress. 'Welcome to the realm that awaits your touch, your reign and your direction. Each of you,' Chhaya spoke, her voice a lullaby laced with authority, 'shall carve your own legend in the annals of continuum.'

Holding all her three children—Saavarni, Shani and Tapati—against her, a profound sense of fulfilment cascaded through her.

She felt the threads of the future and the destinies of her offspring intertwining with those of the world. 'Look at you three,' she cooed, a gentle smile curling her lips despite the lingering pain. 'Saavarni, your wisdom shall be the compass for ages to come. Shani, your depth will challenge the mightiest. And Tapati, your creativity will kindle the fires of inspiration.'

The smile that was unique to Chhaya, not to Saranyu, played on her lips. At least that was how the celestial midwives felt when they gently took the infants from Chhaya, leaving her to recuperate. The Shadow Lady of the Household of Vivasvan could not have asked for any better. She needed this time to plot the future. Not just her and her children's but that of the Guardians of the Cosmos too. And the way they would operate.

Alone in the chamber, Chhaya battled exhaustion, putting her next plan together. It was a surprise for her that her children too bore a strong resemblance to Saranyu's children. Both firstborns promised curiosity and thirst for knowledge. Both the daughters were rivers, and the other two brothers were intense, dispassionate and unmoved in their own ways. Chhaya hoped that the uncanny resemblance did not raise suspicion in Vivasvan's mind. It was with misgivings of this nature that she had politely asked Vivasvan not to be with her in the birthing chamber. She, Chhaya, wanted to be the one uttering the benediction for her children's future rather than their father who was bound to look at her children as second to the children of Saranyu. Was Vivasvan aware of the clandestine rise of Chhaya to fully assume the role of Saranyu? He had never let Chhaya read his mind, and seemed to live in the blissful belief that she was still Saranyu. Or was he letting her think he believed her? Chhaya was not sure and did not want to take any chances.

The shadow of Tvashtra's daughter wanted to be the architect of her children's future in ways different from how Saranyu wanted to shape her progeny's future. To ensure that, Chhaya decided she needed help—from that side of the Universe where the pervasive rays of her husband could not penetrate.

∽

Bhuloka

It was almost like stepping out of a portal from a world that existed in a different dimension. Saranyu opened her eyes and saw nothing of Lord Dakshinamurthy or his disciples. The ancient banyan tree was the sole reminder of her surreal experience. Saranyu lingered on, ruminating on her experience, changing back into her mare form, her hooves unwillingly backing away to resume the onward journey. It was time she stopped running away from her imperfections. And the onus was not just on her. She needed Vivasvan to recognize the unforeseen chasm between them and cover it.

Something stopped her from returning home right away. Would Chhaya agree to relinquish her position? Would her children welcome her back? Would they not ask her why she had not discussed her intent with them before leaving them? Her deepest fear struck her. Would they even recognize her? Would Chhaya admit the truth, or would her own creation, albeit inadvertent, turn against her?

Amidst such disturbing thoughts, Saranyu picked up pace and built that up to a blind gallop, hoping that the physical exertion would bring her back to a calm that would allow her to think. For a while, she was unmindful of the texture of the changing soil beneath her. The foliage of dried leaves gave way to wider clearings, as the sounds of water bodies and birds flocking around them greeted her ears, as though she had entered another dwelling. Only this one was wider and bigger than the other ones in this dimension of existence. A familiar voice made her ears cock up in the direction of the sound. Saranyu turned to canter to a larger clearing where she found someone sitting in a meditative pose. *Was it? No, it could not be!* As if on cue, he turned to looked at her, recognizing her instantly as though the guise of a mare was of no use to hide her true identity. Saranyu backed away, not ready to meet anyone from the family, however distant. He chased after her.

'Sister-in-law!'

'Not a good time, Purandhara!'

'Are you the one who passes through here every night?'

Saranyu nodded, not pausing as she backed away. 'What are you doing here?' She did not need him to answer as her gaze fell upon a *Yajnavedi* and a humble cave dwelling. Purandhara was probably performing a ritual that would strengthen his chances for the position of the new Indra. Or perhaps he was still atoning for the sin of killing Vishvarupa, his Guru and her brother. Saranyu did not care now.

'Just forget you saw me here. Please do not tell him,' she implored, turning around and gaining speed when the youngest son of Aditi said something that froze her to the spot.

'Who is the woman who has taken your place in Surya Mandala? *And has had three more children with my brother.*' Saranyu whirled around while Purandhara trailed off, realizing he had spoken too much. Letting out a sigh, he hurried closer, 'And do you really think my brother does not know?'

Saranyu frowned, trying to hold back the pain building in her chest. She met Purandhara's gaze.

'Things seem to be running smooth and fine there all this time with her in my stead. And you say he knows it all.'

'I–I just think it seems improbable that he does not sense his wife's absence…and worse, bear the presence of an impostor.' He shook his head. 'Sister-in-law, please, I beg you…listen to me and don't assume anything more, or worse, do something rash.'

'Thank you for telling me the truth, Purandhara.' Saranyu

suppressed the sob that was already wracking her bosom, and turned around to gallop away.

'Lo, he has not even caught the wind of my absence all the while! Everything! Everything I did just evaporated into thin air! What else could I expect from the Scorcher of Everything!'

Of Death and the Daystar

'What lies in the South?' Yama stood at the precipice of the cliff gazing at the horizon. *The South stands for death.* That had been his mother's anguished cry ever since they had declared him Dikpala of South. 'Death when there is no life seems strange, doesn't it?' He said to himself more than to Shraddhadeva who stood mostly in companionable silence.

'The end is pre-ordained for everything that is created, Brother,' Shraddhadeva added to Yama's contemplation. 'Not surprising that they want a Deva to preside over death before they can give rise to something that may become uncontrollable.' Yama's lips twitched at his brother's obvious attempt to lighten the otherwise morbid conversation. 'Last time, I heard from Devi Sachi that the terrain of Mother Bhumi has been undergoing a transformation. Life has begun, Brother.'

The tentative smile on Yama's lips faded as reality dawned. 'So, I have to be the end of something beautiful that has finally sprouted.'

'Or a new beginning of something that has lived its course?' Shraddhadeva pointed out. 'Anything that outlives the pre-ordained purpose of its birth for too long is bound to degenerate into something burdensome to the surroundings.' It was Shraddhadeva's turn to be contemplative. 'From what I remember of the corpus of knowledge, the instructions of the Creator seemed clear.'

For the first time in their conversation, Yama beamed, and from the heart. 'The instructions from Brahma's corpus of knowledge!' Yama's smile widened. 'So, they are preparing you to become the Bearer of Order soon, Eldest.'

Shraddhadeva nodded and stilled himself. 'Father cautions against assuming power before one is truly ready.' Yama shrugged as they stepped back from the land and were about to ascend to the skies when his brother pulled at his arm. 'We are here anyway. Why not explore the great expanse of Mother Bhumi?'

Yama liked the suggestion and let Shraddhadeva lead the way. The brothers paused to discern the movement of their celestial father across the sky and then surveyed the landscape. Verdant forests, water bodies, mountains covered with snow and grass. 'Doesn't it feel like…'

'…home? Mother?' Yama completed his brother's thought and both exchanged meaningful glances. They understood each other without words. 'Do you feel the way I do, Eldest?'

'The younger ones need more of her time,' Shraddhadeva countered. 'And she is understandably distracted when it concerns us.'

'Father is never like that,' Yama sighed, sensing the same discomfort in his brother. 'I–I get uncomfortable when she takes her frustration out on Yami.' His brother stood still for a moment before resuming walking.

'There is a change in her,' Shraddhadeva conceded. 'I can't believe we feel more at home here in Bhuloka.'

Yama nodded, feeling the gentle caress of the breeze as they strode down the slope. The once barren land that seemed pale in the light of Vivasvan now seemed to welcome his rays with colourful blooms. The breeze carried the mixed fragrance of dew and blossoms in the creepers that covered the land below them. There was a rhythm in the rustle, in the arresting monotone buzzing sounds of the black six-legged creatures that seemed to suck out from the flowerbeds their sweetness. 'Remember the lullaby that Mother used to sing about Oneness with the Creator?

I can hear her in my mind.'

'I never heard her singing it for Saavarni or Shani…'

They didn't need to tell each other that the changes in their mother had caused both of them more distress than they could express. Instead, Shraddhadeva focused on the new forms of life that had sprung from Mother Bhumi. 'Each creature seems to have a way of its own. Yet, all of them have come from the same source. I should request Grandfather Kashyapa to accompany us the next time we visit.'

Yama was lost in his own thoughts, his gaze lingering on another stream of reddish six-legged creatures, almost invisible to the eye unless one crouched and looked for them. All were scurrying in one direction as though the purpose of their life lay somewhere along the path they had taken. 'So much to observe and discern!' He exclaimed and then turned to his brother. 'No wonder, Devi Sachi is a frequent visitor. The blossoms of Bhuloka are soon going to vie with the Nandana blooms of Deva Loka!'

'Errr… The blossoms might not be the only reason for Devi Sachi's visit to Bhuloka.' Shraddhadeva narrowed his gaze and smiled. Yama's jaw dropped at his hint.

'Uncle Purandhara! Let's visit him!'

∽

Tvashtra's Forge

Vivasvan examined the spherical weapon, and the protruding spikes with carefully sharpened razors. 'Tvashtra, is this what I think it is?'

His father-in-law's response was a silent nod. Vivasvan was aware of Tvashtra's solitary life after the death of Vishvarupa, and of his subsequent separation from his wife Rechana. Saranyu's wedding with Vivasvan was done hurriedly in the hope that

Rechana would come back if the daughter who had betrayed her son left her paternal home. But Virochana's sister seemed to have lost faith in Devas. In the past, Vivasvan and Saranyu had tried to cheer up Tvashtra, and encouraged him to visit Daitya Loka to coax his wife to return. But the Celestial Architect had chosen to keep to himself, treating his work as his sanctuary. The silence his father-in-law wielded this time was almost spiteful, even for Vivasvan's easy-going countenance.

'I can't help feeling a bit insecure knowing that the great Sudarshana Chakra of Lord Vishnu has been with you this long, and that the Protector of the Multiverse is without his invincible weapon,' Vivasvan prolonged the conversation, directing a concentrated ray of heat towards the edges of the chakra. Tvashtra did not respond till the complete burst of his radiance was absorbed by the weapon. He re-examined the edges closely and finally met Vivasvan's gaze. 'Again, Luminous One.'

Vivasvan obliged with another burst of energy followed by another and another. At the end of the almost wordless session of reinforcing the great weapon, Vivasvan found himself falling short of his own radiance but the chakra was nowhere near its former glory. That the great Sudarshana that had sliced open the throats of many Rakshasas and Daityas who had threatened the balance and order of the Universe now lay blunt, and bereft of its sheen, was a disturbing thought. 'What happened to the chakra?'

Tvashtra let out a sigh. 'Much can be attributed to its tussle with Amrita itself.' He turned to his son-in-law, signalling a break from their session. 'During the great churn of the ocean, when Lord Vishnu, in the form of Mohini, distributed Amrita, you exposed Danava Prince Svarbhanu's attempt to infiltrate the Deva hordes to partake of the real Amrita.'

'And I am paying the price for it every now and then,' Vivasvan grimaced.

'So is the Sudarshana,' Tvashtra explained. 'By the time Lord Narayana realized what was happening, and sent his chakra after Svarbhanu, he had almost swallowed the Amrita; the chakra attempted to slice through his throat just when Amrita was passing through it.' Tvashtra filled up a golden goblet with the celestial *Soma* and handed it to Vivasvan. 'The final tussle was between the invincible Sudarshana and the immortality-inducing Amrita. The chakra managed to win, but at a cost to its unparallelled glory.'

Vivasvan smiled his gratitude for the drink and set about infusing the great chakra with his energy once again. After several near-futile attempts, Tvashtra signalled the end of their endeavour. At least for the time being. 'This can't be achieved in one go, Vivasvan,' the Celestial Architect cautioned Vivasvan, holding his arm. 'I shall invoke you again.' Tvashtra's hands came together in a formal salutation which Vivasvan returned with grace.

With a thoughtful glance at the chakra and then at Tvashtra's residence, by the Forge, Vivasvan changed the topic that was fast becoming an awkward stalemate between them. 'Won't you ask after the well-being of your daughter, Tvashtra?'

The Celestial Architect frowned as though he had sensed a deeper meaning in his son-in-law's question. 'Does the Luminous Son of Aditi feel that the bride he lovingly took home needs to be asked after?'

'I thought a father's love and protectiveness overrides these logical arguments, Tvashtra.' Vivasvan gave a knowing smile. 'At least that is how I feel when I think of Yami or Tapati.'

Tvashtra gave up his mask of nonchalance. 'If you knew, why did you not act upon her departure instead of continuing the pretence with that apparition who goes by the name of my daughter in your household, Vivasvan!'

The Luminous Daystar stared incredulously at his father-in-law, taken aback by his outburst. 'That "apparition", Son of Prabhasavasu, is a part of the bride I took to my home.' He backed away by a step, his frown deepening. 'And I am not going to pick and choose the parts of my wife to love or to discard.'

'For all your large heart, Son of Kashyapa,' Tvashtra winced, 'there is a large part of Saranyu that feels "discarded" right now even as you delight in your marital bliss with that other "part" of her.'

Vivasvan smiled sadly, reining himself in from hurling another barb at Tvashtra—on how the Divine Smith had held back from teaching his daughter how to deal with what she felt was her insufficiency. But he knew that the blame game was only going to make things worse, and that the larger chunk of this responsibility lay with him, Saranyu's husband.

Three Overlords of the Universe! How am I going to convince her if she cannot look me in the eye for no infraction of hers? How can I cover the chasm between us if all my love fails to convince her that she is forever my cherished bride?

The Cry of a Sister

The two sons of the Sun faced each other, weapons in hand. Yama stood at a distance from the celestial ring, discerning the opponents—Shraddhadeva and Saavarni—about to face off with each other. Shraddhadeva's and Yama's brief meeting with Purandhara in Bhuloka flashed across Yama's mind. When Purandhara had asked them how their mother was doing, Yama had found an uncharacteristic inflexion in his voice, as though Purandhara knew something about her. But nothing was discussed openly other than them exploring the new forms of life that had taken root around where their uncle had chosen to embark on his long ritual of *Shata Kratu*, to establish his eligibility for the position of the next Indra. The conversation covered everything, including the events leading up to Lord Varaha overcoming Hiranyaksha, the onset of the Great Twilight and others, before landing on little household details of Vivasvan.

'Six children…must be a handful for my sister-in-law!' Something about Purandhara's remark made Yama sit up. 'I can imagine she must have become quite a shadow of herself.' Shraddhadeva caught on to the clue but before both the brothers could ask Purandhara anything directly, he declared that it was time for his evening ritual. The days in Bhuloka passed too quickly!

But the brothers pondered over his veiled remarks and came up with an idea. Yama's lips twitched at the corners as he exchanged a glance with Shraddhadeva before signalling the beginning of the duel. Metal clashed with metal; radiance with radiance. Shraddhadeva had the edge of experience and exposure. Saavarni was just beginning. Yama knew that his eldest was not even unleashing half his capability while facing their little brother. Saavarni, to his credit, defended himself with great alacrity but almost all his moves against Shraddhadeva were miscalculated. The duel went on for a while. Yami, Tapati and their mother came to witness it as the tension built up.

Yama frowned as traces of displeasure showed in their mother's eyes whenever Shraddhadeva dominated. Before long, Saavarni's grip on the sword faltered and Shraddhadeva disarmed him and immobilized him in a vice-like grip before letting him go.

'Good progress, little brother. We need to keep at it, though,' the eldest acknowledged Saavarni's progress.

'I don't see any progress!' Their mother exclaimed, making her way towards Saavarni in the middle of the ring. 'Are you focusing well, Saavarni?'

'Mother, in fact, he applied a lot many new moves and strikes today,' Shraddhadeva interrupted. 'It is just that—'

'That is not enough!' Their mother declared. 'If you find it too cumbersome to teach your little brother, tell me to find another Guru for him, Shraddhadeva.'

'Mother. It is not about—' Shraddhadeva's words hung in the air as she turned about and left in a huff, bumping into Yami and glaring at her as though it were all Yami's fault, before disappearing into the inner chambers. Saavarni gulped and muttered something awkward to excuse himself before following their mother.

Yama gave an imperceptible nod to Shraddhadeva. They were not going to discuss this in front of their sisters. They could seek out their father. But Yama decided to wait it out and find out more about this intriguing transformation for the worse in their mother. He did not have to wait long to find yet another striking example of his mother's transformation.

Of the children who were born later to her, Saavarni showed

promise of being a warrior and a bearer of order. He could stand up to Shraddhadeva while debating the nature of the world, the order of Creation and its sustenance, and the dynamics of everything with respect to passing time. Save for the fact that Yama could sense a growing sense of restlessness in Saavarni—something that reminded him a bit of Bali and Virochana, from the few encounters he'd had with them when he had visited Tvashtra. Yama considered voicing this to their father Vivasvan but his deductions were abstract—something that his inner self felt strongly—with no logical explanation to support them. Shani was the slow one, and declared a planet who would rule over specific aspects of destiny that included personal traits, discipline and fairness. In some ways, Shani seemed to Yama his own spitting image but different in his own way—aloof, quick to anger and argumentative when confronted. But Yama could not see any traces of malice in Shani. He could see that Yami and Tapati got along very well. Both were destined to be rivers when their time came, promising vivacity and empathy. They were the only members of his family who brought a smile to Yama's lips. Many times, when Yama felt weary of unravelling the ways of the Universe, and of its denizens and guardians, he found himself serving as quiet company to both his sisters as they explored Bhuloka and other realms of the Universe with a sense of abandon. So, it came as a shock to him when he found Tapati setting out to explore Bhuloka alone. Yama volunteered to go with her, but she shook her head.

'Talk to Yami instead, Brother,' she pleaded, her eyes betraying a sense of discomfort. 'I fear she is hiding something from me.'

Yama rushed to his twin's chambers and found her resigned to herself, resting her head on her raised knees—a picture of despair so uncharacteristic of Yami! He called out her name and Yami instantly sprang to her feet, a smile, almost a fake one curling along her lips.

'Yama!' She threw her hands around him, almost clinging to him. The protective brother in him scanned the surroundings for any potential danger that might have threatened his sister, making her feel vulnerable and alone.

'Why haven't you joined Tapati?' He asked her, disengaging himself from her embrace while still holding her.

Yami shrugged, saying nothing in response. After a bout of silence, she said, 'Can we go to Bhuloka, just us?'

Yama agreed, finding no reason to deny the rare request of his twin. They had an almost eventless and joyous tour of Bhuloka, with Mother Bhumi greeting their eyes and ears with a fresh offering of life and growth.

'The destiny of rivers is strange, Yama.' Yami spoke suddenly. 'We are supposed to flow, accept everything that comes our way, and yet remain detached. We are meant to be everywhere but nowhere, everyone's but no one's…' Yami drifted off as her glance shifted to a spring bubbling forth from the crevice in the mountain where springs usually originated. 'This one will probably be a tributary that may feed my course. Or it may change its course, leaving me alone.' She cocked her head in Yama's direction as this thought struck her. 'I feel alone. So alone!'

'Sister, you will always have me.' Yama squeezed her wrist, a part of him still trying to make sense of her mixed emotions.

'Will I?' Her words were less than a whisper while he said emphatically, 'Not just me, Tapati, Eldest Shraddhadeva, Father Vivasvan, Mother…' Yama paused at his own hesitation in promising the support of their mother and even that of Saavarni and Shani.

'O Yama!' Yami inched closer. 'I needed someone, yes, but not a whole army!' She giggled through her mysterious melancholy. 'You are enough. More than enough.' She leaned on his shoulder. A part of Yama froze at the contact. Yami was behaving differently. He had never seen her this way!

'You are being… Have you voiced this to Mother, Yami?'

Yami's lips went flat. 'She said we can't fight destiny. Nor can we fight our chosen roles. As though she is fulfilling hers despite not being…' Yami bit her lips and turned away but Yama had caught the drift in her tone.

'Despite not being…?'

'Forget it, Yama. I guess she was just fatigued because Shani was being difficult. And she took it out on me.'

'Yami, tell me everything!' He tipped her chin, forcing her to meet his gaze. 'You told her about how you felt, and she said one must fulfil their destinies like she was fulfilling hers despite not being *what*?'

'She ended our conversation there,' Yami hissed, partly annoyed at his insistence. 'Yama, I just wanted to…wanted you!'

'Wanted me?' Yama frowned, this time mirroring his twin's exasperation.

'By the Trimurtis!' Yami sighed. 'We have been twins, Yama, we shared a womb, and nobody knows me like you do! I am sure not even Father and certainly not Mother! Nobody knows you like I do! Don't just be my twin. Be my mate too!'

They were on solid land, yet Yama felt the earth beneath him wobble. *Was his twin even in her senses?* His hands instantly left her arms and he backed away. Whatever was making her feel this way, Yami was not herself. 'Yami! It is wrong!'

'The wrong that did not apply to Lord Brahma and Mother Saraswati?'

Yama fought the urge to roll his eyes and took another step back. He was not going to give in to the argument of what was done in the past when Creation itself did not exist the way it did now. He was not going to judge the doings of his ancestors of times different from his. 'Yami, this is not you. But you are succumbing to something that will pull you down in a spiral of peril. Whatever in this Multiverse gave you this idea?'

'Fine!' Yami snapped. 'Don't heed my plea. Don't heed my predicament. Just watch me perish in my misery, experience a pain thousand-fold of those who you would punish feel, in your realm. What's that realm of yours going to be? *Naraka*!'

'Yami, you fool!'

'And think about what a fair sentence should be for a brother who lets his sister rot in her misery for eternity, Lord of Fairness. Right, wrong, Dharma and what not?'

Yama looked up to the skies, at the blazing ball that was their father. Yami had been a delight in all their lives, a picture of everything beautiful that Creation had heaped on and moulded into one entity. He wondered how she got these insane ideas in her head. Yes, it was his Dharma to keep his sister happy, but he could not let the code of the Cosmic Order that was being set for the coming cycle of life and world be compromised by her whims.

Something was wrong. Yama's palm shook as he put the idea in his mind into action. Yami was not in a frame of mind to be reasoned with. And he was not going to give in to her fantasies. Yet, he needed her to show him the truth that he sought. He sensed a streak of light emerge from his palms, entwining with the heat of his annoyance. *Something had been wrong with his mother and half of his siblings. And now, his own twin!* He saw Yami look up at the smoke swirling around his, emanating from his frame. He saw her shriek in horror.

'Forgive me, Yami!' He was not sure if she even heard his apology as she became still, like an inanimate rock, oblivious to all traces of life around her. She stared at him, through him, emotion and expression leaving her dilated pupils, frozen at her shock.

'What did you do to me, Brother?' It was not a question. Nor a demand or an exclamation. Just a plain sentence, devoid of fear or anger. 'What do you want me to do?'

Yama took a deep breath. There could be a time in the future he would regret subjecting his sister to this. But right now, he had other priorities. 'Yami, tell me everything that transpired between you and Mother.'

∽

Shraddhadeva cradled a delirious Yami in his arms as she half lay on the couch, her head nestled under his chin. She shivered and screamed at some invisible harm. 'Little sister, whatever it is, it will be over soon!' He promised, glaring at Yama across the room. Oblivious to the sibling drama sat an unaffected Kacha, focused on the medication he was going to administer. The son of Deva Guru Brihaspati was known for his keen interest in healing and curing. Kacha was the closest discretionary physician the brothers could manage, to treat their sister while avoiding the scrutiny of other Gods.

'She will be alright.' The son of Brihaspati smiled, holding up something between his index finger and thumb. 'Please let me.' There was a spark and a glow as he pressed his thumb against Yami's forehead. Both Yama and Shraddhadeva let out a sigh as they saw Yami settle into a peaceful sleep.

'Will she remember our conversation?' Yama stepped forward as Kacha rose.

'She should not,' Kacha replied, casting a compassionate glance at Yami. 'And yes, she has been under the influence of something I find strange. Seems to be *Varuni*. But the potency is different, as though the usual Varuni had been infused with something else that caused a hallucination that made her believe whatever she told you about you and her...' Kacha let the sentence trail off at the look of disgust on Yama's face. 'I just meant to say she was not herself when she said those things. And your burst of power made her admit the truth she was not even consciously aware of. The conflict in her system was too much for her to bear.'

'Thank you, Kacha.' The relief on Yama's face was visible. He saw Kacha nod and take his leave, promising to be available when they needed him again. 'Son of Brihaspati, pray, let this remain between us.' Shraddhadeva need not have added the plea for they knew they could trust Kacha. The elder Devas were more likely to let them off with a reprimand for not using powers discreetly. Yama was not afraid of using his power of *Vashikarana*, or of their reaction. He only wanted to unearth what was happening to his family without exposing his dear ones to any harm.

'What happened?' Yami's feeble voice drew his attention back and he saw Shraddhadeva pat her shoulder, stopping her from rising. But Yami turned and looked at Yama. 'Yama, we were at…'

'Bhuloka.' Yama completed her sentence, forcing a smile on his lips. 'You fainted there. Everything is alright, sister.'

Yami's eyes closed for a moment before they shot open. 'I remember saying something… Yama?'

'Shhh… Something caused you to hallucinate. What you remember may or may not be real. But, thanks to Kacha, you are fine.'

That seemed to calm Yami down. Shraddhadeva rose, settling her in her bed. The brothers were about to leave when Yami called Yama back, and waited for Shraddhadeva to leave. Yama dreaded the moment in between.

'Brother, do you hate me?'

Yama dropped to his knees by her side. 'Never,' he managed to say, fighting back the emotions that choked him. 'Rest, Yami. We will not let any harm come to you, Sister.'

The Flame That Forged the Wheel

Under the crimson sky where the light of the stars had begun to fade, in the ancient realm where luminous entities could no longer witness what happened, stood Yama, cloaked in shadows. He was at the meeting point of two realms bordering the Daitya Loka, his eyes focused on the woman passing through the great gates within a heartbeat, as though the sentinels knew her from long. *Mother, what are you up to?* Yama could walk through the gates as well. It was the time of the Manvantara Sandhya, and ancient rivalries too were suspended. Yet, Yama did not want to alert anyone in Daitya Loka of his arrival right after his mother. Invoking the sky and the spirits of Yakshas, he willed his body to turn invisible before slipping through the gates, hoping that there was no other way in which the realm could alert its denizens of a foreign presence. *Where has mother gone?* He wondered looking at the bustling Daitya streetways.

'Your insights are most enlightening, Devi Chhaya,'

Yama cocked his ears at the voice and turned left towards an alley where a towering Daitya stood before his mother. Yama instinctively stepped back. *Chhaya!*

'I know you are taking a great risk by helping us.'

'Risk?' Chhaya seemed to scoff. Yama could not make out her expression. 'Just doing my part to bring balance,' Chhaya spoke, her tone smooth, yet laced with something that made Yama's spine tingle, betraying a duplicity that he could not ignore.

'Balance?' Yama muttered under his breath, the word leaving a bitter taste. He felt an unfamiliar ache in his chest, a tightening grip of uncertainty. *Who was this Chhaya? Where was his mother? How much did the Daityas know about the household of Vivasvan? Worse, the realm of Devas itself?* Yama clenched his fists. His duty was clear; he was the upholder of Dharma, the Cosmic Balance, and here he was, spying on the woman they all had thought to be his mother. *Not Saranyu, but Chhaya, a spitting image of his mother, of the form, not the heart within.* Had the Daityas imprisoned Saranyu to plant their spy? How could his father not detect the enemy in their amidst?

'Are you certain the Devas will not suspect your...contributions to our cause?' questioned the Daitya, his voice a mix of suspicion and admiration.

'Have I ever given you reason to doubt me?' Chhaya retorted, the steel in her words making the intimidating Daitya take a step back, making Yama clench his fists harder.

Yama exhaled quietly, opening his palms, relaxing his shoulders.

'Should the Devas grow suspicious, they will find no proof,' Chhaya's voice broke through his reverie, oozing confidence. 'After all, who would ever suspect Vivasvan's own wife and progeny? Or at least half of them. Who in their right mind would guess that I was fashioned out of Saranyu's failed attempts to enable herself to face her husband's radiance? And that she left me willingly here to take her place.'

The words and the laughter that followed hit Yama like lightning—blinding and illuminating. His mother had willingly left her household to the care of this woman who was... The facts were growing bizarre by the moment.

'Virochana,' Chhaya's voice, even just a whisper, pierced through the darkness. 'The Devas grow complacent in their celestial abode, blind to the shadows that encroach upon their light. The soon-to-retire guardians feel their responsibilities are just done and the ones taking their places...' Chhaya paused and chuckled again. 'They are far from ready.

'Indeed, Chhaya,' Virochana agreed. 'Their arrogance and complacency will be the cause of their undoing. With your insights, we shall orchestrate their fall.'

Yama's breath hitched. There were forces orchestrating a Daitya takeover of Deva Loka. *By the Trimurtis!*

'By the next eclipse, while Svarbhanu watches over us, we shall strike,' Virochana declared, the firelight bouncing off the amulet—a serpent coiled around a black gemstone—near his throat.

'Strike. War. Come on, Virochana!' Chhaya chided. 'You saw what happened with Vishvarupa. Yet, you cannot give up the old methods!' She counselled him. 'The Trimurtis are untouchable. Their favours must not be lost on us with these rash actions! '

Yama felt his fists clench, his nails biting into his palm.

'If not a swift takeover, then what do you suggest, Chhaya?' Virochana's voice was calmer though his impatience was visible. 'Whatever has to be done, has to be done before Saranyu returns to claim her rightful place.'

Chhaya let out an exasperated sigh and moved to lean against the alley wall. 'Virochana, Virochana! Saranyu, I heard, is pursuing the way of tapasya to "remedy her shortcoming". You know that would take an eternity. The poor thing is not made to be by Vivasvan's side!' It was the mix of scorn and contempt Chhaya had for Saranyu that made Yama's chest churn. And they had let this woman ascend the pedestal by his father's side!

'Leave Saranyu. How about the other Devas? For one, I can never trust Purandhara. His sense of agility is a thousand-fold more than that of the outgoing Indra,' Virochana mused.

'Come on! Purandhara has hardly begun his stipulated ritual of Shata Kratu to establish his eligibility for the position of the next Indra,' Chhaya retorted. 'If somehow we can prevail upon the Saptarishis and the Trimurtis that Bali is ready to take over as the Indra, with my Saavarni as the Manu, this age would belong to the Daityas! Fair and square.' Chhaya paused, letting Virochana absorb her words. 'Daitya Guru would concur if you can consult him on this, Virochana.'

'You make sense, dearest niece! This could take so long!' Virochana let out a sigh. 'Till then, the rest of the Devas should not be able to get a whiff of our motives.'

'Oh! They suspect nothing,' Chhaya dismissed Virochana's concern with a swift wave of her hand, oblivious to Yama's silent presence. 'Yama is preoccupied learning his duties, and Vivasvan... Vivasvan's eyes are blinded by the light of his own radiance.'

Yama was barely able to contain the low growl that rumbled in his throat. He wanted to step forth from the shadows to confront them with the fury of a storm, but held back. It was not yet the moment for revelations.

'Ah, but what of Yami and Shraddhadeva?' Virochana's voice probed, seeking cracks in their façade.

'Yami is lost exploring the Bhuloka, her future realm. Tapati is keeping her busy in that. And the Varuni I keep giving her induces entertaining hallucinations.' She laughed making Yama wince again. The woman in the guise of their mother had nearly driven the siblings apart! 'And Shraddhadeva has not even partaken of Amrita yet,' Chhaya continued with a dismissive wave of her hand. 'They whisper among themselves that he holds the promise to reign as the Manu. But for all practical purposes, he may not even end up being an immortal. Limited breaths and heartbeats. Those two pose no threat to our plans.'

'Be wary,' Virochana cautioned. 'Yama has the eyes of a hawk. Biases and weaknesses don't sway him. If he senses our scheme...'

'Let him come,' Chhaya's laugh was as cold as moonlight on steel. 'That shall be his undoing.'

Yama recoiled as if struck. A cauldron of emotions boiled within him—shock, disbelief, and a burning anger that threatened to consume his very soul. Chhaya had chosen her side, aligned with their sworn enemies—Daityas—against their own lineage.

'Very well,' Virochana nodded, content with her confidence. 'Our destiny awaits. The Age of Daityas shall rise from the ashes of the Devas' folly.'

Yama retreated into the shadows, each step heavy with the weight of the disturbing truth that he had unearthed. Chhaya's voice haunted him, a mocking imitation of Saranyu's in tone and pitch. *Where are you, Mother Saranyu?* He had to confront Chhaya to know the full truth, but not at Daitya Loka. Yama, who would come to represent Time, knew he had to bide his time as he retreated to Surya Mandala.

∽

Vivasvan surveyed his part of the Universe. The expanse of his luminosity lit up. The view of Bhuloka greeted him in new hues at every rotation—a sight that immediately made him crave for Saranyu's presence by his side. He had tolerated the presence of her shadow, respecting her wishes, giving her the space and time to come to terms with the new reality. But it had been too long now. As his children tried to hide their predicament for reasons they alone knew, Vivasvan's chest constricted as they huddled together, feeling orphaned. Shraddhadeva, Yama, Yami.

Yami's sickness, Tapati's fear-filled eyes, Saavarni and Shani's aloofness, Shraddhadeva's clipped replies and Chhaya's absence—it all added up. It was time to bring his wife back, make her understand that she had been away for long enough. But before seeking her out, Vivasvan knew that he had to do something else, something that could make him look her in the eye.

In slow yet determined strides, he came to the doorstep of his father-in-law's forge where he saw Tvashtra immersed in sharpening the edges of the weapon that protected the Universe. 'The chakra has stayed in the forge too long, Tvashtra.' Vivasvan saw the Celestial Smith whirl around, startled at his unforeseen arrival.

'I did not invoke you, Lord Vivasvan.' Tvashtra's brow furrowed. 'The heat you infused it with during our last attempt has enabled me to refashion the razor edges for sharpening. But there is a lot of work to be done before we can have the privilege of knocking on the seven gates of Vaikuntha.'

Vivasvan heard him out with a detached smile and glanced at the legendary chakra. 'Time we tried together again, Tvashtra.'

The Celestial Smith shrugged and waited for Vivasvan to hit the chakra with a burst of his heat. And Vivasvan did. It was not just a burst that he had meant to direct at the weapon, but a part of himself, searing forth from his luminous body, tearing away from the vital celestial limbs that held him together. An anguished roar escaped Vivasvan as his body let out a burning inferno that shook even the skies. Numb with pain, Vivasvan kept feeding the inferno.

'Vivasvan!' Tvashtra's gasp sounded distant as though he was being pulled deep within himself. 'What in the name of Brahma are you doing?'

Vivasvan let the fire whirl around him, letting himself slip beyond conscious existence, towards the steady state of those who exist unaffected, beyond the eras of Manu, beyond the Kalpas. Easing into the new rhythm of sentience, he smiled, letting the inferno whirl faster and expand till it encircled the chakra. The world around ceased to exist. Or so it seemed till the inferno moulded itself into a spiral that struck the legendary chakra of Lord Vishnu, lighting up its edges.

Tvashtra rushed to another part of the forge to witness the unprecedented spectacle, the truth of what his son-in-law was up to dawning upon him. His tongs and hammer reached out through the circle of fire that separated him from Vivasvan and the chakra, pouring out his own experience spanning aeons into fashioning the insentient Creation.

The razor edges glowed, absorbing the spiral of fire.

The chakra turned as though springing back to life.

It turned in tandem with the inferno unleashed by Vivasvan, working itself into a whirl of a larger magnitude.

'That is enough, Vivasvan!' Tvashtra's strained cry pierced the air. 'You have restored the Sudarshana back to its legendary glory!'

The chakra whizzed around, absorbing the radiance of the raging inferno till the blaze gradually thinned to a fine streak and then disappeared. Vivasvan collapsed, partly in reverence for the weapon, partly for feeling lighter in his head and heart. Tvashtra dropped to his knees by his side, supporting him by his shoulders. 'Son of Kashyapa, that was unprecedented. Almost foolhardy!'

Vivasvan laughed, settling into what felt like a rebirth. 'The great chakra needed that chunk of my radiance, Tvashtra. And I needed to see my wife!'

The chakra continued to whiz around, lighting up the skies, letting Creation know that those who dare upset the order, balance and sustenance, will need to face its wrath when the time comes.

The Unveiling of the Shadow

Surya Mandala

Chhaya returned to find Yama at the gates of Surya Mandala. The unwavering Lord of Dharma blocked her way, like a monolith of righteousness that made the shadow within her waver. She forced a motherly smile on her lips, about to fake a pleasantry when his unmoving presence flowed with a radiance of its own, casting an imposing shadow across the ornate chamber. Chhaya felt something stiffen within her, the usual tranquil air of Surya Mandala, now laced with tension.

'Chhaya,' Yama's voice was a controlled tempest. 'Taking the place of Mother Saranyu here, overseeing the household of Vivasvan, and there, conspiring with the Daityas?'

Chhaya stepped back and steadied herself, her cloak of pretence having dropped, like a weight lifting from her shoulders. Her eyes met his, betraying neither weakness nor guilt.

'Yama, finally you found out,' she said with feigned casualness that did little to mask the defiance in her tone. 'What you see and allege as treachery is an act of restoring balance to the Universe. Our people, Devas and Daityas, both stand on the precipice of oblivion. I am only pulling them back to continue this beautiful Creation of Brahma.'

'By plotting with Virochana? By forsaking the Devas?' Yama clenched his fists, the knuckles whitening.

'You seem to forget that "Deva" is a position accorded to

someone deemed worthy of guarding this Universe, not the entitled identity of Adityas alone.' Chhaya's gaze narrowed. 'It is the time of the Great Twilight. Bali has as much of an opportunity as Purandhara to become the next Indra.'

'Just because Virochana promised to throw their lot behind Saavarni, not Shraddhadeva, as the next possible Manu?'

Chhaya smirked. 'You can't blame a mother for securing the future of her children, can you?'

Yama stepped closer, his gaze turning more piercing. 'I would blame a woman for betraying another woman's trust.' He clenched his fists tighter. 'Taking Saranyu's place in the household of Vivasvan and sabotaging the future of her children, and collaborating with Daityas on top of everything!'

'I am still your mother, Yama.' Chhaya scoffed, unfazed at her secret being revealed.

'Not anymore, since you made Yami hallucinate things that don't even make sense.'

'That worked then!' Chhaya whispered, pleasantly surprised.

'I know of the war that you plan to wage against us!' Yama's voice boomed, echoing through the chamber. The wind around them whirled, as if shuddering at his fury. 'I have overheard your clandestine conversations with the enemy. And you have not an ounce of regret?'

'Regret? No.' Chhaya's lips curled into a semblance of Saranyu's smile, though it held no warmth. 'But understand this, dear Yama, not all battles are fought on the field. Some are waged in the shadows, with whispers and alliances.'

'An alliance with darkness is annihilation,' he countered, his tone laced with sorrow beneath the anger. '*Anartha.* It bodes no good, Chhaya.'

'Or perhaps it is you who cannot see beyond the light. There is strength in darkness, Yama, strength that the Devas have long forgotten.'

'That is not strength, but hunger for power.' He took a step closer, the air between them crackling with unspoken power. 'Hunger that makes Daityas threaten the order and balance of the Universe. Hunger upsets the equilibrium of Creation, putting its sustenance into jeopardy. I will not stand by idly while you, posing to be the wife of Vivasvan, put Dharma to risk, Dharma that we are sworn to uphold.'

'Then what will you do, Lord of Dharma?' Chhaya challenged, stepping forward so that they were mere inches apart. 'Will you pass judgement on me as you are supposed to over the souls of mortals, if and when mortal life actually begins?'

'Judgement is reserved for those who stray from the path of righteousness,' Yama said, his gaze piercing her like a lance. 'You leave me no choice but to act as my duty commands.'

Chhaya looked into Yama's eyes, searching for signs of faltering, but found none. 'Choice, dear son,' she whispered, her voice carrying the weight of inevitability, 'is but an illusion for both of us.'

Yama's mind churned with conflict as he walked away. To protect the Cosmic Order, he would confront even his own. Chhaya was his mother's creation, a reflection of his mother's own self. Perhaps Saranyu trusted them all to protect her as she trusted Chhaya to nurture them. What would Saranyu do if she came to know of Chhaya's machinations? A part of Yama wanted to invoke all the Devas and expose Chhaya. *'But Father must know,'* he resolved, his jaws clenched, before hurrying to catch up with his father. He felt something hit his foot. But Yama had too much on his mind to care for petty wounds.

'Brother.' A gentle voice broke the silence. Yami, his twin, caught up with his fleeting self, her eyes brimming with concern. 'Where are you going? Your spirit is troubled.'

'Yami,' he said, turning away, unable to meet her gaze. 'There is no point hiding the truth anymore.' And he revealed the truth about Chhaya replacing Saranyu. Surprisingly, Yami took the news more calmly than he had expected. The grimness of the reality, though, marred the characteristic spark in her eyes.

'Did Father truly not know of Chhaya? Don't you find it hard to believe that the Lord of Light and Knowledge had little knowledge of what was going on in his household?' Yami seemed to ask herself more than anyone else. Yama hurried ahead, finding no answer even as her frank question troubled him. 'Or did he let her have a free run of his realm despite knowing everything?'

'Yami.' He halted, not willing to let her voice troubling possibilities. 'Father lights up Surya Mandala. Bhuloka, that was ravaged and rendered near barren due to Hiranyaksha, heals and has begun to nurture life again, thanks to his steady presence, a hope to one and all that Dharma, the Cosmic Balance, is what will ultimately prevail. Let us not jump to hasty conclusions.'

Yami pursed her lips, unconvinced, but did not argue further. 'Go forth and tell him what you have discovered, Brother.' Her words were a genuine attempt to comfort him. 'Let the deceit not fester further, poisoning all we hold dear.'

'Deceit...' Yama echoed, the word tasting of venom on his tongue. 'It is not deceit I fear, but the upheaval it will bring.' Finally, his eyes met hers, a storm of anguish brewing within them.

'Upheaval can also be cleansing. Fresh cycles of reinforced Dharma take birth from upheavals. Is it all not a cycle, Yama?' Yami assured him, placing a comforting hand on his armoured shoulder.

'Perhaps. The Trimurtis alone should know,' Yama conceded, reconciled to playing his part in the greater scheme of events. 'Let's go to Father. He must see the darkness that lurks behind the guise of light.'

'For your path is Dharma,' Yami said, her voice a soothing balm to his frayed nerves. 'So be steadfast, Brother,'

With a nod, Yama continued, with his twin sister falling a step behind him as they sped towards the path of the Cosmic Order that their father took in his chariot driven by the half-bird Aruna, another son of Prajapati Kashyapa. One look at their father and the twins realized that something was different about him. The forbidding blazing radiance of his midday form now seemed like an overstatement. The luminous eldest son of Aditi did not need to calm his gaze as he would earlier when he met his children.

'Father,' Yama began, then hesitated gazing at what he thought was a diminished form of his father. If this was indeed a diminished version of his father, it only enhanced the affable resplendence of Vivasvan.

'You look different,' Yami remarked as she followed Yama in kneeling before Vivasvan to seek his blessing.

The father did not hide his surprise and gathered his children in an embrace. One look at Yama's rather troubled face made Vivasvan squeeze his shoulder. 'So you came to know.'

Exchanging a shocked look with his twin, Yama turned to his father. 'So you knew? From the start? Of the truths that lay buried in the shadow, truths that threaten to upset the very balance of the Surya Mandala you command.'

Vivasvan showed his twin children towards his throne, willing them to be patient. 'Speak, Yama. About everything you have discovered. Let your heart not be burdened with any element of the truths you have unravelled.'

'The woman taking Mother's place at home is Chhaya,' Yama started, the name a fissure splitting the foundation of their lineage. 'She has cast her lot with the Daityas. All in a bid to groom Saavarni to be the next Manu.'

Vivasvan sighed inwardly. 'I feared things would go this way—out of hand.'

'Isn't it time you stopped being a mute witness, Father?' Yama's words were laced with pain. 'And Mother, wherever she is—' Yama broke off midway as something struck him. Suddenly, he alternated his gaze between Yami and Vivasvan. 'You know where she is, don't you? If you don't, I think Uncle Purandhara has a clue. Perhaps Lady Sachi too might know.'

Yama saw Vivasvan's lips twitch at the corners. The next sentence elicited a little more than a gasp. 'She is in Bhuloka!'

The light in his father's eyes and the lack of shock said everything. 'You knew it all, Father? And yet you remained as though—' Yama struggled to find the right word, '—nothing happened. Whatever is happening with Mother?' For a moment, he wondered if his father even loved his mother.

'Your mother is on her own sojourn, Yama,' Vivasvan explained. 'I am surprised you did not feel the caress of her love when you visited Bhuloka.'

Yama looked up, remembering the pleasant transformation of the face of the earth, the emergence of life forms of various shapes and colour. They had welcomed the transformation as a sign of Mother Bhumi's healing and getting ready to nurture civilization again. 'Does Mother Saranyu have anything to do with life sprouting out on Bhumi?'

Pride shone in his father's radiant gaze when Vivasvan nodded. Yama let himself revel in the memories of their past trips to Bhuloka. 'How did we not guess? Will she come back ever, Father?'

'About that…' Vivasvan inhaled deeply, his fiery breath indicating an air of determination. 'I think it is time she returned.'

'What about Chhaya?'

'Saranyu installed Chhaya in her place.' Vivasvan spoke in a tone that betrayed no emotion. 'It is up to your mother to now decide what to do with the being that is her own shadow.' Vivasvan rose, light from his being piercing through the veils of doubt in his children's minds. 'But let us try and bring her back before it is too late.'

The Mare and the Stallion

The terrain under her hooves had transformed beyond recognition over the countless earth years that she had covered its circumference multiple times over, taking care to stay by the dark side of the land. Saranyu realized that the weather around has settled into predictable cycles, each lasting a specific time period. Dwellings of those divine beings seeking to perform tapasya and Yajnas had grown denser over the pleasant foothills of the majestic snow-capped peaks that were once known to be the birthplace of the Great Goddess Uma Haimavati, who was the incarnation of Adi Shakti herself. Saranyu would slow down as she passed through the vicinity just to overhear conversations of the usually quiet Rishis about happenings at Deva Loka, their interactions with Devas and about those who had met Lord Brahma Himself. The Rishis too had begun to notice the rhythm of the weather. They called each phase a *Rtu* or season. They classified an earth year into six Rtus: Vasanta, Spring; Grishma, Summer; Varsha, Monsoon; Sharad, the pleasant early Autumn of clear skies; Hemanta, the colder dry Autumn of falling leaves; and Shishira, Winter. Streams and rivulets had begun to take shape from the glaciers far North. Life had multiplied in the flowing waters, and on land.

Left to her, Saranyu would have gladly spent the rest of her existence at these foothills. She wasn't even sure if the effort to stay on the darker side was worth it. There were no signs of Vivasvan having detected the presence of her shadow in his household. Was he still blissfully unaware or had he just reconciled himself to her departure and settled in with Chhaya? Did her children not miss her presence, or had Chhaya's play of illusion kept them in the dark even in the very household of the blazing sun?

Saranyu tried shaking off these thoughts. A tapasya was undertaken for an end. Hers was to build sufficient radiance of her own to be able to meet the gaze of her husband. But how was she to know if she was on the right trajectory with her tapasya? Who would tell her if she was even doing it the right way. The King of Gods would know. But before she sought out Indra himself, Saranyu remembered Purandhara performing his own stipulated ritual of Shata Kratu to prove himself worthy of Indra's throne. Purandhara was bound to know at least something even if he was not yet Indra himself. Saranyu cantered along to the location where she knew her brother-in-law was engrossed in the ritual, chanting away, oblivious of his surroundings. Thanks to Saranyu's keen observation, she spotted another intruder in the vicinity. Without any further sound, Saranyu transformed herself into her divine form. She was about to invoke the mantra to render herself invisible when she sensed who the intruder was. A smile broke on her lips. 'Sachi!'

The daughter of Puloma pulled her into a teary embrace and was in no way apologetic about stalking Purandhara, an infatuation she had never denied. A few days later, Saranyu told herself that she would check with Purandhara on what kept him from reciprocating Sachi's affections.

'What are you doing here?' Sachi asked her. 'And I heard something disturbing about the woman taking your place in the household of Vivasvan!'

Purandhara seemed to pause his chanting in front of the ritual fire for a brief moment. The two women quietened down too. Saranyu decided to talk to him after she had caught up with what had transpired at Surya Mandala since her departure. She looked askance at Sachi, while the Danava Princess pulled her away from Purandhara's earshot.

'Firstly, what came over you, Saranyu? To leave a vibrant household like that? Your children, all at the mercy of that dark apparition!' Sachi's questions poured forth without respite till Saranyu sighed deeply.

'Which means he has settled for my eternal absence, has he?'

'Even if he has, why would you let him do that?' Sachi countered. 'Saranyu! Your shadow, that Chhaya, is plotting to strengthen Bali's case to become the next Indra, based on the tacit understanding with the Daityas that her son Saavarni would be made the next Manu!'

Saranyu leaned against the tree trunk, letting her fatigue show. 'How did you come to know?' Then it hit her, the last sentence spoken by Sachi. She straightened grabbing Sachi by the arm. 'What did you say? Chhaya's son Saavarni?'

The pain in her face made the Danava Princess step back. 'Saranyu!' Sachi gasped. 'I never meant to—'

'But you've done the damage!'

The women almost jumped at the third voice.

'Purandhara.' Saranyu greeted her brother-in-law while Sachi bowed in mock reverence, making him roll his eyes.

'You are letting this Danava woman fill your ears about your husband, sister-in-law?' Purandhara asked even as he returned the respectful gesture.

'She though speaks the truth, doesn't she?' Saranyu narrowed her gaze. 'I have never known Sachi to lie, not even in jest.'

'Pray, come into the *Ashrama*,' Purandhara showed them to his dwelling. 'Saranyu, there is much that you need to know. But first, allow me to play a decent host to my sister-in- law.'

Refreshments were the last thing on Saranyu's mind after it had been numbed by the bitter fact that Chhaya had not limited herself to remaining the caretaker of her household, but had even indulged in marital bliss with Vivasvan and had children of her own. 'How many children does she have?' She stared at

Purandhara when he offered her an earthen goblet filled with something she did not bother to check.

'Three, and strangely, they also look like reflections of your children,' came Sachi's ready reply before Purandhara could say anything.

Saranyu tried saying something, then decided against it. Her limbs shaking in frustration, she held on to restraint and drank up the whole refreshment that Purandhara had given her. 'Three children,' she repeated. 'All of them in a strange way reflections of mine.'

'Not just that. I overheard my father Puloma talk to King Virochana,' Sachi continued. 'Something about Bali becoming the next Indra through some ritual Yajna that would take only one hundredth the time and effort of the Shata Kratu that Purandhara is performing.'

'Trust the Daityas to take shortcuts!' Purandhara scoffed. 'What Yajna is it anyway?'

'*Vishvajit Yajna*,' Sachi mentioned. But its details are inaccessible even to the great gurus Shukra and Brihaspati. 'Apparently, only the Lord Creator Brahma can guide the procedure.'

'And the Manu would have access to the Creator's corpus of knowledge!' Saranyu inferred, pressing her temples. 'By the Trimurtis! The order of cosmic events is being tampered with! And I happen to be the root cause of it all!' Saranyu felt her sight blur and held on to the wooden log that served as a pillar for Purandhara's dwelling. Innumerable circumventions of the earth at her celestial speed in her transformed body had kept fatigue at bay, only for both to break down on this tragic realization. *Her absence did not make a difference to Vivasvan!* The already dark world went darker. 'Purandhara! I feel…' Words would not come out of her mouth. Saranyu felt Sachi rush to her side, supporting her. She saw Purandhara loom before her

'I never asked for your forgiveness after killing Vishvarupa, Sister.' He slowly knelt as Saranyu struggled to keep her eyes open. 'And I pray with all my heart that you will forgive me now.'

Saranyu wondered if she was even comprehending Purandhara's words, when Sachi gasped. 'You mixed Varuni in her goblet!'

Saranyu backed away but staggered back glaring at Purandhara. He looked apologetic but did not betray any hint of regret.

'Forgive me, sister-in-law. This is for your good!'

And the world went completely dark.

∽

When she opened her eyes, brightness greeted her like a warm cloak that sheltered her from the rest of the world. *The familiar sense of comfort, the same intimacy that she had torn herself away from, the same touch!* Saranyu awoke with a start and sat up. Daylight had broken. And she was no longer in the Ashrama of Purandhara but on a hilltop that overlooked a rioting bloom of flora that spread across the breathtaking valley. Before she could turn around to sense another presence, a familiar palm covered her eyes.

'Vivasvan!'

'Devi!'

Saranyu shrank back and turned around. 'I am nobody to you, am I, Deva?'

'Saranyu!'

'You carried on as though my absence didn't even bother you all this while, and now, you seek to trick me along with that brother of yours, Vivasvan!' She shrank back, trying not to look at him. She was not sure if she could do that and then bear to live with the truth, the truth that was born out of her!

'Saranyu, come back and listen.'

Instead, she hurried away from his presence, summoning

the very form of Ashvini, the mare, that had kept her moving all through these past years. Ashvini broke into a gallop, away from the Lord of Light, for in that ironical moment, darkness seemed a better refuge!

'You were the one who seared your shadow out of your own self! You can't escape to the shadows now, Ashvini!'

'I guess you were happier with that shadow, Deva! Go back to her!' The mare galloped faster till the speed of the wind against her blinded her, but her hooves did not falter. They clattered against the steepening earth; she could hear the echo of her own hooves. No, hold! It was the clatter of two more pairs of hooves chasing her. Ashvini continued even as the earth grew steeper still, the wind grew harsher, and the parched wilderness that had arisen out of nowhere stopped yielding new paths for her to escape. An unseasonal dust storm blew around her, ruining any sense of direction and navigation that was left in her. It looked as though suddenly the very elemental beings stood against her.

Anger and frustration replaced her usual celestial speed with an uncharacteristic sense of fatigue. Or maybe the effects of the Varuni were still fresh. 'Let me go, I beg of you, Deva!' She turned around and found the dust storm rise higher. A tall white stallion entered the dust storm and galloped closer to her, its silvery mane fluttering, untouched by the whirling particles of dust. She had not seen anything this handsome. The radiance was soothing and imposing at the same time, the orb of resplendence surrounding the stallion reaching out to her, encircling her, holding her in its thrall.

'You don't need me anymore, Deva!' A part of her wailed, torn between the magnetic pull of his aura and the reality of her not being missed during her long absence.

'I needed you all the time! Chhaya was all that was left of you!' The stallion came close enough to not allow her to bolt away. 'Chhaya played you in your absence but could not be you completely. She is you, and you are her. But neither of you are complete without the other, Saranyu! Accept that. Not just accept but cherish and celebrate the real you, that is both Saranyu and Chhaya—radiance and shadow. The true Guardian Goddess of the Twilight, of dawn and dusk! Come back to your rightful place!'

The mare nuzzled against the stallion and the orb of light encircled them both, as did the storm of earth and wind.

The Lord of Light had finally reunited with the Goddess of Twilight.

Sṛṣṭi, Sthiti, Laya

Amidst the tranquillity of the fragrant grove, adorned with blooms and fruits that presented a visual tribute to the rhythm of Rtus, Saranyu relaxed against the fibrous grass beneath her. Her gaze was fixed on the two boys, divine and vivacious, as they hopped from tree to bush to shrubs, observing the flora, drinking in the wisdom of Mother Bhumi with their sheer power of retention. Naasatya, the fairer one seemed to show something of interest to his twin of dusky hue, Daasara. The twin sons of their union mingled their lessons with play, the wisdom of their father and the grace of their mother, their swiftness a reminder of her reunion with Vivasvan in the form of Ashvini.

'What's with their obsession with herbs and roots!' Saranyu smiled to herself.

'They are curious about the vibrant forms of life that their mother helped sprout on the face of Devi Bhumi with her tapasya,' Vivasvan remarked. His gaze turned serious, though Saranyu could spend a lifetime looking into the golden orbs. 'It is time we returned, Saranyu.'

She pursed her lips, bracing herself for the conflict that lay ahead. 'Chhaya will not take my return lightly,' Saranyu remarked, shifting her gaze towards the horizon.

'This conflict is with your own self, Saranyu,' Vivasvan sighed. 'The more you regard Chhaya as something different, the more she gets aligned with the Daityas—a legacy you have been trying to deny.'

Saranyu pondered over the futility of her past endeavours.

'Perhaps,' she mused aloud, 'there is more to this Daitya blood of mine than I have dared to admit.'

'Have you ever wondered what causes the difference between the progeny of the same father, the great Prajapati Kashyapa? Those born of sisters, Diti, Danu and Aditi, born of the same parents?' Vivasvan took her hand in his. The fingers of her other hand traced intricate lines on the long leaves of the creeper that lay by her side, feeling the coolness of the dew.

'I have wondered much about this, trust me.' She looked at him. 'You take examples of cousins and half-siblings, Deva. What about me and Vishvarupa, twins by blood? Sachi and Svarabhanu, one fiery and steadfast, the other with a personality that creeps up behind from the shadows of deceit. We are from the same source and yet so different!'

'Brahma's Creation, Vishnu's Sustenance, Maheshvara's Annihilation, all are a part of the cycle of this Universe,' Vivasvan said, his voice resonating with the serene gush of spring waters in the background. '*Srishti*, *Sthiti* and *Laya*, my love. There is significance and uniqueness in each of these phases.'

It was not new to Saranyu. But Vivasvan's mention of the eternal cycle with respect to the two lineages was profound. 'Save for a handful, Daityas and Danavas have always resented Vishnu, the Guardian of Sustenance and Continuum. They stuck to worshipping and idolizing Creation and Annihilation, but not Sustenance,' Saranyu pondered aloud.

Vivasvan's brow rose and fell at her prompt observation. 'Look at the form of Dharma, the Cosmic Balance, and Rta, the Cosmic Order, during each of these stages, Saranyu. Lord Brahma would marry the very Goddess born of Him. The rules of the latter phase would deem it horrific. Take the phase of Laya—the Great God, the benevolent Shiva who drank the Halahala to save the Universe, will himself burn and devour what he protected.'

'Dharma assumes a different dynamic with each phase, Deva.

But the Daityas' affinity for Srishti and Laya, their resistance to the stable Sthiti, as opposed to the Devas' obsession for Sthiti as they rally behind Vishnu, is that what causes the whole rivalry spanning yugas and Manvantaras?' Saranyu's resplendent mate nodded in agreement. She continued. 'I heard that the great Daitya twins Hiranyaksha and Hiranyakashipu were conceived in the prohibited phase of twilight, and ended up being sworn rivals of Vishnu. Their rivalry was in fact not against Lord Vishnu, but against the very principle of Sthiti.'

Vivasvan nodded with a solemn frown. 'They rebelled against the order of sustenance with little or no understanding of the need for Sthiti. Their misplaced restlessness over rules and codes, misdirected sense of righteousness casting the whole to Sthiti dharma as oppressive or stifling, made them go astray with their power. We all know how their reign ended. But in their wake, rivalries sprouted and clashes erupted, though dialogue and diplomacy too were used, alliances forged to put off the imminent if only for a short while.' Vivasvan paused in between his monologue. 'Amrita was the fruit of the labour of both Devas and Daityas. But sustained existence supported by Amrita would never fit in with the Daitya philosophy, though they may hate us till today for being tricked by Lord Vishnu. Daityas are better off with Guru Shukracharya's gift of *Mrita Sanjeevani*, the skill of bringing the dead back to life. That sits better with their dynamic Srishti-Laya cycle without Sthiti.'

'Are they conscious of their choices, Deva? Without giving Sthiti its place, how would even the Daityas rule over the Universe if they ever supplant the Devas?' Saranyu pondered aloud. As much as the discussion seemed like a long commentary on the macro cosmos, understanding its crux was what would help her strike peace with Chhaya, or at least find a starting point without going for a direct conflict.

'That's where the cycles of Manu play a great role.' Vivasvan smiled. 'Those are the cycles of the Cosmos when mortal life sprouts on Devi Bhumi, flourishes enough to establish civilizations, sustains itself through periods of peace, strife, intrigue and so on, figuring out the dynamics of Dharma. Mortals, with their limited life span, teach us Devas and Daityas important lessons on the consequences of siding with Dharma and Adharma.'

'Mortals teach *us* lessons?' Saranyu raised her eyebrows, a half-amused smile touching her eyes. 'Is this Vivasvan attaining newer heights in humility or your humour, Deva?'

'A mortal life, lived in accordance with Dharma with its complicated dynamics, with an unwavering focus on the intransient Parabrahma, would indeed not just be a great lesson for Gods but also an inspiration and reference in protecting the Cosmic Order. That is an eternal truth, and not born of my humility. Some may say the mortal world is a playing field for Devas and Daityas, for they are born with the characteristics of both.'

'And the dominant characteristic shall lead to their choices and the consequences,' Saranyu drew up her knees to her chest, her attention briefly shifting to the twins chatting about their newly discovered subject. Vivasvan's infinite wisdom as well as his resplendence seem to have flowed into them. 'That means Devas and Daityas will witness order and chaos clash through mortals, and hopefully appreciate the zones and phases of complexity and transformation.'

'That's the hope,' Vivasvan smiled. 'Shraddhadeva and Saavarni both show promise of sprouting mortal life on Mother Bhumi. Their gifts are not anomalies but necessities for the cosmic dance to continue. They will shape destinies and carve paths for the stars themselves. But…' The momentary pride in his eyes dimmed as a line of concern etched itself on Vivasvan's forehead.

'But there can be only one Manu,' Saranyu said, drawing a glance from him that said that she had spoken his mind. 'At least during a single Manvantara.'

'Indeed, Saranyu,' Vivasvan affirmed, placing a hand over hers, a comforting warmth quelling her doubts. 'Each of them will get a term of Manu. The question remains as to who goes first. One will be selected and the other will have to bide his time, observing, recording, and learning from his brother's reign as Manu.'

In her heart, where fear and wonder often dwelled side by side, Saranyu felt a burgeoning sense of purpose. 'Then let us guide them to embrace their destiny, Deva,' she declared with newfound conviction, rising from her seat.

'Time we returned, Saranyu.'

'Time our little ones too met their siblings and the larger family.' Saranyu was about to call upon the twins when Vivasvan shook his head. 'No, let the twins remain here and prepare to carve their own roles.'

Saranyu's jaw dropped as she gazed at Naasatya and Daasara trying to gather an armful of leaves and heap them on the earth. The mother was not ready to leave her youngest ones even though their celestial lineage equipped them to survive for a while. And she had not even discussed their destiny with Vivasvan.

As if he had read her mind, the Luminous Daystar rose and helped her up. 'When a mortal life starts, there will be forces that will impede and threaten its progress. Mortal limbs don't retain celestial strength. Disease is a constant company of a mortal's body, often a harbinger of death. Our younger twins shall rescue distressed mortals from their predicaments, with their unique knowledge of medicine—Mother Bhumi's home-grown remedy for future crises.'

'They will become physicians who will heal the afflicted?' Saranyu's gaze misted over with a mix of pride and pain at the thought of the upcoming separation. 'But Deva...'

'Only for a short while, Saranyu. They will be safe.'

Saranyu had to remain content with that assurance of her

spouse. Besides, they would be under his watchful eyes, probably with the Rishis, and at times, Purandhara would watch over them too. The conditions at her home demanded much more of her attention now. As Saranyu tenderly kissed the foreheads of the twin brothers, her mind went to Chhaya. Her shadow self was not going to be the one who would bother with the detailed commentary on the complex dynamics between Deva, Daitya and Martya nature, and the evolving nature of Dharma. She, Saranyu, would have to assert herself this time and have patience too in convincing Chhaya.

'Will you stand by me, Deva?' she asked, although in her heart she knew his answer even before he said anything.

'Always, Devi.' His word carried the weight of eternity. 'Together, we shall watch our children, all of them, rise to their own destined heights, and become the architects of the Universe of tomorrow.'

Their hands clasped, an alliance sealed by their shared vision and love, Saranyu looked up at the skies, feeling her spirit soar. In the union of sun and twilight, a promise was made, under the watchful eyes of the realm of Devas.

Cosmos at Crossroads

Vivasvan's golden chariot sliced through the cerulean paths of the Deva realm, its radiant beams piercing the darkness like molten streams of pure dawn. The arrival of the Luminous Son of Aditi and Kashyapa was heralded by sounds of conch shells, their echoes reverberating with the mystical hymns of the Vedas. The denizens of Surya Mandala saw Saranyu, the embodiment of celestial beauty and mystery by his side—a vision of ethereal grace returned to the fold of divinity. They murmured among themselves about the Goddess who ruled in Saranyu's stead. They knew that something momentous was about to happen.

While her dusky complexion was a perfect reflection of Saranyu's, the tempest that brewed in Chhaya's cloudy irises gave her away. The moment Vivasvan descended, she erupted, 'Saranyu, happy now? You forced him to carve out and discard a piece of himself like you did.'

'Chhaya!'

'They accuse me of allying with the Daityas. But even I know that a wife, a companion for eternity, would never cause her mate's downfall! And you, on the other hand…' She shook her head and turned to Vivasvan. 'Deva, you promised me that I, whoever I am, would always have a place in your household! Yet you bring her back, only to disrupt the harmony that was finally shaping up in our lives?'

Vivasvan's face remained impassive like the golden orb that encircled him, yet within, he felt the stirrings of an inner tumult. It was the heat of confrontation, not warmth, that he had brought back to his realm today. 'Harmony?' He echoed, his tone a mix of compassion and reproach. 'Harmony was never going to be possible in her absence, Chhaya. You know that better than me.'

Chhaya stepped back even as the couple approached her, her firm hand raised as if to keep the distance.

'Chhaya, I am not your rival.' Saranyu braved another step forward.

'Your mind weaves fantasies even after your so-called long-drawn tapasya, Saranyu!' Chhaya scoffed. 'You sliced me out of your own self because you could not bear my presence within you! Your heart knows it. Further, you resented the fact that you needed me to even stand in his presence. Wasn't that rivalry, sister dearest?'

'I admit I didn't take well to the Daitya part of my lineage, Chhaya.' Saranyu tried to explain. 'Yes, I hated the fact that I needed you to even withstand Vivasvan's presence. I failed to accept that you are a part of me.'

Chhaya remained unmoved and turned away. 'The moment his radiance decreased, thanks to Vishvarupa's machinations, which you exposed, Saranyu, thanks to me,' Chhaya's outburst grew louder with each word, 'you began to ignore me! You were happy to not need me! You would have been happier if you could have relegated me to oblivion!'

'But that is not to be, Chhaya,' Saranyu implored. 'Treating each other as rivals and pitting our children against one another—that's not how it is supposed to be now.'

'You installed me in your place because you could not continue, Saranyu,' Chhaya pointed out with an air of finality. 'And you thought I would meekly continue to be a nurse to your children. No, I have an identity and ambition of my own. And my children shall ascend to those positions of power and rule over the Universe! They will be the ones Creation would bow down to.' She turned to Vivasvan. 'And you owe me this, Deva.'

Vivasvan held back Saranyu from stepping further ahead and shook his head. 'The positions of guardianship over the Universe are not my legacy to bequeath, Chhaya. I don't owe you that, neither do I owe Saranyu that. But,' his words were softer, 'to me, you were never different from Saranyu, nor is your identity distinct from hers. Neither are your children distinct from hers.'

Before the women could say more, Vivasvan considered the other denizens around them, baffled at the familial confrontation. 'Shraddhadeva has been destined to don the role of Manu for the coming Manvantara. And it is Lord Brahma's declaration that he has proven himself fit for the role.'

'How is this justice?' Chhaya's voice thundered, slicing through his passivity, her stark silhouette rigid with fury against the radiant backdrop of Surya Mandala. 'You know Saavarni is ready, he is destined. He must ascend as Manu before Shraddhadeva.'

'Destined...' The word lingered in Vivasvan's mind, fraught with the weight of aeons and the burden of celestial duty.

'His time is now!' She stepped closer, her visage contorted by the vehemence of her plea. 'Have you forgotten the power he holds? The Daitya clan backs him fully and he is of *your* lineage. He is an Aditya too! Your people should not have a problem supporting his claim!'

'Is it about clan support for him over merit, Chhaya?' Vivasvan let out a wry chuckle as he exchanged a glance with Saranyu. 'Well, your words...they are not without a point though,' admitted Vivasvan, his own voice betraying his inner conflict. The future balance of the Cosmos lay upon his shoulders, on how he would resolve this contentious claim by Chhaya.

'Point?' Chhaya laughed, her laughter as bitter as the darkest of moonless nights. 'It's not about merit. It's about what's right, about what was promised!'

'Promise,' he whispered, almost inaudibly amidst the divine onlookers' murmurs. Promises had to be upheld. 'Chhaya, you thought you tricked me into promising you the same power to your children. What I assured you was not an unquestioned ascension to power but the knowledge and wisdom necessary to be worthy of it.'

'Look into my eyes, Vivasvan,' demanded Chhaya, her form commanding despite the lack of a celestial glow. 'Tell me you will not go back on your word. Tell me you stand by your queen and her progeny.'

Her gaze bore into him, fierce and unyielding, a challenge that pierced deeper than any weapon. Vivasvan's heart wavered between the firmness that was required to do things the right way and the emotions that piled up over Chhaya's contention. *She is but Saranyu's shadow!*

Chhaya's lips seemed to quiver as though something had struck her. 'With Saavarni as the Manu and Bali as the Indra, Daitya support will be won over and they will no longer be a threat to the Cosmic Order, Deva. You would be correcting aeons of continued imbalance by installing Saavarni as the Manu!'

'Chhaya,' Vivasvan paused, the gravity of the moment making him search for words. The Trimurtis had served up a fine puzzle by declaring both his sons as Manu designates. The Purandhara-Bali dynamics was an added complication.

'Say it,' she pressed him, her voice as sharp as the edge of a blade.

'Time will reveal all,' Vivasvan finally said, the decision still hung in balance. He offered no promises, only the enigmatic certainty of fate.

'Your return changes nothing, Saranyu,' Chhaya declared, her voice a tempest that carried the weight of her authority. The ethereal court watched, the indignation of her words echoing through the silence.

'Does it not?' countered Saranyu, her presence like the gentle dawn juxtaposed against Chhaya's twilight fury. 'Shraddhadeva, though in my absence, has grown under the light of Dharma and jnana—Wisdom.'

'Virtue? Wisdom?' scoffed Chhaya. 'They are luxuries of this realm, this fast-fading realm, Saranyu. The term of the current Devas is soon to end! Power is the language of Daityas, and Saavarni has been forged in its fires.'

Vivasvan could feel the divide, as if the very ground beneath them was cleaving to create a chasm between the aspirations of the two mothers. Their gazes locked, one a blaze of solar flames, the other a cool, shadowy steel.

'Power without restraint begets chaos,' Saranyu argued, her figure radiating calm defiance. 'Shraddhadeva will bring order, balance.'

'Order and balance! Saranyu, you amuse me.' Chhaya's laugh was scornful, 'You think the future race of Martyas is going to be swayed by your Dharma, Virtue, Balance, Order…' Her brow furrowed and jaws gritted. 'They are going to be driven by their instincts—Hunger, Desire, Strength, Weakness. The stronger shall overpower the weaker. That is the law of the mortal realm!'

'Wrong, Chhaya!' Saranyu chuckled like she would at a child's claim. 'Martyas, though under the influence of everything you say, will find sustenance in order, balance and togetherness. It is not the stronger over the weaker. It is not even the stronger for the weaker. It is about the strength each one lends to everyone's survival and wellness, the flourishing of their progeny and, hence, the whole civilization.'

A soothing breeze seemed to carry the conviction of Saranyu's words. Chhaya, though, seemed to roll her eyes.

'Creation favours the strong, Saranyu and Vivasvan,' Chhaya retorted, her eyes alight with a fierce challenge. 'Deny it if you dare.'

'Strength...' Vivasvan murmured, his thoughts a maelstrom. 'True strength lies in the harmony of all things.'

'Harmony,' Saranyu echoed softly, her hand reaching out to brush against his arm—a silent plea for support.

'Words,' Chhaya lashed out, her disdain palpable. 'Pretty words that mask indecision. Choose, Vivasvan, before your hesitation rends what little order remains in the period of this Great Twilight. Your dear balance and order are in your hands, for you to shape, as you always have. By naming Saavarni as Manu, you honour the pact between Devas and Daityas. You ensure balance.' Her lips curled into an uncharacteristic smile. 'Remember the chaos that the Daitya clan is capable of unleashing. Can the Cosmos handle a war at this delicate moment?'

'Resorting to threats now, Chhaya?' Vivasvan scoffed. 'All for power!' It was one of the rare times that he was on the brink of losing his cool. 'The choice is not mine to make, Chhaya. The decision on Manu is Lord Brahma's alone.' He moved closer to Saranyu, beckoning Chhaya closer to him as well. 'I shall now leave you both alone to reconcile whatever your differences are.'

Before Saranyu could say anything, Chhaya stepped back, turning her face away as if the suggestion did not warrant even a verbal rejection. Saranyu made an unsuccessful attempt to call her back. Then she followed Vivasvan to the inner chambers. It was when Saranyu was about to cross the threshold that Chhaya said, 'She and I can't stay under the same roof, Vivasvan.' On seeing them turn around, Chhaya drew herself to her full height. 'And do not fear that I shall go to Daitya Loka. I am going to be at the Celestial Architect Tvashtra's place till Brahma and your Saptarishis give a decision about the future of my son. My children will follow me.'

∽

Vivasvan would have liked to be with Saranyu to help her assume once again the role due to her. But he chose to let Shraddhadeva, Yama and Yami have a quiet reunion with their mother and sought out the realms that were not in his usual path

Soaring through the skies, Vivasvan chanted the syllables that opened portals between realms. The realm of Devas was separated from Satya Loka, the greater realm of Lord Brahma. Vivasvan dared not cross the portal and step over to the other side to spend even a short period at Satya Loka—that would result in his prolonged absence from the lower realms that needed his presence. But he could always call out to the Great Grandfather. Vivasvan's father was Kashyapa, the Prajapati who was born of Rishi Marichi, the Manasaputra—the mind-born progeny of Brahma Himself.

The Creator Great Grandfather, Vivasvan knew, would manifest Himself only as a result of a long tapasya. But the pressing issue of the moment did not allow Vivasvan that luxury. Waiting at the threshold of the portal that connected the realm of Devas to that of Brahma, he waited for the Great Ancestor to sense his dilemma and grace him by his presence.

The issue that burdened the Lord of Light was not his alone. It was going to be that of the whole cycle of Creation and life that was to follow in the coming phases of the Universe. The Manvantara was set to start, and the position of the next Manu had two contenders—both Vivasvan's sons. An impartial father, he had followed the progress of both his sons. They could compete with each other in the retention of the knowledge of Dharma that they had received from the Prajapatis and Saptarishis. They could vie with each other in valour, holding onlookers spellbound. But *knowing* and *being* were different. While Shraddhadeva had always been the calmer one, Saavarni was outspoken in discussing the ways of various realms, the rights and wrongs, with great passion, at times betraying lack of objectivity. Could the first progenitor of mortals afford the dispassion of Shraddhadeva or the excessive investment of self that Saavarni was capable of?

Vivasvan thought of the preceding Manus of the Kalpa—

Swayambhu, Swarochisha, Uttama, Tapasa, Raivata and Chakshusha. Each of them was unique, and yet became one with the continuum of Dharma.

'It is the uniqueness brought to the continuum that makes Manu the leader of the times that lay before him, Vivasvan.'

Shaken out of his thoughts, Vivasvan gazed at the approaching orb of white light that dwarfed his, and yet spread around him with the familiar warmth of security that only a grandfather could offer.

'Salutations, *Vidhata*!' Vivasvan knelt as the shape of the orb morphed, first letting him see a radiant swan that carried the one who made the Universe happen. Lord Brahma looked at His great grandson, His four heads, believed to represent the four Vedas, nodding in synchronized assurance. 'Two sons with merit to contend for the position of Manu would have any father's heart brim with pride.' The Great Grandfather smiled, compassion and indulgence reflecting on all His four radiant faces. 'And I see your otherwise luminous face clouded by concern?'

The hint of indulgence drew a smile from Vivasvan. 'But the Universe needs one Manu, *Lord Grandsire*. And the Daityas threaten rebellion if Saavarni is not chosen. Life has barely begun to spring on Mother Bhumi. Now is not the time for war between Devas and Daityas.'

'War will indeed unleash chaos while the need of the hour is stability,' the Grandsire mused. 'We can influence one of your sons to abdicate this term of Manu for the other, for greater peace. But Vivasvan, something tells me you had already decided against that when you sought me out.' Lord Brahma's words reverberated far and wide, with the skies above them carrying their echo to unexplored distances.

The Lord of Light hesitated for a moment before voicing his reason. 'Indeed, my Lord. But it would be unfair to ask Shraddhadeva to wait out his term as much as it would be futile to ask Saavarni to do so, for right now, his mind is clouded with ambition sans the weight of responsibility—the fruit of Chhaya's and Virochana's counselling.' Vivasvan's broad forehead creased. 'I cannot help but blame myself. The one whose very purpose is to dispel the darkness of the worlds could not sense the shadows hovering over his own household.'

'Your function is also to shed light and bear witness to the eternal truths that unfold in their own ways, Son of Aditi.' Brahma remarked. 'Intervention when the course of events turns against Dharma is the function of the Indra and others. But your hesitation springs from elsewhere. The balance that has eluded your household all this time cannot be achieved by antagonizing Chhaya and her progeny.'

'And yet, I cannot let Chhaya or her newfound Daitya supporters hold a universal decision hostage to their claim to power, *Pitamaha* Brahma.'

Brahma nodded, His glance narrowing, each of His four faces responding in different facets of knowledge of the future—gravity, intensity, indulgence and determination. 'The Universe shall indeed bear witness, Son of Aditi.' He smiled. 'The decision on Manu shall be announced not just for the coming seventh era of Manu but for the era that follows too.' Vivasvan listened intently, this idea having struck him earlier too. 'But just to let the Daityas know that they have to bide their time, both the upcoming Manus shall spar to decide their order of ascension.' The Creator smiled.

'My sons should spar with each other so that Devas and Daityas are spared a war.' Vivasvan reflected, his crimson irises more a reflection of his inner turmoil than of his characteristic luminosity.

'Small sacrifices, Lord of Light.' Brahma raised His hand that held the prayer beads. 'The next Manu shall ascend with an assurance by the other that he would bide his time.'

The golden shades turned to crimson in the distant skies. Chhaya tried to not focus on the course of her luminous spouse in the skies. Instead, she made her way to the reluctant Celestial Architect working alone in his forge. Tvashtra was not too eager to let her stay in his abode. But Chhaya gathered that a part of him was happy to let Saranyu and Vivasvan reunite in peace, if it meant him sheltering Chhaya for a while. She was happy to note Shani's interest in metals and Tvashtra not discouraging him from working in his forge. Now, if only she could see Tvashtra in the eye and push her plan a step further.

Chhaya entered the forge and saw Tvashtra pause, sensing her presence though he had his back to her. After a moment, the Celestial Architect resumed his work, letting his tongs hit the metal weapon—a scythe or something similar. Chhaya was not interested in learning about the weaponry of Devas. She was not a spy of Daityas like Yama and his siblings thought her to be. She had only found a potential ally in Daityas, and she could not fathom why the descendants of Diti would not handle responsibility if actually entrusted with it and given the role of guarding the Universe, like Devas, under the watchful gaze of the Trimurtis. Chhaya flitted past rows of covered weapons, closer to where Tvashtra stood. Clearing her throat, she started with what she knew would catch his attention. 'I saw her during my last visit to Daitya Loka.'

Tvashtra stilled this time for a while before his hammer tapped the sharper edge of the scythe again. 'If you mean Rechana, she is not bound to any role with allegiance to Devas like I am.'

Chhaya pursed her lips at the finality in his tone. The Celestial Smith was going to be hard to manipulate. 'At least she got to grieve for her son. It just feels unfair that you cannot even do that openly, Tvashtra.' She saw him turn towards her, his pronounced frown signalling his scepticism. 'Deva, I just feel guilty. I was instrumental in exposing what Visvarupa did. I was a nascent

formless being under Saranyu's control, eager to do what pleased her, so that…' She paused, shrugging, willing him to understand.

'Is that all?' Tvashtra set aside his hammer and glared at her. 'I don't blame you for my son's death if that is what is bothering you, Chhaya.' It was evident that he wanted her to leave his sanctum, treating his query as her dismissal.

Chhaya stood her ground for a full moment and then stepped closer. 'What bothers me is Shraddhadeva's closeness to his uncle, the killer of your son, Purandhara.' Chhaya saw Tvashtra flinch at the name of the youngest son of Aditi. She knew she had scored a point. 'If Shraddhadeva is made Manu, though he is not the decision maker on who will rule over the Gods, the odds swing in Purandhara's favour to ascend the throne of Deva Loka.'

'Chhaya.' Tvashtra's face contorted with pain and helplessness but the Celestial Architect quickly managed to regain his composure. 'We all concede the fact that the Grandsire, Creator Lord Brahma, sees the destiny of the Universe and His vision surpasses ours. The decision of making one a guardian of the Universe is His alone.'

Chhaya nodded, the tilt of her head conveying that she had nothing to disagree with Tvashtra. 'Indeed, Deva.' She smiled. 'And the Lord Grandsire would of course see beyond choosing this hot-blooded warrior God as the next Indra. I mean this Purandhara would make for a great commander but would need to be reined in by someone more level-headed.'

She turned around in a fleeting moment, enjoying the changing hues on Tvashtra's face. She would return sometime later to impress upon him how Saavarni as Manu and Bali as Indra would reign over the Universe a thousand-fold better than Shraddhadeva and Purandhara. But before that, the Celestial Smith needed to dwell on the possibility of becoming an attendant to the killer of his own son. 'It is time for me to quiz Saavarni a bit on the knowledge of the ways of mortal life that he attained during his tutelage under the Saptarishis and other learned ones.' She brought her hand to her chest as though it was her duty as the mother to ensure the capability of her son. 'The reputation of the Lord of Light too is at stake.' She added, before leaving the Celestial Forge.

The Eternal in the Perishable

'Mother,' whispered Shraddhadeva, seeking comfort in her presence. His eyes, pools of innocence, searched hers for reassurance.

'Shraddhadeva,' Saranyu whispered back, her touch a feather's caress on his cheek. 'Trust the stars that guide us; they waver not, even when clouds obscure their sight.'

'Stars...' Shraddhadeva frowned. 'Aren't they distant and cold? It is the sun that nurtures and the earth that sustains.'

'Both have their roles, as do we all,' Vivasvan interjected, his words a gentle assertion of Saranyu's observation. 'A ruler must embody not just the strength of the sun but also the patience of the earth.'

Shraddhadeva took in the weight of his father's words, though with some scepticism. 'At times, Father, patience can be the harbinger of decay.'

'Only if pacifism masquerading as patience clouds the mind into inaction,' countered Vivasvan. He found his wife and son reach out to him for they seemed to empathize with the pangs of emotion that seemed to twist in his chest.

Saranyu felt tears unbidden welling up in her eyes. Had she not given in to desperation and forked out Chhaya's being from her own, had they figured out a solution by themselves together, the household would have been spared from this strife. *Chhaya's children are mine too!* That was the thought that crossed her mind when her gaze locked with Vivasvan's for a moment. He responded with a tentative smile. But the solution given by

Lord Brahma now seemed as though it would deepen the strife between Shraddhadeva and Saavarni. They exchanged a look of understanding before Vivasvan broke his gaze lock with her to turn to their firstborn.

'The *Martya Tattva* or Mortal Nature is determined by the Panchabhutas, the five elements of earth, water, fire, air and space. Their perception of the world around them, made of these elements, is driven by their five senses.'

'The *Pancha Indriyas*,' Shraddhadeva responded to Vivasvan's explanation with a smile. 'While these five senses help mortals perceive the transient world around them, they also make the Martya mind vulnerable to the whims of these senses.'

Saranyu brushed aside Shraddhadeva's curls, partly proud and partly relieved that her prolonged absence did not seem to have affected his learning process. She had Vivasvan and the Rishis to thank for that. 'Desire.' She echoed the word that was forming in Shraddhadeva's mind. 'A double-edged sword that can either make a Martya a slave to the senses or can mould it to connect with the intransient that exists above the visible worlds.'

'We cannot wish away double-edged swords, Mother.' Shraddhadeva smiled a warrior's smile. 'One needs to figure out how to deal with desire. Forget the Martyas yet to be born, even Devas and certainly Daityas find themselves trapped in these cycles of desire.' He turned to his father with a shrug. 'Easier said than done, isn't it, Father?'

Vivasvan beamed as Shraddhadeva left his seat to come and kneel closer to his parents. The Lord of Light delved into the history of Creation as he knew it. 'Aeons ago, an innocent Gandharva maiden Varudhini desired a mortal householder Pravara who, unfortunately for her, could not return her affections. Her desire made her a victim to another wily Gandharva called Kali who deceived her by assuming the form of Pravara.'

'This was during the first Manvantara Sandhya,' Saranyu

pointed out. 'While Varudhini's blind desire made her fall prey to Kali's advances, her love and devotion for Pravara turned her into a determined mother who birthed a son of the deceiver, but brought him up to imbibe the nobility of the man who truly owned her heart.'

'Swarochi!' Shraddhadeva exclaimed. 'The father of Dyutiman Swarochisha, the second Manu.'

Vivasvan and Saranyu exchanged a smile, marvelling at his knowledge of the history of worlds that existed long before he was born.

'Think of the more recent Hiranyakashipu.' Vivasvan resumed. 'The thirst for controlling the worlds was so strong that he would stop at nothing to get what he desired. The desire to lord over the Universe blinded him with hatred for Gods who stood in his way, including the Great Sustainer Narayana himself.'

'And the hatred drove him to harass Rishis, and devotees of Lord Vishnu, including his own son Prahlada. At last, even his unique boons granting him near immortality could not save him from Vishnu who assumed the form of Narasimha,' Shraddhadeva mused aloud.

'The sons of Prajapatis and celestial beings too fall prey to the effects of desire, Shraddhadeva. What then can be said about poor mortals?' Saranyu interjected, seeking her son's response.

'Perhaps, mortals are not as "poor" as we think them to be, Mother.' Shraddhadeva was gentle in his disagreement. 'While they are indeed vulnerable to the ravages of desire and lust, they are also capable of Varudhini's devotion and determination.'

'And what can empower them to wield this devotion, Son?'

'The knowledge of Dharma, of the intransient, and of the transience of the world around them,' Shraddhadeva replied and then looked at Vivasvan.

'The Manu must rise from unity, not division. He must rule with consciousness and not just with control. Mortals represent the glorious promise of rising to the status of Gods, provided they gain mastery over their innate, invaluable qualities: Shama, control over mind; Dama, control over limbs; Uparati, withdrawal from sensual instincts; Titiksha, equanimity during trying times; Shraddha, faith in self and in Gods; and Samadhana, focus on the intransient, the Parabrahma.'

'Live in the world. Fulfil your role. Yet, remain conscious of what lies beyond it.' Shraddhadeva spoke, gazing into the vacuum before he met the gaze of his parents. 'The Manu must be capable of steering his people through this cycle and leave the knowledge of this cycle to his progeny, the knowledge of Dharma, the Cosmic Balance, of Rta, the Cosmic Order that maintains the balance and harmony that uphold the Order.'

'Shraddhadeva, this position of Manu is the fulcrum on which this harmony and balance rest. And this is the lesson I shall bestow even on Saavarni if he seeks me out.' Vivasvan's tone was grave.

His father's moment of melancholy reflected on Shraddhadeva's fading smile. 'Father...' he stepped forward, his small frame suddenly seeming to hold a weight beyond his years. 'I will strive to be worthy...of all.'

'The coming trials, and the sparring between you brothers, shall determine the course of the Universe, my son.' Saranyu held him by his shoulder. 'The trials are to be decided by the Saptarishis in consultation with the Grandsire Brahma Himself. And your father has left the decision to their wisdom.'

Shraddhadeva gave an almost imperceptible nod and waited for anything else that his parents would have to say. After a few moments of companionable silence, he bowed low at their feet.

'What is the blessing that you seek of me, Shraddhadeva?' Vivasvan asked, raising him with a tender grip on his shoulder.

'Bless me so that I neither disappoint you, nor hurt my brother.'

∽

'Does Bali know that I have nothing to do with the decision on his ascension to the throne of Deva Loka?' Saavarni frowned as the Daitya messenger left after conveying Bali's and Virochana's best wishes for his upcoming face-off with Shraddhadeva.

Chhaya nudged his arm to keep his voice low till the messenger was completely out of their earshot. 'Is it really in my hands to make you the Manu of the upcoming aeon, Saavarni? But I am sitting here doing nothing?'

A part of Saavarni wished that she would consider doing something. It was a privilege he could not deny—having a mother who drove his ambition and went to any length to secure it for him. He had asked Chhaya why the choice of the next Manu mattered when both he and Shraddhadeva were anyway destined to become Manus of their stipulated aeons, and she had scoffed at what she called his 'weakness'.

'These descendants of Aditi, don't go by their outward radiance, Saavarni.' Chhaya had warned. 'Their glow and luminosity, their long sermons and debates about Dharma, harmony and balance are but for the sake of appearances.' She recounted her own experience. 'Saranyu created me as a tool to shield herself from the intense radiance of Vivasvan, something she was not capable of facing by herself. But when I acquired my own voice and being, she shunned me. The moment I was not needed, she was more than happy to relegate me to oblivion!'

'Hope you also remember that Daityas don't have a great record of helping uphold Dharma.' Saavarni had countered. Chhaya had simply ended their conversation by saying he needed to revisit their history from a perspective different from the biased one of Saptarishis. Saavarni had given up after that. Willing himself to return to the conversation they were having at the moment, Saavarni followed Chhaya back to the residence of Tvashtra. 'Should I seek out Father once before the grand event?'

Chhaya halted in her tracks as though she considered his

question. 'You need the benedictions of your Sire, Saavarni. You need them indeed. But,' she paused again, betraying her own hesitation and then shook her head, 'you should seek them just before your and Shraddhadeva's trials begin. Seeing you after all this time, a benediction is bound to slip out of his soft heart.'

'Why not before that?'

'I don't want him confusing you when we are so close to our goal.' Chhaya raised her finger with an air of finality. 'Shani has tested a sword fashioned out of a new metal that he managed to forge under Tvashtra's direction,' she added. 'You must test yourself with that and keep up your strength too.'

'I shall, Mother,' Saavarni assured her, swallowing the retort he had in his mind on Shani's rather slow way of working with things. It was a boon of destiny that the contenders of the upcoming trials were him and Shraddhadeva, close equals, and not between Yama and Shani. The God of Death would have bested Shani in no time though Shani kept talking about his ability to slow down the destiny of others even if they as much as approached him. 'But you never told me about what drives you to ensure that the Daityas maintain a close alliance with us.'

Chhaya remained quiet for a while, betraying her inner turmoil. 'You know about the marriage of Tvashtra and Rechana, the princess of Daityas and sister of King Virochana,' she started in a low voice.

Saavarni nodded and shrugged as though that was common knowledge. 'One of the diplomatic attempts to maintain peace, I guess. Or a wise game by Prahlada to keep an eye on the kind of weaponry and armoury that Devas were building.'

'Tvashtra guards his forge as though it were dearer to him than his own children.' Chhaya let out a contemptuous chuckle. 'But yes, diplomatic effort it was. And the children of Tvashtra, Saranyu and Visvarupa, bore the characteristics of both Devas and Daityas.'

'I know what happened with Vishvarupa.' Saavarni attempted to stop Chhaya from recounting another known event so that she could come to the point sooner.

'Vishvarupa resorted to nurturing the Daitya side of his strength to weaken the Devas and eventually met his tragic fate. But Saranyu, a part of her detested the Daitya side of her. She blamed it for rendering her incapable of bearing the radiance of Vivasvan, her fated spouse.' Chhaya narrated as her eyes narrowed. 'What she did not know was that it was the Daitya half of her that actually knew how to hoodwink her luminous mate and make her look at him without flinching. But then she got too ahead of herself.' Chhaya chuckled. 'The result today is that she remains the daughter of Tvashtra, the Deva. And I, the daughter of Rechana, the Daitya.'

'You are, in fact, the creation of Saranyu,' Saavarni frowned but backed away when his mother glared at him. 'But you identify yourself as a Daitya.' He shrugged. He did not offer her any rejoinder about his lineage having the Deva line through Vivasvan.

'One term of Manu. Just one!' Chhaya pleaded, collapsing into the nearest seat. 'One term of Manu on our terms, on those of Daityas, so that the Prajapatis, the Saptarishis, the Trimurtis, and even those half-brained sons of Aditi realize that we are capable. Far more capable than those raised to the pedestal across the previous Manvantaras.' Chhaya sat up, beckoning Saavarni close. 'And you show the promise of fulfilling that goal, Saavarni. You could correct this historical wrong. Show everyone what true balance looks like. Promise me you will give it your best, Son.'

His mother's dusky silhouette against the crimson skies summed up the struggles she had endured. Saavarni knelt before her, taking her hand in his, 'I shall not disappoint you, Mother.'

The Great Trial

The congregation of celestial beings was abuzz with anticipation, their divine forms and auras glowing against the dusky backdrop of the placid and eternal space. At the centre of this otherworldly assembly stood Lord Brahma on his swan-shaped throne, flanked by Prajapatis and then Saptarishis. The air seemed heavy with the gravity of the announcement that would decide the fates of two worthy contenders, and with that, the fate of Creation.

'Beings of the three worlds,' Lord Grandsire Brahma's voice resonated, echoing through the expanse of existence, 'the time has come to witness a contest of valour, wisdom and wit, a competition to determine the precedence of the Manu term for Shraddhadeva and Saavarni.'

Shraddhadeva's eyes had a luminous glow reflecting the will to lead and protect during his tenure as Manu. Saavarni, equally determined, had a quiet confidence, his keen mind already wading through the possibilities of the challenges they were to face.

'Let the fourteen realms bear witness,' declared the Creator, His voice heavy with the wisdom of countless Kalpas, 'as we unveil a world crafted from the very essence of Maya. A virtual domain, vibrant and alive, awaits our champions.'

With a flourish of cosmic energy, the vision of the virtual world unfolded before them. It was a landscape that defied imagination, a reflection of the whole Creation interwoven with threads of fantasy. Lush greenery blanketed rolling hills, giving way to towering mountains that pierced the heavens.

'Behold,' whispered Shraddhadeva in awe, his heart racing with the thrill of the unknown. His gaze followed the silhouettes of mystical creatures that soared and roamed—majestic centaurs, horned whales, bejewelled creatures with wings and tails.

'Indeed,' replied Saavarni, his thoughts probing the depths of this new realm, already mapping out strategies and contingencies. 'An intricate illusion, but an illusion nonetheless.'

'Let not your senses deceive you,' advised Brahma, His eyes twinkling with mirth. 'For the trials here are as real as the virtues that will be tested.'

Shraddhadeva clenched his fists, feeling his warrior spirit surge. He was ready to scale the highest peak, to face the fiercest creature if need be. Casting a reverent glance at Vivasvan and Saranyu, seated at a distance, he felt for the virtual anchor. The knowledge imparted by his father would be his compass, guiding him through the mirage of reality.

'Remember, it is not merely about being the swiftest or the strongest,' intoned Lord Brahma, capturing the attention of the two contenders once more. 'It is about wisdom, compassion, and the will to lead. All these shall be scrutinized.'

Saavarni nodded, a plan already crystallizing in his mind. Raw power was not the only key to triumph. The ability to discern the subtle currents of this world, to adapt and overcome were perhaps more important.

'Let the challenge begin,' decreed Lord Brahma. The air thrummed with His command that set destiny in motion.

As the contenders stepped forth into the virtual expanse, their spirits steeled for what lay ahead, while the Gods watched with bated breath.

∽

The first challenge loomed before Shraddhadeva—a mountain path that twisted upward like the coiled body of a slumbering serpent made of stone and soil, with fatal sharp precipices and treacherous marshes. It was a monstrous spine against the sky, where even the clouds seemed to hesitate, parting around its indomitable peaks.

'Behold the Path of Peaks,' boomed a formless voice from space, 'where only the enduring shall not falter.'

Shraddhadeva's gaze ascended along the serrated edges of the mountain path, his pulse quickening at the sight. The rocks were jagged and unyielding, as if they were challenging him to dare their heights.

'Ancestors, guide me,' he whispered, tightening the grip on the rudraksha beads that graced his brawny arm. Inhaling steadily, he began the ascent, his muscles contracting with each calculated heave upward.

'Watch your steps, Shraddhadeva!' called out a familiar voice, melodious and soothing. *'These stones have been the downfall of many aspirants.'*

'Mother, is that you?' Shraddhadeva looked at the skies, expecting to find the congregated divine beings, but he saw none. As though he was all alone in this treacherous expanse.

March on, Son. Saranyu's voice resounded in his head. *This is a test of will and perseverance.*

Shraddhadeva's hands found holds in the cold crevices, his fingers tracing the script of the ages in every grain of the rocks. He moved with a dancer's grace, a warrior's precision.

'Remember,' he thought, recalling the wisdom imparted by sages long past, 'the body achieves what the mind believes.' With this mantra fuelling his spirit, he pushed forward, his breath syncing with the rhythm of his climb.

The higher he climbed, the thinner the air grew, yet his lungs seemed to expand to embrace the challenge. His form was a silhouette against the expanse of a sky painted with the hues of twilight—a celestial dance of purples and oranges.

'Is this all?' Shraddhadeva spoke to the wind, half in jest. 'The trial ends when I manage to scale the peak? Or does something lay in wait?'

'Careful what you wish for,' the wind seemed to chuckle. *'The mountain might hear you. Worse, it might oblige you!'*

'Then let it hear my defiance,' Shraddhadeva retorted, a smile playing on his lips. 'For I am Shraddhadeva, Son of Vivasvan, and I bow not to fear.'

'Careful, Shraddhadeva!' Saranyu's voice echoed in his mind, like a stable anchor tugging him back to reality. *'Conquering nature is a grand ambition. Resonating with it is a grander vision. A true leader is not just a conqueror.'*

'I am obliged for this insight, Mother,' Shraddhadeva responded, focusing on the crest of the mountain now within reach.

His hands grasped the final ledge, hauling himself over the precipice with a triumphant heave. Standing atop, he surveyed the world below, the virtual realm stretching infinitely, alive with possibilities. The sight was the reward of the indomitable force of his will, as though the earth bestowed a vision of the realm that was to be his in future. The moment passed and Shraddhadeva remembered his mother's words. The trial could not have been this simple. There was something more, something beyond the pristine expanse that lay before him. The task was yet to be accomplished. Shraddhadeva's muscles burned with a glorious fire atop the conquered peak, the wind an echo chamber for his pounding heart. Yet, even champions know the treachery of complacency, and as he prepared for descent, Saranyu's voice bloomed in his mind, a lotus unfurling in still waters.

'Shraddhadeva, Son of Vivasvan,' her telepathic touch was both balm and spur, *'your victory is half-won. But gaze not too long at your triumphs lest they become your pyre.'*

'Indeed, Mother,' he returned to reality, the connection

between them pulsing like the rhythm of ancient drums. 'Your words steer me truer than any compass.'

'Remember the eagle,' she encouraged, her presence a beacon in the mental fog of fatigue. *'It does not conquer the sky by merely flapping its wing, but by knowing when to ride the currents.'*

'I am the sun's heir; I claim my victories in the light,' Shraddhadeva declared.

'True,' Saranyu's voice resonated within him, *'but do not scorn the shadows. They too serve those who know their worth.'*

'Then, with your blessings, Mother, let us be masters of both realms,' he resolved, accepting the challenge of duality. His body may have ached, his spirit may have wavered, but his will remained unbroken, tempered in the forge of Saranyu's wisdom.

'Onward, then,' she urged, her confidence a lance piercing through his doubts. *'For every mountain bowing to your might, there are many valleys yearning for your tread.'*

∽

Saavarni examined the formidable mountain range before him, his gaze not one of fear but of calculation. His fingers traced a map in the air, his keen vision identifying patterns in the terrain. 'Every peak has a brother,' he murmured to himself, his eyes twinkling with the sharp light of strategy. 'And every path, a hidden twin.'

Saavarni's intellect carved a different journey. He studied the orography, noting the subtle cues of nature that whispered secrets lost to the brute-force approach. Where Shraddhadeva saw obstacles to overcome, Saavarni saw puzzles to solve.

'Well done, Son. Let your mind work the magic,' Chhaya's voice sounded in his ears.

'The way the wind courts rocks,' Saavarni spoke, more to the mountain than to anyone else. 'It skirts it, never fighting head-on.'

'Your mind is as nimble as a charioteer evading capture,' Chhaya responded. *'But you must be sure that it carries you all the way*

to the summit. Conquer the peak and see the world at your feet, my son.'

Saavarni smiled thinly, already stepping towards an innocuous crevice, a mere shadow to the untrained eye. 'The summit will come to me.'

∽

Shraddhadeva's lungs heaved, drawing in the scents of damp earth and ancient wood as he stood at the threshold of the forest. The climb down was more exhausting than the ascent, for he had to watch out for treacherous crevices that could lead to a fall. Now, the labyrinthine woods beckoned with its deceptive calm, the leaves whispering secrets only the wind could understand.

Realization struck Shraddhadeva. It was here that the real ordeal awaited him—the Enchanted Forest of *Mayavi*, a realm where reality bends to the whims of illusion. Saranyu prompted him, breaking through the daunting silence of the woods. 'Trust your heart, Shraddhadeva.' Her voice echoed in his mind, a melodic murmur. 'The eyes can be deceived, but the *Atman*'s compass veers only towards the truth.'

'Deceptive serenity,' he whispered, stepping over the gnarled roots that clawed at the earth like the hands of spirits long past. His gaze swept across the dense foliage, each leaf saturated with the verdant glow of life, yet shadowed by the unknown.

'See beyond sight,' Saranyu advised, her words entwining with his thoughts, a telepathic exchange that fortified his resolve. 'Let intuition guide you through this web of illusions.'

He nodded, though she could not see, and began navigating the treacherous terrain. With each step, the forest transformed itself. Paths closed in with a sudden onslaught of creepers. Roots grew from under his feet, causing him to stagger as his toes grappled for a foothold. Trees twisted into grotesque shapes, their branches reaching out like spectres craving touch. The path forked and coiled back upon itself, a serpent eating its own tail.

'Mother!' The cry emerged as he nimbly jumped out of the path of a branch that swept across where he stood.

'Stay alert! Stay patient!' Saranyu reminded him as he halted pushing against an enormous truck of a rapidly expanding banyan tree. *'Rashness invites folly. Measure each breath, each stride.'*

'An enigma wrapped in riddles,' he muttered, extending a hand to let his fingertips graze the illusion. 'How does one unravel such a knot?'

'Unweave it, thread by thread,' she counselled. *'Start with the simplest truth and build from there.'*

'Simplest truth...' he echoed, closing his eyes to focus on her voice, allowing it to anchor him in a sea of deception. When he opened them again, the trunk blurred, revealing a narrow passage obscured by its overgrowth.

'Well done,' Saranyu praised him, her delight palpable even within the confines of their shared consciousness. *'Now press forward, Shraddhadeva.'*

'Forward,' he affirmed, taking cautious steps. The forest seemed to watch him, its myriad eyes hidden among the leaves.

'Each choice,' Saranyu continued, her confidence a balm to his unease, *'brings you closer to destiny. Embrace the uncertainty; let it sharpen your senses. Do not pause for the seduction of tranquillity.'* She cautioned, *'The allure of false peace is a snare that has incapacitated many otherwise valiant heroes into self-destructive pacifism.'*

'Then I shall be the storm that breaks the stillness,' Shraddhadeva declared, striding across the clearing with renewed purpose, leaving behind the comforting lush bed of lies for the harsh embrace of truth. *'When the forces of Adharma challenge the Cosmic Balance, true heroes don't look for the false lull of peace and tranquillity. Move ahead, Shraddhadeva!'* Each revelation, guided by Saranyu's unwavering support, propelled him deeper into the heart of *Mayavi Vana*.

'Your faith in me is a wellspring, Mother,' he admitted, feeling her placid smile resonate within the shared sanctuary of their minds.

'For in you I see the dawn of a new era, Shraddhadeva,' Saranyu replied, her voice a tender caress on his psyche. *'Build upon the strengths and fight against the weaknesses of mortal life, Son. Remember your father's teachings.'*

Shraddhadeva navigated the treacherous turns of the maze-like forest. The bond between mother and son shone like a beacon, guiding him through the dance of shadow and light. His footsteps were hushed whispers against the forest floor, while the earth below him gradually became softer, making him wobble at times. The heavy scent of wild blossoms was replaced by a foreboding stench of decay. *Death!*

'Who is that? Help us,' a voice murmured from the shadow, frail as a dried leaf.

Shraddhadeva cocked his head in that direction, his keen eyes piercing the dimness, and found them—beings that he had only heard of but never seen, beings that were spoken of as existing in forbidden shadowlands. *Pisacha*s—spectres bound by invisible fetters, their ethereal forms flickering like dying flames.

'Who binds you to this sorrow?' he asked, reaching out not with his hands but with the kindness that swelled in his heart.

'Lost...we are lost,' they chorused, their voices a haunting lament that stirred the leaves.

'Why?' The word did not quite slip through his lips but it seemed as though the beings understood his question.

'As mortals who encounter death in the wrong circumstances, we are stuck in our journey, for our *self* is still in the world while the *body* has decayed beyond existence.'

'How can I help you in your onward journey?' Shraddhadeva offered, his voice a soothing balm.

One Pisacha scoffed. 'If only I knew!'

Shraddhadeva looked ahead and saw the path thinning, as though the enchanted forest had grown its own walls to close in upon him.

'And now, you too will be trapped with us!' The pisacha laughed.

'The world is transient, my friend. The self, the Atman, is capable of journeying onward.' Shraddhadeva extended to the spectres the warmth of his spirit—a beacon of hope amidst despair. 'Look within the maze of your own bindings. Therein lies the path to release.'

'Compassion will be your strength,' Saranyu's thoughts intertwined with his, a gentle nudge towards the destiny they shared.

'Let go of your bindings…' Shraddhadeva encouraged the Pisachas, unmindful of the fast-closing path that threatened to trap him in the jungle forever. 'I know not what caused your death and when. But reach out to the power of your own self that can overcome what holds you back. Even the forest closing in upon us cannot hold you back.' The rustle of the rapidly approaching wilderness grew louder. And louder.

'Fool! Leave at once!' The pisacha hissed.

Shraddhadeva's lips twitched, and he glanced at what looked like impending death that would trap him along with that undead being. 'Mother!'

'The power of the self, Shraddhadeva, as you rightly pointed out.' Saranyu's voice did not waver at the so-called danger. Shraddhadeva's smile widened. The roots and branches swished like flames and spikes, baying for his blood. Yet he stood firm.

∽

Saavarni surveyed the labyrinthine forest, his eyes reflecting a vision that went beyond the naked eye. The hilly trek was eventless much to his surprise, and he had decided to stay away from the easier paths which he was sure were camouflages of slippery slopes. Navigating the forest now seemed relatively harder despite the even terrain. Saavarni's senses were on their highest alert.

'This is Mayavi Vana, Son,' Chhaya's husky warning rung in his ears. *'It brings further illusions in this already illusory world!'* Saavarni could not help laughing, and ducked just in time as the wind shifted, signalling a sudden impending attack by a being he had never seen till then.

'Another mirage,' he murmured, scrutinizing the path where *vetalas* or phantoms capered enticingly. At the dismissive wave of his hand, they dissolved into space. Saavarni's gaze landed on a series of suspended flora with invisible stems—geometrically and physically impossible in nature.

'Patterns reveal underlying truths,' he deduced, tracing with his fingertip the spiral of a creeper blooming with saugandhika, feeling the pulse of the forest's heartbeat synchronize with his own analytical rhythm. 'Nature's riddles speak only to those who listen.' Saavarni whispered to himself, the ciphers unravelling before his mind's eye. Where others saw chaos, he discerned order—a map written in the language of the forest itself. 'Only the keenest will perceive the underlying order,' he thought, a smile playing on his lips as he navigated the web of deceit with ease.

'Indeed, Saavarni!' Chhaya's presence brushed against his consciousness, an affirmation of his methodical approach. Her belief in him steeled his resolve.

The lattice of shadows thickened as Saavarni stood at what he thought was the heart of the forest. Before him the river roared—a tempest incarnate, as though she was protesting the intrusion of her privacy. If Yami and Tapati defined his understanding of rivers, this body of water was something Saavarni would put on an aggressive or even destructive side of the line. Amidst the cacophony of water against rock, he sought the soothing whisper of tranquillity through the telepathic bond he shared with Chhaya.

'Patience, Saavarni,' Chhaya's voice echoed in the recesses of his mind, smooth and steady. *'Your keen vision deciphered the patterns in the wilderness. Now, observe the currents closely. Listen to the message they want to give you. They dance to a rhythm known only to the elements.'*

'I am grateful for the guidance, Mother,' he responded mentally, closing his eyes and enhancing his audial abilities, focusing them on the raging river before him. The torrents twisted and turned like a serpentine deity hissing in unbridled fury. 'This is hardly a river! How could one possibly cross such a perilous embodiment of a deluge?'

'Calm down, Son. Your greatest asset has always been your intellect,' Chhaya's chain of thought interwove with his own. *'Use it now. The river's wrath is but a mask; seek the path it conceals.'*

Saavarni inhaled deeply to calm his pounding heart. 'Each obstacle is but a veiled opportunity,' he mused aloud, his gaze dissecting the pattern of the frothing waves, searching for the hidden order within the chaos, the still point in the storm of the relentless waters.

'Indeed,' Chhaya affirmed telepathically, her cunning infusing his senses. *'But beware, for hesitation breeds disaster.'*

Saavarni took a measured breath, studying how the whitecaps of the waves clashed and parted. As Chhaya had indicated, there was indeed a rhythm—a brief lull between two currents—a bridge of relative calm. That was the crossing. Anyone else would have missed it, overcome by either terror or shock at the river's aggression.

'The time is now!' he whispered, as if sharing a sacred secret with the river itself. With the nimbleness of a horse, he leapt forward, each footfall a silent testament to not just his swiftness but also his analytical prowess.

'Come on, Saavarni, faster!' Chhaya urged in his mind. *'Embrace the speed that complements your intellect. Trust your judgement.'*

'Courage, speed and intellect,' Saavarni repeated, feeling the spray of the river on his skin as he navigated the invisible path he had discerned.

'The river is not your enemy. Remember that, Son!' Chhaya continued, her guidance a beacon in the labyrinth of his thoughts. *'It represents a challenge. It tests the mettle of those who dare to cross it. Lunge forward. Leap. Swim ahead! Victory lies just beyond,'* Chhaya promised, her confidence in him unwavering. *'One final leap, and the challenges of this virtual world shall yield to your determination. And the lordship of the real world will be yours.'*

'Lordship of the real world,' Saavarni let the words echo in his ears. 'Courage, intellect and speed. One was insufficient without the other two.' He affirmed, sensing Chhaya smile as he readied himself for the final bound. His muscles tensed, and with a burst of energy born from the fusion of the very characteristics—intellect and bravery—his mother had egged him on to imbibe, Saavarni leaped. The river's roar reached a crescendo around him as air and water became indistinguishable. In those moments of being suspended in time, he was the living embodiment of resolve. *'The final bound. The lordship of the real world.'*

And then, he felt it, the solid ground beneath his feet. He had emerged triumphant on the other side. The river's roar faded to a respectful murmur, acknowledging the passage of one who had bested its wild heart.

'Excellently done,' Chhaya's praise resonated within him, a harmonious chord concluding the symphony of their joint endeavour.

'Onto whatever end awaits,' Saavarni thought, his chest heaving with exertion as he cast a final glance back at the conquered river. Ahead lay the culmination of all his trials in the virtual realm, the determining moment of his destiny as Manu.

∽

The river lay before Shraddhadeva, a snarling beast of frothing currents and churning eddies. Its roar was deafening, drowning out the cries of those caught in its merciless grip.

'Help us!' they cried, their voices carrying over the tumultuous waters to where he stood on the bank—a call to action that resonated with the very core of his being.

'Stay calm!' Shraddhadeva shouted back, his words slicing through the dissonance. Without a moment's hesitation, he dove headlong into the river, cleaving the water with the force of the momentum his body could generate.

'Push through,' Saranyu's voice urged him telepathically, her presence a guiding star in the mental fog that threatened to cloud his judgement. 'Their lives are now entwined with your destiny.'

'Destiny can wait; duty can't,' he thought fiercely as he reached the first struggling soul. With strong, sure strokes, he pulled it to the safety of a jutting rock, then plunged back into the fray.

'Another awaits,' murmured Saranyu in his mind. He knew that. Yet, his mother's voice was an assurance that he was not alone at the mercy of elements in this virtual maze of a world.

'I am going right back for them, Mother,' he panted, locking eyes with another victim, terror etched upon its features. 'Hold on!' he called out, swimming powerfully against the current.

He pulled soul after soul to safety, without as much as having time to think about their origins. Becoming Manu, the Lord of the Mortal World, came with a huge responsibility. Shraddhadeva realized that only the Adi Kurma, the Primal Tortoise which had borne Mount Meru for the Great Churning of the Ocean, could understand the weight of a moral imperative. If saving those caught in the torrential waters in a virtual world seemed impossible, how would he even begin his reign in the real world? The question kept his tired muscles functioning.

Amidst the torrents, another being caught his eye. Shraddhadeva frowned, straining his sight that was blurred by the incessant currents thrashing his face. Caught in the whirls was a tiny being with a wing and a tail. A fish. Before he knew what he was doing, Shraddhadeva reached out for it. The creature swished its tail with an ethereal grace, creating a soft ripple around it. The moment seemed suspended in time, its spell broken only when another frantic voice reached Shraddhadeva's ears. He turned back and battled the currents, reaching the person in trouble, just before the waters engulfed him. 'Hold on!' Shraddhadeva panted, keeping himself afloat along with the one he was rescuing. A part of him surveyed the waters for the fish again, wondering what the tiny creature's presence in this illusionary world meant.

∽

Saavarni surveyed the scene from further downstream, his gaze analytical. 'There must be another way across this watery labyrinth,' he murmured to himself, scanning the treacherous landscape for a solution.

'Indeed,' Chhaya's voice echoed in his mind. *'Look to the patterns of nature, dear son. There you shall find your path.'*

'Patterns...' he mused, eyeing the rhythm of the river's flow. A series of stepping stones, partially hidden by the violent spray, revealed themselves to him—a precarious but promising path to traverse the river.

'Brilliance,' he whispered, a smile flitting across his lips. He leapt from stone to stone with the grace of a dancer, each movement calculated, each breath measured. The river snapped at his heels, hungry to claim him, but he was always one step ahead.

'Shraddhadeva plays the hero,' Saavarni observed with a mix of admiration and strategic detachment as he watched his opponent's selfless rescue from afar. 'But the hero's journey is not always the quickest path to victory. Shraddhadeva heeds the temporary, the illusionary denizens of this illusory world.' He smiled to himself. 'For all your knowledge of the ways of the Universe, Gods and Rishis, dear eldest...'

With a final agile leap, he landed on the opposite bank, his resourcefulness having carved a safer, swifter route through the river's chaos.

'Each to his strengths,' Chhaya's voice resonated within him, pride colouring her mental embrace. *'Now press forward, Saavarni. Don't look back, for the endgame is close.'*

∽

The air at the edge of the virtual world shimmered like a mirage, the mystical boundary between the illusionary and the real, as abstract as the veil between worlds during the Great Twilight. Both Shraddhadeva and Saavarni stood at this threshold, their chests heaving with the exertion of their trials, the final portal pulsing with an otherworldly glow.

'In the name of Brahma, the Creator, what a journey that was!' Shraddhadeva gasped, his eyes reflecting the celestial light of the portal. 'Real and unreal. Perhaps close to the worlds that we would be leading.'

'Indeed, Brother, it has tested every fibre of our beings,' Saavarni replied, his tone level, his gaze fixed on the passage that marked the culmination of their quest. He flexed his fingers, still feeling the ghostly pressure of the river's current against his skin. 'Yet, I find your investment in the temporary amusing, Eldest. Why battle what doesn't exist?'

'Existence is a relative question, little brother,' Shraddhadeva smiled. 'What's real for one is unreal for another. What is a lifetime to someone might be a blink of an eye for someone else.'

'Yet, you mingle and merge with something that you find unreal?' Saavarni frowned.

'No, Saavarni. I mingle and merge with something where I am to prove my mettle. To treat it not as an obstacle to the end, but as the stage for my role, that deserves my reverence rather than finding ciphers and shortcuts.' He regarded the son of Chhaya. 'Whichever way this ends,' Shraddhadeva said, turning to Saavarni, 'your mind is as sharp as the Sudarshana Chakra itself.' He offered a respectful nod, acknowledging their disparate paths to this singular moment.

'And your heart,' Saavarni countered, 'is as boundless as the ocean from which Varuna reigns.' There was no mockery in his words, only genuine admiration for Shraddhadeva's courage and compassion.

Shraddhadeva chuckled softly, the sound mingling with the ethereal hum of the portal. 'One last step, then?'

'One last step,' Saavarni confirmed, and together they moved toward the pulsating gateway, their rivalry giving way to a shared sense of anticipation.

With each stride, Shraddhadeva's thoughts churned like the waters of the endless sea. *Have I proven myself worthy?* The question of self-doubt echoed within him. Saranyu's silent encouragement lingered on in his consciousness, her telepathic touch being the only compass that kept him conscious of the ethereal nature of the world that engulfed him.

Saavarni's mind worked like the intricate patterns of a *Yantra*, tracing the labyrinthine possibilities of outcomes. Chhaya's counsel resonated within him, her whispers shaping his resolve. *Is victory ours to claim?*

'Sons of Vivasvan!' The voice of Lord Brahma boomed around them, magnified by the divine echo of the virtual realm. 'Step forth and seal your fates.'

Shraddhadeva cast a knowing glance at Saavarni as they readied themselves to cross the threshold to step back into the world of the divine that they always had been a part of. Both of them looked back at the realm of illusions—the battlefield on which they had to prove their mettle.

'Everything is indeed temporary! Including our reigns,' Saavarni mused softly, though audible enough to reach Shraddhadeva who was observing the illusory world melt into the vast nothingness of space, including the treacherous topography, the furious river and the curious beings that he had saved. *And then it caught his attention!*

Shraddhadeva stilled at the sight of the fish traversing the currents. 'I'll be back!' He turned around and raced into the fast-obliviating world.

'Eldest!'

'Shraddhadeva!'

'The portal is closing!'

Chaos erupted among the celestial denizens.

'Where did Shraddhadeva disappear?' murmured the sages among themselves, their voices a hushed whisper beneath the celestial dome. Suspense hung in the air, heavy as monsoon clouds awaiting the command to release their bounty. Did his sudden action, beyond anyone's comprehension, leave his brother free to covet the title of Manu?

The Dawn of Manu Vaivasvata

Shraddhadeva sensed Saranyu's silence; her usual words of advice were missing. He was aware of the closing portal. And unaware of what would follow if he did not spring out from the illusory world. Would the deluge consume him into the vacuum of Dyaus? But something within Shraddhadeva refused to turn back. Not when there was a struggling creature that needed his help. Would he consider himself successful with a task left incomplete? Shraddhadeva put an end to his thoughts as he reached the bank of the river and hurled himself headlong. The tiny creature seemed to battle the waters well. But would it make any sense to save it with the fast-approaching oblivion? The deafening silence from his mother told him that Saranyu was as confused as he was. Or did the forces that connected her to him give up and condemn him to oblivion along with this illusory realm?

'Mother?'

Shraddhadeva? He could sense the anxiety in her voice. And then nothing. Her presence! That was enough. All was not lost!

'There is a task that needs fulfilling, Mother!' His eyes frantically searched for the fish that seemed to lure him deeper into the waters. As long as this realm existed, and his task was to save all beings from the currents, illusory or real, he had to complete the task.

'Do your best son.' At this point, she could only nudge him to do that.

'Eldest!! I am stepping out!' Saavarni's words seemed distant. His stepbrother seemed like he was already out of this illusion.

And Shraddhadeva plunged into the waters. The currents thrashed him about, testing his will to its limits. Even as the world faded, the currents kept testing him. The fish seemed to only pull him deeper and deeper, towards the approaching oblivion. Shraddhadeva extended his right hand to hold the creature. He needed to keep it in the waters and yet away from the currents. He needed to spot a safe space within the water. Shraddhadeva looked around for anything that could contain some water to keep the fish alive even as he figured out the safe space. His mind furiously mapped out the flora of the realm, trying to spot the right container. *Shells!* As soon as the thought struck him, he dived to the bottom, hoping to find a shell big enough to contain the water that could keep the fish going. Meanwhile, the creature seemed to whirl towards its end. Shraddhadeva grabbed the biggest shell he could find and swam back to the surface. Nothing else mattered now. Not even the reign of Manu. For the failure to save the fish would anyway disqualify him from reigning over the Manvantara.

Holding the enormous shell between his teeth, he battled the currents to reach the fish. With a thrust that tested his limits, he paddled hard, his hand just catching the fish before it was swallowed by the whirlpool of oblivion. Thrusting himself above the waters, with a relieved sigh, Shraddhadeva placed the fish in the shell, swimming his way back to the bank. Voices of many dear to him protested at the sheer vanity of what he was doing, at the approaching oblivion. Yet, there was something about the role he had to stand by and fulfil, without which even the reign of an *aeon* would make little sense. The fish, contrary to the cyclone that raged around and within Shraddhadeva, seemed to have found its calm in the safety of the shell. Shraddhadeva continued to battle the currents, heading towards the bank, where he could ferry anyone in danger, where he could fulfil the very purpose of the test, the very purpose for which this world had been created.

And then the world around him stilled.

He looked up to ascertain that it was not just in his mind. The waters had frozen, mid-current. The air seemed immobile, as though he was contained in a painting where he was the only one mobile against the background of the whole world. 'Mother.'

He felt her anxiety like a ripple down his spine. But Saranyu did not breathe a word. Why did the world stop in its stride? Why did everything around him freeze except… It was Shraddhadeva's turn to freeze when he saw the fish swimming in the placid waters of the shell that he held. Almost as though the creature looked into his eyes and locked his gaze.

'What? Are you?'

As though it had heard him, it flapped its tiny fins—an acknowledgement of his question. It was not the creature that had been caught in a deluge rapidly spiralling into nothingness just a moment back. It was more like someone who was delighting in the play of the forces around it.

Unaffected.

Distant.

Yet indulgent.

The orbs around its eyes. Shraddhadeva found himself drawn to the play of hues and the ethereal reflection of light against its scales. As though a glow was building up around the creature. Only to become brighter. And brighter. Till the light consumed his entire vision for a moment when Shraddhadeva was reminded that even Time surrendered in the presence of Eternity.

And then his vision cleared, revealing the gathering of denizens from celestial and nether realms—his father, his mother, his siblings and those from his other mother. And the rest of the cosmic pantheon. And those contending to occupy positions in the pantheon.

Then Shraddhadeva beheld his Great Grandfather whose gaze

was tinged with pride and joy. He knelt in front of the Lord Creator Brahma.

'Arise Manu Vaivasvata Shraddhadeva. Seventh of his order.'

All those assembled let out a deep breath. Loud cheers erupted, as vibrant as the first rays of dawn. From the corner of his eyes, Shraddhadeva saw Saranyu breathe a sigh of relief and lean on Vivasvan's arm, awash with joy and pride.

Shraddhadeva had triumphed, not by sheer might, but by embodying the essence of what it meant to lead. The significance of this moment went beyond the bounds of the competition. It was the heralding of an era in which Shraddhadeva, as Manu, would shepherd humanity with wisdom gleaned from both divine counsel and the depth of his own heart. His victory was more than personal; it was the promise of a future built on the pillars of justice, compassion and unwavering resolve.

'Today, you have witnessed not just my victory but the affirmation of our path forward,' Shraddhadeva addressed the gathering, his voice resonating with authority and gentle assurance. 'As Manu, I shall forge our civilization with these hands—hands that fight, hands that heal, hands that hold us together,' he declared, his eyes alight with the fire of purpose. 'Together, under the guidance of the divine, we shall rise to heights untold, our spirits unbroken, our legacy immortal.'

And as the crowd roared in approval, the heavens themselves seemed to nod in silent, sacred agreement.

The air was thick with the fragrance of a myriad celestial blooms and incense as Shraddhadeva stood amidst the grandeur of Surya Mandala, the newly ordained centre of the life force. A brilliant riot of colours unfurled in the sky, heralding the divine beings who descended to witness the consecration.

'Behold the dawn of a new epoch,' Vivasvan, the resplendent solar deity, proclaimed. His voice, thunderous yet warm, reverberated through the Universe. 'In the heart of Surya Mandala will beat the pulse of Creation, a beacon for all civilizations to come, under the watchful gaze of Dyaus, in the nurturing lap of Mother Bhumi.'

Saranyu, ethereal and serene beside her consort, radiated a gentle luminescence. Her eyes met Shraddhadeva's, conveying a silent message of pride and fortitude. The bond they shared, transcending words, filled him with an inner calm amid the splendour of the ceremony.

'Your wisdom has been our guiding star, Mother,' Shraddhadeva continued, his gaze softening. 'Our gratitude is as boundless as the Cosmos itself.'

Shraddhadeva watched as Saranyu inclined her head gracefully, accepting the acknowledgement with a humility that belied her immense wisdom. He felt the weight of his own destiny, knowing that her telepathic guidance had been instrumental in his path to becoming Manu.

The assembly of divine entities began the rites, their chants melding into a symphony that seemed to stitch the very fabric of reality. As they moved, the ground beneath them hummed, resonating with the cadence of primordial energy.

'Through fire, water, earth, air and space, let the elements converge,' intoned a celestial sage, his hands weaving intricate patterns in the air.

Shraddhadeva felt the surge of power beneath his feet, a testament to the forces at play. Closing his eyes, he allowed himself a moment to connect with the life force pulsing around him. In his mind, Saranyu's presence whispered encouragements, bolstering his resolve to lead with compassion and insight.

'Today, we stand on the threshold of greatness,' he said, his voice steady and clear. 'Let us embrace this gift, the vitality of Surya Mandala, and nurture the seeds of our future.'

The crowd echoed his sentiments, a unified chorus that sang of hope and ambition. Shraddhadeva opened his eyes to see Surya

Mandala's core begin to glow, its light expanding like the birth of a new star.

'See how it thrives!' exclaimed a wind deity, her form fluttering with excitement. 'This is the true essence of life—unyielding, ever flourishing.'

Surya Mandala's energy swelled, a radiant spectacle that painted every onlooker in a sheen of golden brilliance. The Mandala's heart, now ablaze with divine fire, sent ripples of power across the land. As if the Universe itself had exhaled, bestowing its breath upon the world humanity was destined to build.

In the midst of it all, Shraddhadeva stood firm, a conduit between heaven and earth. Feelings of awe and humility coursed through his veins, yet there was a steadfastness that anchored his spirit.

'Let it be known,' he declared, his conviction echoing through the realm, 'that from this day forth, Surya Mandala shall nourish our souls and our soil, as we journey through the ages.'

Vivasvan nodded, the warmth of his approval as potent as the sun's rays. 'So it shall be, Manu Shraddhadeva. Under your stewardship, civilization shall flourish anew.'

'Indeed,' Saranyu's voice resonated in his mind, her telepathic touch as gentle as a zephyr. 'Your vision, Manu, will be the compass that guides our civilization.'

Shraddhadeva turned towards the gathering, his eyes meeting those of Saavarni, who had been a formidable challenger but now stood as an ally in this grand design. Together, they looked at the assembly of divine beings, each emanating their own ethereal glow, their faces aglow with expectation.

'Let us stride forward,' his voice carried the strength of mountains, 'into a future shaped by our collective will, bound by the wisdom of the past and the promise of tomorrow.'

A murmur rose among the deities, a harmonious blend of assent and excitement. They began to disperse, their forms merging with the elements around them—fire, water, earth, air and space—all essential in the Creation that was to come.

As the echoes of the proclamation faded, Surya Mandala continued to pulse, its rhythm promising rebirth and endless possibilities. And in that instant, the future seemed not just bright but infinite, with Shraddhadeva at its helm, ready to guide humanity into a new dawn.

'Manu,' Saavarni spoke, his voice firm yet filled with camaraderie, 'the challenges we faced have made us stronger. Together, there is nothing we cannot accomplish.'

'True strength,' Shraddhadeva replied, clapping a hand on Saavarni's shoulder, 'lies not only in power but in unity, little brother.'

As the last of the divine beings vanished into the skies, Shraddhadeva stood alone for a moment. He closed his eyes, allowing the inner symphony of his thoughts to rise to a crescendo. Doubts still flickered like distant stars in the night sky, but his resolve burned brighter than any uncertainty.

We are the creators of destiny, he thought, *the builders of worlds*. The burgeoning panorama of the morrow unfolded before him—lives intertwined with the cosmic dance, each thread vibrant with potential.

'Come,' Saranyu's voice beckoned once more, invisible yet omnipresent. 'Let us begin the work that awaits us. There is much to be done, and time, though eternal, waits for no one.'

'Then we shall waste not a moment longer,' Shraddhadeva declared, opening his eyes to the view of a nascent world. With a final glance at the luminescent Surya Mandala, he took a step forward, his heart brimming with conviction.

'Forward,' he murmured with a smile, 'to the dawn of a new era.'

And so, with the echoes of a new age whispering in the winds, the stage was set for the saga to continue. Under Shraddhadeva's leadership, hope unfurled like a lotus at daybreak, its petals stretching wide to embrace the coming days. The future was theirs to mould, a canvas vast and vivid, ready for the first strokes of their shared dream.

Yama took a deep breath, feeling the power of his role as the God of Death coalesced within him. Each step he took was purposeful, each thought clear and focused.

'May my judgements be just,' he intoned, his voice resolute. 'May the cycle of *Samsara* flow unimpeded.'

With that solemn vow, Yama felt a connection to every soul that traversed the realms of existence. He was their guide, their final companion on the journey to what lay beyond.

'Let the Cosmos pay heed,' Yama proclaimed, his words carrying the weight of eternity. 'I embrace my destiny.'

As twilight descended upon the forest, the stars began to twinkle, one by one, in the canvas above. They bore witness to the momentous occasion—the birth of a new era.

'May the guardians uphold their sacred duties,' Yama said, his voice a soft echo amidst the enchanting symphony of nocturnal life. 'And may the Universe thrive under our watch.'

Turning his face to the heavens, Yama allowed the celestial light to wash over him, sealing his pact with the Cosmic Order. And as night enveloped the world in its velvety cloak, the Lord of Dharma stepped forward, ready to fulfil his divine purpose—to maintain the equilibrium of all things, in life and in death.

Epilogue

It was an atmosphere of mixed emotions in the Celestial Forge. Tvashtra continued with his work, trying to crown the disturbance in his mind with the slew of tasks he had been entrusted with by Lord Brahma. With a definitive clang, his hammer broke the metal rod into two. His work had piled up with the recent turn of events—the announcement of Manu, his grandson Shraddhadeva Vaivasvata, who would herald the end of this very eventful Great Twilight between the two ages of Manu and begin the seventh age. Tvashtra should have been with his daughter's family at Surya Mandala, celebrating alongside Lord Vivasvan, Saranyu, the apple of his eye, his grandson, the new Manu and his other grandchildren. But then Brahma's announcement to the denizens of the Cosmos that followed the crowning of Manu held a deep significance for him. *A rather dark one.* Tvashtra played the events out in his mind.

The denizens of Deva Loka celebrated, cheering Shraddhadeva's crowning as Manu, the progenitor of this era's mortal kind. Chhaya and Virochana did put up a feeble resistance, citing that Saavarni's performance in the illusory world was worth considering as well.

'Of course, Saavarni shows promise!' The Great Grandfather agreed. 'His consciousness of the transient and intransient, his ability to see beyond what is visible speak of a keen perception that a leader needs.' Brahma stepped forward as Saavarni knelt before him. 'Son of Chhaya, stay by the side of your brother and witness for yourself his reign. That would equip you to herald your own reign at the end of your brother's.' The Great Grandfather turned

to everyone present. 'The Surya Saavarni Manvantara shall follow the one ruled by Shraddhadeva Manu Vaivasvata.'

The Devas cheered and the Daityas who had supported Saavarni's ascension had to be content with the long wait. Tvashtra saw Saranyu approach Chhaya. He saw the 'sisters' argue a bit before the rest of the family gathered around them. Perhaps they would reconcile with each other. Chhaya had little to be unhappy about. She had a household she could share with the ever-accommodating Saranyu, and children whose destiny had been chalked out. Tvashtra was about to join them when lightning pierced the skies. And then he saw the one against whom his heart bore a deep grudge.

Purandhara Kashyapa.

'Saaho Shata Kratu Purandhara!'

He heard the other sons of Aditi and Kashyapa cheer. Eyes full of concern, he turned to face the King of Gods, Manojava Vasava. The Indra pursed his lips and responded with an imperceptible nod before approaching him, frozen as Tvashtra was in his steps. 'Forget the past, dear cousin.' Lord Manojava counselled him. 'Larger ends need sacrifices. And yours will be counted among them.'

That was when Tvashtra took his leave from the cosmic gathering. He was to forge weapons and build dwellings for Devas under the command of the new Indra. The name struck like a bitter aftertaste on his tongue. 'Purandhara! The killer of my son, Vishvarupa.' Somewhere in his heart of hearts, Tvashtra had hoped that Bali would be appointed the next Indra, but like the son of Chhaya, the Daitya Prince had to be content with the long wait of another Manvantara before he could ascend the throne of Deva Loka. The fate of the Daitya Prince was not on the top of Tvashtra's priorities. It was the thought that none in the Universe, including the Trimurtis, seemed to care about the death of his only son, Vishvarupa!

Unfortunately, the three-headed being was too ambitious for his own good. His treacherous actions warranted punitive measures from the Gods. Tvashtra had no problem with that. But then the killing… It happened under the watch of Indra, at the hands of the incumbent Indra. The tongs in Tvashtra's hands shook and the hammer struck at the wrong place! The Celestial Architect groaned and let go of his tools. If the Devas did not care for the emotions of a bereaved father, well, he was entitled to avenge Vishvarupa's killing—Tvashtra promised himself, his estranged wife and their departed son.

ᔕ

The flames of the Yajna rose like the heads of a timeless serpent. The Celestial Architect paused his chants, his mind conjuring up the vision of a serpent devouring the head of that Purandhara. Notwithstanding him becoming Indra or anyone else, this Yajna had to bear fruit. Tvashtra poured all his energies into the ritual. It was ordained by the timeless Rishis to bless the *Yajamana* with the kind of progeny he desired. It was known to not disappoint.

Tvashtra could sense the Cosmic Balance tilt. Yes, the birth of a son who would kill the Indra would cause this. Tvashtra remained unperturbed.

Rather, *overjoyed* was the word.

The ritual progressed.

It was the call of a father.

And that of the Smith and Architect of the Gods.

The cosmic forces had to heed it.

And the purpose had to be articulated. Tvashtra chanted. The skies quaked. The flames bore a shape. The father was overjoyed.

Vritra! Welcome to the world, my son!

ᔕ

Saranyu pursed her lips, her fingers curling around Vivasvan's wrist. 'I knew it! He was uncharacteristically reclusive after

Shraddhadeva's coronation!' Saranyu exclaimed. 'First it was my brother, and now...'

'It is your father!' The completion of the sentence was needless but from the sarcasm lacing the tone that reflected her own, Saranyu knew that her shadow could not resist the glee and suppressed her urge to roll her eyes.

'Do the higher forces of the Cosmos not know of this, Deva?' Saranyu tugged at Vivasvan's arm. The Lord of Light seemed to stare at the horizon, most likely aware of the facts that no one else knew. After what seemed like an eternity, her luminous spouse turned to her.

'Purandhara can handle what is in store for him.' Vivasvan almost chuckled before solemnness took over his placid face. 'It is going to be a long battle for the Gods.'

Saranyu closed her eyes in silent prayer and let the moments sink in. Her luminous husband was omniscient. The eternal witness. His unperturbed state of mind was something she could only aspire to have. As if reading her mind, Vivasvan gently turned her in the direction of the cosmic ball in glowing green and blue hues—Mother Bhumi in her newly discovered bloom and life.

'We can take a break from the conflict of the immortals and delight in the rise of the mortals for a while, Devi. And let these conflicts play out their course. The age of Manu Vaivasvata begins now.'

The words brought a smile to her lips. Saranyu gazed into space, at the celestial forces aligning themselves to herald the age of her son's reign. She hoped that Shraddhadeva was ready for it. And then she remembered someone who she should have long ago. 'About time I asked after Sachi.'

Acknowledgements

Penning a story that is alluded to in multiple source texts including Rig Veda, Mahabharata and a number of Puranas is a celebration as well as a challenge. The making of this novel would not have been possible if not for the blessings, support and encouragement from many people.

My foremost note of gratitude goes to my Spiritual Guru Sri Karunamaya ji. Initiation to Sri Vidya under Your abundant blessings have transformed my relationship with Divinity and hence, with the texts, stories, thoughts, prayers and interactions with them. Cannot thank you enough, Guru ji.

Team Rupa—Rudra Narayan Sharma, Padma Pegu and the rest—we have built this relationship over three books and discussions over multiple other books. From ideation to editing to marketing, it is a pleasure to work with them all. A heartfelt thank you to Amrita Chakravorty for the work on cover illustration and design.

My mother Smt Usha Krishna Swamy's unwavering push to keep me writing new and new stories is a constant source of rejuvenation. A connoisseur of top-quality Pravachanas by a whole cosmos of scholars, her inputs and brainstorming are my starting point of work on every story I write. My father P. Krishna Swamy Kumar, the silent and yet steady witness to my evolving thoughts and views. His almost clinical interventions through my writing journey watch my back. Arvind, the Sun of my life, my light when things go dull, my sturdy pillar of support, is actually a standing inspiration every moment. Like Saranyu, when I retreat to my creative shell, he assures me of my space and promptly pulls me out of it when I need that too! Abhirami, my daughter, thank you for that occasional 'Amma, how long will you take to write the next book' reminder that keeps me going.

Among the luminaries whose encouragement kept me going through tough times, the late Shri Bibek Debroy's name tops the list. I still remember his affectionate chiding when we met about two years ago at Bengaluru, asking why I had not written more books. I told him I was working on the story of Devi Saranyu and asked him for his support and blessings. Bibek Da, though you aren't with us today, you are another Lord Vivasvan, lighting up the world with your translations of Hindu source texts. I owe a large chunk of my research to you!

The nurturing ground of creative reimagination and the foundation as well as platform for my literary journey has been Indic Academy (INDICA) and the wonderful people associated with it. Sri Harikiran Vadlamani, your association is the fruit of punya of many past births. My brainstorming friends, Shivakumar GV whose works on Srishti Sthiti Laya framework have helped me look at the Deva-Daitya dynamics in a new light, Abhinav Agarwal for that continuous focus on craft and process, Pranshu Saxena, those long info bits which make us all think you are the human version of GPT, and the whole extended fraternity, cannot do without any of you.

The book was conceptualized, researched and written when I was working at Chanakya University, Bengaluru. My humble words of gratitude for everyone there, right from the leadership to younger colleagues who took a personal interest in my writing journey along with my professional one. A special note to students too, for interacting with you all has opened up new ways of engaging with the audience.

To all those forces of support who I may have missed naming, and to you, the reader, praying to the one Visible God of the skies and the Invisible Goddess of the Multiverse to shower Their light and love upon you. May the quest for knowledge and divine engagement grow.

Glossary of Sanskrit terms

Adhvaryu: The priest responsible for physical performance of rituals in a Vedic yajna

Anartha: Misfortune, calamity, or meaninglessness

Annam Brahma, Raso Vishnu, Bhokta Maheshvarah: 'Food is Brahman, essence of that food is Vishnu; the consumer is Lord Shiva (an amalgamated statement from the Upanishads symbolizing the Srishti, Sthiti and Laya cycle of food)

Ashrama: Abode of a hermit/alternatively, life stage in Hindu dharma (brahmacharya, gṛhastha, vanaprastha, sannyasa)

Atman: Self, soul, inner essence

Avidya: Ignorance (especially spiritual ignorance, opposite of *vidya*)

Charaiveti: 'Keep moving/Keep walking forward'; from *Aitareya Brāhmaṇa*, exhortation to persevere

Guru Hatya: 'Killing of the guru'; considered one of the gravest sins

Iha: Here/In this world

Jnana: Knowledge, wisdom (usually spiritual knowledge)

Kratu: Ritual yajna

Laya: Dissolution (cosmic destruction/absorption)

Maṇḍapa: Wedding pavilion or ritual canopy

Martya: Mortal, perishable being (opposite of *amaṛtya*)

Mayavi: Illusionist, wielder of *maya* (delusion, magical power)

Mrita: Dead; opposite of *amṛta* (immortal)

Naraka: Realm of afterlife suffering in Hindu cosmology

Padmasana: 'Lotus pose'; a meditative yogic posture

Pancha Indriyas: Five senses (sight, sound, touch, taste, smell)

Para: Beyond/Transcendent/Supreme

Pitamaha: Grandfather

Rtu: Season; also denotes order, rhythm of nature

Samsara: Cycle of birth, death and rebirth; worldly existence

Sanjeevani: Life-restoring herb; a plant capable of reviving the dead

Shata: Hundred

Soma: Sacred ritual drink and Vedic deity; also associated with moon

Srishti: Creation (cosmic origination)

Sruk-Sruva: Ritual ladles/spoons used for offering ghee into fire during yajna

Sthiti: Preservation/Sustenance (cosmic maintenance)

Tapasvi: One who practises *tapas* (austerities)

Tapasya: Austerity, penance, discipline performed for spiritual progress

Tattva: Principle, element, essence; philosophical category

Vana pisachas: Forest spirits, often malevolent beings in folklore

Varuni: Goddess of wine/liquor, consort of Varuṇa; also refers to intoxicating drink

Vashikarana: A tantric practice; also 'enchantment' or 'bringing under influence'

Vetala: Ghostly being/ghoul inhabiting corpses

Vidhata: Ordainer, creator, or destiny-maker

Vishvajit yajna: Ritual yajna meant for universal conquest

Vivaha: Marriage, the samskara (rite of passage) of wedding

Yajamana: Patron/sponsor of a yajna (the one who commissions the ritual)

Yajna: Sacrifice/ritual; offering to deities through fire, with hymns

Yajnasthala: The sacred ground/altar where a yajna is performed

Yajnavedi: The fire-altar/platform where yajna is performed

Yantra: Sacred diagram or mystical device denoting a deity used in rituals